Explosions near and into the sky, as if light armour of the darkness, 1 seams. Kathleen was sayin arm. Charlotte shook her off. She would wait for Robert; wait until death if that were required.

Robert emerged from the darkness before her, carrying Alice over one shoulder like a rolled up rug. *Oh, thank you, merciful Father,* Charlotte thought in gratitude. *Thank you for this gift.* "Take her!" Robert shouted, slinging the limp girl into Charlotte's arms. His eyes were stark in the illumination of the lights. "Get under cover!"

Charlotte collected Alice, who stirred in feeble protest. "Sir, you must hide—"

"No," he shouted again, and she realized the explosions had deafened him. "I must help dig out the bunker!" He squeezed her hand, too hard, but she did not notice the bruises until later, and he was gone into the night.

from *The Old World*

I found myself "finding," "creating," and "needing" time to read after I began **The Old World.** Being an historian, I have studied The Great War, now called World War I; however, that front line horror of war is hard to tell. Griffis brought the story right to me with words that created characters whom I quickly came to enjoy so much I had to read. The story delivers fear, horror, love, salvation, humour, friendship, honour, and death all meshed together to create a book I won't soon forget.

Novelist C.M. Huddleston

Cover art and design by Cedar Sanderson

Copyright 2023 by Roy M. Griffis
All rights reserved

By the Hands of Men

Book One

The Old World

by

Roy M. Griffis

The Casualty Clearing Station

The new girl was peering about the tent when Charlotte and Kathleen stumbled in at the end of their shift that July day in 1917. The work itself was exhausting—twelve hours of standing, bending, folding, feeding, bandaging, debriding, cleaning, and sterilizing; only to repeat it all again. Add to that the effort of presenting cheerful countenances to the hundreds of wounded men they passed each day, and it may be understood that their labours were truly Herculean.

Giving a smile to men who might not live through the night, and who knew this to be a fact, was begrudged by none of the nurses. But after long hours of facing down death, with men who had not seen a woman's smile or felt the gentle touch of a feminine hand in months, the most fervent desire to be of service could transmute into mere stoical endurance under the simple grinding toil, as if turning gold into lead. Know this, and understand the depth of the two nurses' fatigue as they tramped into their temporary canvas-covered home.

The camp had been in place for over a year, and this was fortunate for the weary women. They were able to trudge directly to their tent without sparing it conscious thought. When the hospital was reorganized the previous spring to accommodate the ever-increasing flow of the wounded, the nurses' tents and their few belongings were placed haphazardly around the new hospital location. The nightly blackout would force the two girls to creep along, whispering for directions from equally worn-out nurses who were fortunate enough to already be abed. More than once, Charlotte and Kathleen had tumbled unknowing into strange cots, only to be awakened for their shifts by bemused nurses ready for their own beds.

"Hullo," the new girl said politely as they entered the tent that had been their home these last twelve months.

"'Lo," Kathleen the plain-faced nurse from America allowed, heading directly to her bunk. They'd been fed the infernal hospital soup along with the unexpected treat of fresh plums at the end of their short shift. There had been a lull in the continual contest over the same yards of churned, bloody French soil, and thus the number of causalities pouring into the hospital had slowed. A 12-hour day was a comparative luxury, compared to their experiences after the Battle of the Somme less than a year ago.

The American dove toward her pillow with almost lustful abandon. "Kathleen," she said, indicating herself, and then flapped a weary hand toward Charlotte. "Cheri," she added, giving the nickname the wounded French soldiers had bestowed on the other girl.

"Charlotte," the other corrected, and observed on the

new girl's face an eyebrow flick, registering the faint accent her voice still carried.

The new girl extended her hand primly. "Alice." Charlotte shook the offered hand. Alice had prominent bones in her hand, and very fine, pale skin, unlike the olive of Charlotte's more foreign complexion. Alice's English diction was precise, her speech dancing with the tones that only birth and wealth and High Church could provide.

"Take that cot," Charlotte said, trying not to resent the time the new arrival kept her from her own waiting pillow and blankets. "We'll get you sorted in the morning."

"Oh, thanks, much!" Alice said. "I slipped over on a mail packet, and one of the boys driving the ambulance made some room for me in the back."

Charlotte smiled wanly and grunted in a way that only indicated acknowledgement, not interest. Nurses came over in all kinds of ways now, so hopping one of the little boats that plied mail across the Channel was nothing special. Nor was catching the ambulance. Most of the drivers were boys, and they'd not turn down the opportunity to flirt, however shyly, with a young Miss in the horse-blanket ugly, dark blue serge uniform of a nurse.

Kathleen had already turned into her blankets, her back to the two of them. Charlotte sat on her wooden and canvas cot, eased off her boots. There was so much to tell this young slip of a Lady-to-be...but she'd learn it soon enough. "We'll get you sorted out in the morning," she repeated mechanically.

Alice looked at her blankly. "I beg your pardon?"

"Nothing," Charlotte replied. "Be a dear and try to get some sleep. We're knackered. We'll be woken before dawn with our breakfast." Lord, she hated being so short with the girl, but it had been weeks since she'd been able to sleep more than 6 hours, and she fully intended to immerse herself in the opportunity now.

Even as fatigued as she was, Charlotte's mind fretted first over the day that had passed, and then it roved to the duties that would be waiting in the day to come. After a time, much too long a time it seemed to her, she was warmed by the coarse wool blanket and she began to grow drowsy. She turned her head to the other cot, wondering why the new girl had not yet extinguished the lantern.

The new girl's uniform was neatly folded and placed at the end of her bunk. The bulky, distinctive, ugly garment, with its large black buttons down the front and shoulder pleats giving it a wholly military appearance, would soon be Alice's constant companion. The other nurse sighed inwardly, realizing another thing the new girl would need to be taught in the morning. Alice had tied her hair up in clean new ribbons, draped her feet in thick woollen socks, and buttoned up a nightdress to her throat. She didn't look round at Charlotte or Kathleen as she did so. There was an air of an unexpressed sniff of distaste at her companions' slovenly behaviour of climbing into their rough cots still fully clothed save for their hats and shoes.

Her eyes burning from fatigue, Charlotte was too weary to give the girl's hauteur much consideration other than a brief stab of sympathy. *What idiot is instructing these women?* she thought in English as she descended toward sleep, unable to resist her body's aching need for rest. She was thinking in English almost exclusively these days, a result of the long and blood-filled hours among the British doctors and nurses. She remembered to spare a glance at the floor of their tent, to ensure nothing cluttered the centre, and then she closed her eyes.

There was no bombing that evening, which allowed Charlotte to sleep almost ten hours. Even so, it seemed she had merely closed her eyes only to open them again immediately. The weariness she felt transcended sleep...she swore she would never again take rest for granted.

Having forsworn stockings, Charlotte tugged on clean socks and her boots. Huddled in blankets on the edge of the cot, Alice was awake and smiled nervously at her. "I couldn't sleep," the new girl admitted. "I was too eager!"

"Come along, then," Charlotte said in a low voice, so as not to awaken Kathleen. "I'll show you the loo."

The new nurse drew on her great coat over the nightdress, slipped into her own boots, and followed Charlotte. There were few about that morning, save for the sentries on patrol round the perimeter of the hospital camp, and the nurses were either on duty or still asleep. To Charlotte's surprise, the girl sensibly kept quiet as she tottered along the duckboards behind the other nurse. The latrine lay toward the rear of the camp, and Charlotte led her down the path toward it. As they slipped and stumbled on the uneven pieces of wood laid upon the ground in the usually forlorn effort to create a more secure surface upon which to walk, the new girl lifted the hem of her nightdress in some long-ingrained habit to prevent the mud from soiling it.

Alice halted at the sight of the wooden privy. A shack with ill-fitting doors, it was like something you'd find on a farm. Charlotte had seen many on her family's estate, and most of them had been in better shape than this one. It was unlikely a well-brought-up young lady, such as Alice obviously was, had ever used such rough accommodations, or in such a public setting.

Charlotte tugged her forward, and Alice resisted. "But the common—the soldiers...won't they look?"

The question struck Charlotte as largely idiotic since

there were no men actually in sight. "No," Charlotte answered firmly, urging the girl into the dank interior and pulling the door shut after them.

An unwelcoming vista of four seats separated by wooden partitions confronted them. Slits high overhead let in some of the faint early morning light and, more importantly, fresh air. "The soldiers are most gentlemanly," she said as she began to perform the necessaries. Beside her, she could hear Alice lowering herself with reluctance to the seat. "They are a queer bunch," Charlotte went on in a conversational tone, trying to make this awkward moment less so for the girl. "The boys will queue up to see a bare ankle…yet they give us every bit of privacy we require."

Alice didn't reply, so Charlotte stepped outside to allow the girl a bit of solitude, perhaps even a moment to gather herself together. The more experienced nurse turned to the trough of reasonably fresh water that was outside the privy. She found the greyish slab of soap and took the opportunity to thoroughly scrub her hands. Alice slipped out of the latrine, and joined her. She noted with approval the fastidious care the young girl used when washing up.

They both shook their hands to dry them as they walked. "Come along," Charlotte ordered. "If we miss breakfast, you'll faint before mid-morning." She debated a trip to the hospital buildings for a hurried sponge bath, but a glance at the brightening sky turned her from that thought. No time. "Madame will bring us breakfast. She usually has extra, so don't worry, you'll get something."

"Madame?" Alice asked, labouring in her wake. The young girl had not yet acquired the near sprint of a stride the other nurses assumed without thought, even over the variable surface of the duckboards.

"That's what everyone calls her, just 'Madame',"

Charlotte replied, forging ahead. Already, there was a kind of clock running in her mind as she reviewed the work ahead: the dressings to be changed, the equipment to be cleaned. "She's a lovely old French woman. Both her children and her husband were lost to German bombs. We pay her a few pennies a day, and she brings us breakfast. Fresh bread, tea, jam. It's just the thing to give you strength for the day." Actually, they paid Madame a few pennies a week, but Charlotte was willing to allow Alice (a complete stranger to poverty if one were to guess by her speech and her fine clothes) to pay the old woman more. Feeling a tinge of guilt at this small dishonesty, as well as at her harsh judgment of a young girl she hardly knew, she added, "Oh, she takes in washing as well."

Alice merely nodded behind her, a bit breathless from keeping up, focusing on her feet. She'd hate to tumble into the mud before her first day began.

Madame was outside their tent when they arrived, a rather forbidding woman with a thick mane of white hair framing a seamed face. When she smiled at the two young nurses, her forbidding nature receded like a cloud on a sunny day. "Bonjour!" she cried merrily, swinging a sack from her back and holding it open for them. She chattered at them in a refined French which Charlotte could follow only by focused concentration, an expenditure of energy she was loathe to allow. She listened long enough to introduce Alice and procure the girl a hefty, still-warm length of bread and jam. Kathleen, who was upright if not entirely awake, rounded up an extra mug, and Madame poured a draught of hot tea for Alice.

The two more seasoned nurses sat on the bunks and ate their breakfast while Alice dressed, shivering a bit in the morning chill. "You have never worked as hard as you will here," Charlotte warned.

"Yep," Kathleen agreed. "And you can't go wasting your energy."

Charlotte took another bite of the baguette. How did the old woman manage to make such delicious, fragrant bread under these circumstances? Had she found a dwelling amidst one of the ruined farm holds? In Charlotte's far-distant land, the bread was black, thick and grainy. She turned her attention back to the immediate moment, and the need to impart useful wisdom upon young Alice as quickly as possible. Base Hospital No. 12 needed good nurses. "You must learn to become as efficient as possible. Never take two steps when one will do."

The American nurse drank her tea loudly, and added, "When you're feeding the boys, relax your whole body except for your hand. When you feed them, sit on the beds instead of bending."

Alice stole a glance at them, her porcelain blue eyes widening. "On the bed? Is that really proper?"

Charlotte snorted into her own tea. "Those poor lads in hospital—many of them are going to die. Most of them worry about their families, their mothers especially. None of them have ever made an improper suggestion to me."

"Or me," Kathleen added. "Girl, you don't want to end up like some old, blown draft horse with bad knees and a back that aches in the winter."

Alice looked dubious. It seemed she was still considering the implications of sitting on a strange man's bed. Charlotte tried another tack. "You must learn to save your energy, Alice. The shifts are long. If you do not take care of yourself, you won't be able to help anyone."

Outside, there came the sound of boots hurrying along the duckboards. The steps halted outside the tent. Both Kathleen and Charlotte stood, while Alice hurriedly covered herself with the greatcoat. "Miss?" came a young boy's voice. "Miss, er, Bran. Bran—Brannie…"

Kathleen glanced at her friend, the mangled pronunciation of the last name a sure sign it was she they sought. "Yes, one moment, please," Charlotte called, loosening the laces on her boots. Fourteen hours of standing and walking would cause her feet to swell, and tight boots would be an agony.

The runner spoke again from outside. "Beg your pardon, Miss, but Doctor Hartford needs you right away. There's a big push at the front, and the CCS is being overwhelmed."

Doctor Hartford was the Senior Physician, the Medical Head of Base Hospital No. 12. It was the boy's information about the CCS that induced Charlotte to stop looking for her nurse's hat. The thing was a nuisance, anyway, and required large pins to keep in place. At the look on Alice's face, she explained, "Casualty Clearing Station. They're very close to the front." She raised her voice to the waiting runner. "I've not served at one before. Am I to bring anything?"

"No, Miss. Doctor H told me all the supplies would be in the lorry. But, please hurry."

So, it must be bad. It was always bad, but this must be worse than usual.

She found an old fur hat, a gift from one of her father's troopers when she was younger. It would keep her warm on the drive as the skies threatened rain. Kathleen held out Charlotte's heavy coat and helped her into it as Alice watched with an expression of great unease.

"Come along," Kathleen said to the new girl. "If they need Charlotte at the CCS, that means we're going to be busy as a one-armed paper hanger very soon." The American nurse was fond of such strange sayings. She gave

Charlotte a rough kiss on the cheek. "Hurry back, Cheri."

Charlotte purposefully shoved the fur hat a trifle askew over her thick black hair. She knew it made her look ridiculous, like a little girl playing dress-up. She hoped it would lighten the fear on Alice's face, and might mask her own uneasiness at the new assignment. "I should be back in a day or two. These things are usually over quickly."

Over quickly, yes. The assaults burned through men's lives as if they were the driest tinder thrown into a furnace. She slipped out of the tent into the purplish dawn where the runner was waiting. He was a boy of sixteen or seventeen, with bad spots on his face, and scars from the pox. She'd seen him before, usually with a cheerful smile, but now his mouth was small and pinched.

Later, historians would record the whole of the confused contest as the Battle of Passchendaele. In the space of little more than eighty days, three hundred and ten thousand British Expeditionary force soldiers died attacking a single village, while another quarter of a million German soldiers died defending the roughly five miles of land. It worked out to a cost of perhaps one hundred thousand souls per mile.

The number of those wounded, ruined, or maimed during that spasm of carnage was impossible to accurately calculate, but it was surely twice those who had perished. Later, most often in the night, Charlotte would imagine wearily that every one of those wounded men had passed through her CCS. It was hard to recall individual faces, and for the longest time, all but impossible to forget the pain that came with them.

However, there was one man she would remember very clearly.

Charlotte and the other members of the CCS team drove to the front in an ambulance, sitting in the back of the swaying lorry. The driver and his fellow medic sat exposed to the air on a bench seat, while the rear of the ambulance was a kind of large enclosed metal box that had glassed ports fore and aft. At least the lorry had a motor, and they were not being drawn by a team of dray horses, she thought as she clutched her seat, the better to keep from being propelled into the air while speeding along over what had once been a road.

Besides the CCS team, the ambulance was crammed with hastily assembled equipment: sterile tins of bandages, basins, tourniquets, adhesive tape, safety pins, iodine, disinfectants, medicines, ether, a folding bed, even an extra operating table. There were also gas masks and helmets, a tacit acknowledgment that no one, even doctors and nurses, was safe from the attack of the enemy.

"Very sensible," the Captain shouted over the crash and bang of the supplies as the ambulance toiled toward the fighting. Charlotte had never worked with him before. He was one of two doctors who had been selected for the team by Dr Hartford. The Captain was a red-faced, stout Englishman with oddly thick arms and a grey walrus moustache like that worn by the Kaiser.

The other physician, a tall, thin, wry Major by the name of Johnson, an American volunteer, gamely took the conversational bait. "How's that, Captain?"

Charlotte and the orderly held onto their benches as the ambulance lurched over the cow path that passed for a road. "They need this wagon at the front, Major. Best way for us both to get there without being shot to pieces by the Boche."

The boy orderly squeaked, "That's right, sir. The Huns would fire on a regular army lorry." He was the runner who had summoned her from her tent, a red-haired boy, just an inch or two taller than Charlotte, with crooked legs and pale skin that only made his spots more apparent.

The Captain turned a frosty eye on the boy orderly. The Captain's accent was a very precise, educated English. He didn't normally associate with those of the orderly's class.

The American Major patted the spot-faced boy on the knee. "Yes, they would, George. We've all seen it."

George, that was the orderly's name. She recalled it as soon as the American Doctor had said it. Charlotte shifted her body on the bench seat, trying to avoid giving herself a concussion by allowing her head to bounce off any of the metal parts around her. She and Major Johnson had already seen the bombed-out hulks of previous ambulances. The enemy didn't strafe humanitarian transport as a matter of course, but they had been known to do so on occasion.

The four medical personnel had been riding for six hours, only making hurried stops to attend to the necessaries before scrambling back to the scant safety of the ambulance. Charlotte's normally sturdy constitution was beginning to rebel from the jolting ride and the close quarters. She leaned forward to try to snatch a glance of the passing countryside through the dirty front windscreen.

She expected countryside, at least but beheld only a broken world, a landscape that might have been painted by Hieronymus Bosch. Instead of bird-headed imps torturing the damned or winged monstrosities flaying sinners, she saw bloated corpses of horses and lorries blown inside-out scattered like broken toys along the way. Abandoned artillery pieces littered the side of the road, barrels pointing to the sky like dead men's fingers. Greyness hovered over the world in spite of the sun that fought to shine through the clouds. It would rain soon, she thought, pitying the troops of soldiers marching along the road, heads down, smudged charcoal figures moving over the glutinous surface.

The air reeked, too, and Charlotte would never again be able to view one of poor, twisted, insane Bosch's canvases without feeling her nostrils prickle with the memory of that awful stench of petrol fumes and smoke, and the persistent undertone of decaying flesh.

Yet, she knew it would get worse.

George had followed her gaze outside the ambulance. He'd probably never seen the original Bosch, as had Charlotte, but no one could look on that shattered land and feel confident in the sanity of man, nor the mercy of the Almighty.

The young orderly blinked, trying to hide his nervousness. He was probably only a year younger than Charlotte, yet she felt like an elder matron next to him. She had been a Voluntary Aid Detachment (or VAD) nurse for three years, and George had only been at the hospital for a few months. And that facility was an oasis of order and stability compared to what they passed through.

"How close to the front will we be, sir?" George asked, trying to sound conversational.

"Anywhere from three to five miles from it," Major Johnson replied.

"Oh," George admitted. "I thought we would be right up among the fighting. I wondered why the Sister was coming with us."

Charlotte felt herself warming to the boy. He was terrified and trying so hard not to show it. "No, George," she told him. "Sisters can go no closer than a CCS."

"For their own good, lad," the Captain intoned. "We don't trust the bloody Hun around our nurses." He caught himself. "I beg your pardon, Miss, for my indelicate language."

She restrained a smile. The English and their illusions of the frailness of women. On her father's estate, she'd seen the peasant women in the fields, working as hard as the men and swearing with equal fluency. She nodded at the Captain. "Of course, sir. These are indelicate times."

Major Johnson extracted a pencil and scrap of paper from the breast pocket of his jacket. "See here, George," he said leaning forward, the paper in one palm, sketching a few lines on it. "There are front-line stations, usually less than an eighth of a mile from the front. The wounded are taken there first. The primary task is to keep the soldiers alive there. What kinds of actions would we take there?"

Charlotte wondered if the American doctor had been a teacher in America. He was trying to educate young George. The boy answered rotely, "Stop the bleeding. Make certain they can breathe proper. Splint the breaks, I think."

The Captain rumbled, "Stuff the internal organs back into the body cavities, very likely."

"Indeed," Major Johnson agreed mildly. "Some of the care we provide will be of the roughest kind. Only the most dire surgery will be undertaken, and only to save a life." He pointed to his sketch. "Bearers take the wounded men to the Advance Aid Station—about here—and the evaluation continues."

"I wanted to be a bearer," George blurted. The others looked at him, politely waiting for him to go on. "I had the rickets in my legs. The Army didn't think I'd be able to carry the stretchers."

He seemed as ashamed of this disease as if it were a moral failing. Charlotte wanted to comfort him, pat him like the little boy he seemed to her, but propriety forbade that gesture.

The bluff Captain surprised her by saying warmly, "Their error, lad. We'll get plenty of good use out of you, eh, Major?"

Dr Johnson nodded. "Of that, I have no doubt, Captain McDougal."

George blushed, and Charlotte did give him a sisterly nudge. There was a particularly hard lurch of the ambulance, and the Major lost his pencil. It skittered around their feet. Captain McDougal trapped it under a large boot, then handed it the American.

The Major nodded his thanks and pointed to his sketch. "And there is us, at the CCS. We will perform the major surgery there; stabilize the patients for transport to Hospital."

"And from there, England," Charlotte added.

The Captain leaned forward, turned his gaze first on Charlotte and then young George. "You'll be helping save lives. Did you ever think you'd do that when you were a boy, eh?"

"No, sir," George admitted. "Did you, Sister?"

Charlotte's mouth quirked. "No," she said, and then threw a hand forward to brace herself as the ambulance gave an especially powerful shuddering jolt.

"What did you want to do, Sister?" George persisted.

"My parents wished for me to be a ballerina," she said dismissively, thinking of those times so long ago in both miles and years, and of the terrifying dance classes when she was a tiny slip of a thing, called by her parents' serfs "Kisa", which was a word in the common tongue for a little kitten or the runt of the litter.

"Oh, my," George replied. "You are so very beautiful, Sister, you would have looked like a lady out of a painting up there on stage. Wouldn't she, sir?" he added, asking of the Captain.

"Well, yes, quite," the English doctor agreed uncomfortably.

She looked away, embarrassed by the unexpected praise. An awkward conversational lag filled the rear of the ambulance. Charlotte could not speak, lest she be seen as inviting additional flattery. The two officers remained silent, to avoid the appearance of paying court to this young woman who was under their protection. And poor George, Charlotte noted, his face grew red and his spots stood out in harsher relief as he realized the breach of good manners he had committed.

The Captain and the Major turned to one another and began an earnest discussion about the best way to resect a bowel. Charlotte risked a pat on George's knee and a whispered, "It's all right."

Distant booms reached their ears. The American doctor put away his pencil and the scrap. "We're getting closer now. Put on your helmets."

George leaned over and found the tinpot helmets in a musette bag next to the gas-masks. He passed them to the others without a word. Charlotte reluctantly removed her wonderfully warm cap and settled the heavy, cold metal of the helmet on her head. The straps dangled on either side of her face. The Captain leaned over and fastened the buckle for her. "Don't want that coming loose just when you need it, Sister," he said.

"Thank you, sir," she replied, pulling back. She hadn't liked the feeling of him brushing her skin. His fingers were thick and blunt, not what one would expect of a surgeon. It wasn't the Captain himself that had made her uncomfortable, as much as the way he'd done it…mechanically, without a care or warmth. She had not been touched with compassion in such a long time. The poor wounded souls she tended each day grasped at her, clutched her arms and hands, but it was with their own need for comfort, for reassurance. In so many long months, no one had held her; no one had been strong that she might, just for a while, be weak.

Feeling the prickle of tears, Charlotte looked down at her lap, angrily blinking her eyes. Where was this coming from, this morbid outbreak of self-pity? Poor little Charlotte, away from home and estates in a strange land. It had been nearly seven years since her parents, fearing both the ineptness of the Tsar and the dangerous unrest encouraged by the Bolsheviks, had installed their youngest daughter in one of the better boarding schools in England. Charlotte forced the unseemly thoughts from her mind in a few moments by castigating herself, cataloguing all she had when compared to the brave lads she'd seen with their horrifying wounds and their hearty cheerfulness. Thoroughly chastised, she took a deep breath and straightened her back. Enough of that.

The others had not noticed her silence. The three of them instead were peering anxiously through the windscreen of the ambulance, consulting a map, then looking outside once again.

The distant booms were louder now. She could both hear and feel them vibrating through the sheet metal sides of the ambulance. The driver, a lad not a year older than George, called back over the back of the bench seat, "We'll get you as close as we can. The Huns are playing merry hell with their big guns."

The doctors stared at the driver dumbly, as if laboriously translating his speech from a language they had not yet mastered into something they could comprehend. Another blast from the road and the sides of the ambulance shivered like a tuning fork.

Charlotte turned to George. "Where did you pack the

surgical supplies?"

The orderly answered with a feeble gesture toward the front of the compartment, to the shelves and bins on either side. "There…" he replied uncertainly.

She addressed the two doctors. "Sirs! Gather up your surgical tools. George, pass them out. With a will, George!" The sharpness of that last sentence stung the boy into action. He scrambled forward on his knees and began shifting parcels until he uncovered two sturdy wood cases, the surgeon's personal operating tools. The resemblance of the wooden cases of fine surgical steel to a carpenter's toolbox would not occur to her until long hours after their tour of the CCS had passed.

The sight of George in motion brought the two officers out of their state of stricken contemplation and back to themselves. The Captain tore open a paper-wrapped package of supplies and began filling the pockets of his own greatcoat with catgut and bandages. The American Major seized on the idea and began shoving ampoules of morphine at George, who took them and began securing them about his person with enthusiasm.

In the space of three more bomb blasts, a kind of gunpowder metronome, the four had stuffed as many supplies as they could into their pockets, aprons, boot tops, and even, in the case of George, under his helmet. They crouched in the back of the ambulance, additional tools clutched very tightly in their hands: surgical cases for the medical officers, with drainage basins and a bone saw under their arms.

The ambulance shuddered to a halt. Another bomb exploded, somewhere behind them. The rear doors of the lorry flexed. Everyone inside the vehicle cried out at the punishing pressure change hammering at their eardrums. The wind screen in front of the drivers shattered, ripped forward by the vacuum of the passing blast. Charlotte instinctively threw her hands over her face against the possibility of shards of glass

The driver scrambled out of his seat and wrenched open the rear doors of the ambulance. "Road's gone!" he shouted, himself a bit deafened by the nearby explosion, grabbing the folding operating table and hoisting it to his shoulder. The other ambulanceman appeared beside him. "Follow me! Reggie will bring the rest of your kit!"

George hopped out first and extended a hand to assist Charlotte. It was faster to allow him help her down than refuse, so she took his palm and lowered herself to uneven ground. It was nearing dusk, and a cool moist wind was blowing, bringing the strange scent of muddy earth and another acrid, burnt odour she would soon enough learn was the sign of a bomb blast. Reggie, the other ambulance man, shoved a random parcel into her arms before clambering past her into the lorry. Her clothes stuffed with supplies, and now this paper-wrapped package in her hands, she wondered how she would be able to run. At least she had resisted the temptation to strap packages to her legs under her skirt.

There came a high pitched, sharp sound that teased at the edge of her punished hearing. Major Johnson and Captain McDougal scrambled out of the back of the lorry, one thin and spindly, the other shorter and stout, a sight that in other circumstances might have raised a smile. Not at this time, however. Each was rewarded with additional packages shoved into their arms by Reggie.

"Come along!" the driver shouted again, and now Charlotte could distinguish the sound of gunfire and muted explosions. The driver plunged down the muddy road, head turning from left to right just above the table balanced awkwardly on his shoulder.

"How close to the line are we?" she asked as she followed him.

"Too damned close," he answered, before adding in an encouraging shout, "Look lively there!"

She looked as lively as she could, blundering along with vials clacking together in her bosom, bulging from her pockets, and packets of catgut and needles stuffed into the tops of her ugly boots. The high-pitched noise of which she had only been partly aware suddenly precipitated into machine gunfire that sounded perilously close, and she was sprayed with a dusting of mud and dirt from an explosion whose source was out of her sight. Both sensations spurred her to new levels of liveliness, and, she presumed from the harsh breathing behind her, the artillery and weapons reports had a similar effect on the other members of her team.

She followed the ambulance driver up a muddy path that was scored two or more feet into the ground. Debris lay underfoot and when she stumbled she was thrown against the side of the path. Pushing herself upright, she saw that her hand had come to rest beside the decaying face of a corpse that half-jutted from the earth like a large stone. English, French, German, she could not tell. A small sound escaped from her and then was bitten off angrily before it could turn into some useless, girlish shriek. Charlotte stood, resisting the sudden urge to spit like a consumptive as she realized the very air she breathed was full of death.

From behind, another explosion rocked the ground, and she realized she was on her knees. She looked up. An older, bespectacled man in a heavy jacket, rubber apron, and over-sized rubber boots came shambling heavily toward them. Everything he wore was splashed and speckled in blood. Seen on a Piccadilly street corner, he might have been a butcher out for a pint. Here, it marked him as a surgeon. "Come along, Sister," the white-haired surgeon said, taking her arm and pulling Charlotte to her feet. "You're needed."

"Of course, Doctor," she replied. "The driver was leading the way." She gestured with her head toward the driver, struggling along with the folding surgical bed. She didn't look back down the path. She could not bear to know what might have happened to the rest of her team.

Nodding at the driver, the surgeon said, "Yes, good lads, those." He led her further up the path. They crested a slight rise to reveal a depression in the ground that contained a tent which spanned perhaps forty feet across. "We are most glad to see you," the man said, "the rest of the CCS staff are played out."

For a moment, Charlotte faltered. During her training, she'd seen a model Casualty Clearing Station. It had been a clean, straight structure, with wooden walls and a canvas roof, equipped with electric lights, glassed windows, operating tables in neat rows. It had also been blessedly empty, calm, and quiet.

Here was simply a large canvas tent staked to the ground with heavy iron pegs. Linens were draped over the stay lines, apparently drying. Wounded men were piled around the tent before her. They sprawled on stretchers, or slumped in the mud, their bandages caked with blood. The sight of the blood struck her…she was seeing it as if on a magic-lantern show, the life cycle of blood outside the body. From the bright red seeping steadily into a bandage wrapped around an arm (likely a severed artery), to the darker hue of older haemoglobin drying on a wad of bandages across a misshapen face, to the flat brownish of clotting and scabbing. It was all there before her in the mud of France. And even as she watched, more wounded were coming, carried by bearers, stumbling under their own power, or being led by their less-seriously wounded fellows.

God alone knew how many wounded soldiers already crowded the interior of the tent. There was nothing for it but to plunge in. She turned to the unnamed doctor who'd led her thus far. "Which table is ours?"

"There's an empty one toward the back of the hut. No one wants it…too close to the trenches. Bursting shells have been known…"

"We'll take it. Send the others there." She clutched the various medical supplies closer to her and waddled toward the tent. Her ungainly and most indelicate stride reminded her incongruously of a peasant woman she'd seen smuggling chickens back to her hovel by stuffing the poor creatures into her leggings beneath the skirt.

The wounded men brightened at the sight of her, and they murmured among themselves as if she were a special visitor. One of the soldiers, a younger man in wet clothing, with old eyes and a drawn face, a crude splint on his upper left arm and a filthy sticking plaster upon the left cheek, knelt in the dirt beside the man with the misshapen, bandaged face. "There's the Sister," the younger soldier said in a clear, calm voice to the bandaged man. "She'll set you right." Then, strangely, the young soldier climbed to his feet in a gesture of unmistakable respect. "Sister," he said formally, lowering his head. "It is a pleasure to meet you, Miss."

She blinked at him in astonishment. Amidst the noise, the moaning of the wounded, the shrieking of the shells, the ground rumbling at the explosions, his behaviour was absurd, if not insane. He seemed to be waiting for her to say something.

Perhaps it was the blood all around her, a metallic

stench she could clearly smell over the tang of gunpowder and decay. Perhaps it was the vials of morphine digging into the tender flesh of her bosom, but she snapped at him, "This is no time for chivalry!"

There were explosions further behind them. She glanced back and noted the path was heaped with clods of dirt. George the orderly risked a peek over the mound and waved reassuringly at her. The rest of the team were still among the living but delayed for the moment.

The young soldier with the old eyes never flinched. He gazed on her, not staring exactly, but seeming to look deep into her. "Why, Sister," he said with gentle courtesy, "this is when we need chivalry the most."

It was the strangest thing he could have said, but it brought her back to herself and to her immediate duty. She had no time to regret her sharp words now. "Then, Sir Knight," she said, "help me with this man." She was already moving toward the soldier with the severed artery.

Her Knight merely said, "Yes, Miss," and strode over, dropping to one knee.

For a moment, she thought the man mad and kneeling to her in his delusion of chivalry and knighthood. But no, he called over his shoulder, "Climb aboard, there's a good fellow. Our Lady Sister is here for you."

The bleeding soldier crept forward and draped himself over her Knight's shoulders. The Knight stood, surprising her with his strength, and said, "Lead on, my Lady Sister."

Clutching the precious supplies to her, Charlotte threaded her way into the tent, skirting patients slumped on the floor or supine in rough stretchers. The operating tables had been laid out in two rows of five, and every one of the tables, save the one farthest from the entrance, were in use. There was gore everywhere, blobs and chunks of what had been men's flesh and sinew and bone. Their boots made sucking sounds as they trod upon the sticky fragments.

Four-person teams crowded around their own tables, bloody to the elbows if not higher. At least one person from each table spared them a hasty glance, evaluating the condition of the two soldiers with her, and then dropped their eyes back to the more grievously wounded men on the tables before them. The sound inside the tent was a symphony of pain, unlike anything she'd heard before. Moans, sharp shrieks, weeping. And under it, the sound of the physicians at their frantic work—steely directions, rasp of saws, snick of scalpels, reassuring words faint under the din.

She hurried to the passably clean table at the front of the tent, where she could clearly see the small holes in the canvas, the fabric rent by passing shrapnel. She swept her arm across the table, wiping away the pebbles and dirt that had landed there from previous blasts.

"Place him here," she said to the Knight. The chivalrous young man's face was a bit white now, moisture on his brow. He took a breath before easing the other soldier from his back and laying him on the table. The wounded soldier gave a grunt of pain.

"Are you well, Mister—?" Charlotte asked, trying to examine both men at once.

"Fitzgerald, my Lady Sister, Lieutenant Robert Fitzgerald at your service," he said with a slight smile through the sweat on his face. "Our friend here needs your attention much more than I."

How odd, she thought. When her Knight spoke, she could hear him clearly and plainly, even through the sounds of pain that surrounded them. "As you wish, Mr. Fitzgerald." She leaned closer to him, lowered her voice so the man on the table would not hear. Fitzgerald cocked his head to Charlotte as she went on, "You must help me, sir. It will not be pleasant."

Fitzgerald nodded, leaning over the wounded man. When he did, she could see the blood on his back, shed by the soldier he'd carried. "See here, old thing, the Sister will help you now. You'll be a brave lad, eh?"

The soldier replied in a thick voice, "Yes, sir."

She reached into her boot top, found a packet of catgut. A quick glance back through the tent told her every physician was busy, and there was no sign of her team at the entrance. She edged over to the closest operating table. "Needle," she said in a tone that carried no request. The aged nurse at the table glanced up, saw the situation in a moment, and slipped two curved needles to Charlotte without missing a beat.

Charlotte took a slow breath, gathering her thoughts, ignoring her fear. If she gave in to her lack of courage, her patient would die. "Hold him still," she said to Fitzgerald, who complied without question, taking the bleeding soldier by the shoulders. Her Knight, curiously, turned his right ear toward her, rather than look directly at her.

She needed a tourniquet to slow or stop the man's bleeding long enough to repair the vessel. She unwound a bit of the bloody bandage from the man's arm, tore a length of it free. She took Fitzgerald's nearest hand, pressed it over the wound. "Squeeze here." The solider on the table stiffened at the sudden pressure but made no sound.

"Good lad," Fitzgerald murmured, his thumb pressing against the artery and keeping the soldier from bleeding to death. While he did, Charlotte deftly took several turns of bloody bandage around the upper arm of the wounded soldier above the gash, then cinched it tight with a broken scalpel scooped from the floor before tying off the ends to prevent the tourniquet from unravelling.

"Now, sir," she said, tearing the fabric of the sleeve and laying the wounded arm bare, "You must hold the ends of the blood vessel so I may sew it up."

"My hands are vile, Sister," Fitzgerald said softly.

She had almost forgotten. Her own hands were covered in the noxious mud of the battleground, as well. She located a glass jug of mentholated spirits under their table. She splashed the clear, shockingly cold liquid over their hands, allowing it to dribble on the floor at their feet. She rubbed her hands briskly, actions which Fitzgerald copied. "This will sting," she said apologetically to the wounded man, who gave the slightest of nods—a nod which suddenly stopped when she poured a draught into the wound, partially to cleanse it, and partially to clear away the blood.

She could see the gash inside his biceps clearly. Some of the muscle has been cut, but most dire was the slash in the brachial artery. Her hands were small, her fingers delicate, and in a moment she had fished the artery out of the wound and gently stretched it clear of the man's arm. She had seen the surgeons do this, and knew the arteries of younger men possessed some elasticity. Of course, the surgeons she had observed had the benefit of years of training and were being assisted by skilled nurses.

"That feels bloody odd," the wounded man said between clenched teeth as she teased the artery into position. Tears of pain carved trails in the dirt on his face. Remembering himself, he said, "Miss."

"Mr. Fitzgerald," she said in a much steadier voice than she expected. "Please hold either side of the vessel as close to his skin as you can. Do not put any additional tension on it. Do not stretch it any further."

"Yes, Miss," he answered. His hands were much larger

than her own, and with his fingers clamped on either side of the artery, there was just barely room for her to work. She took the curved needle, threaded it with the speed born of years as a nurse, and began to carefully suture the side of the drooping reddish cylinder before her, her face close to the open wound. She could not rush, nor could she jerk when an explosion sounded worrisomely close outside. The delicate stitching brought to mind some of the mindless "lady's work" she had been forced to do as a young Countess in training, embroidering pillows and other frippery while the older women gossiped about the Tsarina and Rasputin. None of what she had done had been as important as this, and she was grateful for the skill the meaningless work had provided her.

She glanced up once at Mr. Fitzgerald, whose face was close to hers. His skin was blanched, and she thought he was squeamish at the surgery. He gave her a fleeting smile. "Looking splendid, my Lady."

She returned her attention to the artery. In a few moments, she had closed the gap in the blood vessel. She slipped her smallest finger behind the artery. "You may let go now, Mr. Fitzgerald." He opened his fingers gently and eased them away from the wound. His fingertips were sticky with blood. "Please, loosen the tourniquet. Slowly."

A wince of pain flashed across his face as he straightened from the crouch he had assumed over the table. Without comment, he loosed the ends of the bandage around the soldier's upper arm and unwound the scalpel a turn or two. Beneath her finger, the artery expanded and began to pulse. She wiped at the stitches with her finger. No leakage.

"Excellent work," a familiar voice said behind her. It was Captain McDougal, face red, moustache dusty, but otherwise intact. Behind crowded George and Major

Johnson, equally as winded and dirty. "I'll close up now, Sister."

Fitzgerald bent over the prone soldier, whose face was ashen grey. "Bravely done, lad."

The soldier tried to speak, licked dry lips, and managed to rasp out, "Thank you, sir. Thank you, Miss."

Captain McDougal boomed, "Well, our little respite is over. Let's put our backs into it, shall we?"

Around her, George and Major Johnson began to empty their pockets of supplies. Charlotte knew she must organize the equipment on the table so the team might begin helping the wounded hordes outside, but felt she must spare a moment for her Knight.

She moved around the table and took his blood-spotted hands in her own. "My thanks, Mr. Fitzgerald." She wanted to add *You were truly my knight,* but that sounded giddy and foolish in her mind, so it went unsaid.

Fitzgerald raised her hand and bent over it, but was enough of a gentleman not to actually press his lips to her skin like some of the crass French nobles she'd dodged at court in Saint Petersburg. "Then I take my leave," he said, addressing them all. The three men gave him searching looks, for his manner of speech was so unexpected in this place as to seem disordered. "There are a bevy of the lads who need you much more than I. Perhaps I'll take the evening air." He dropped her hand and walked unsteadily toward the rear of the tent, stepping over stretchers and around huddled men.

"Odd fellow," Captain McDougal commented, taking his position by the side of the supine soldier.

"Splint on his humerus," observed the American doctor. "Must've hurt like blazes to have held his arm in that position when he was assisting."

Oh, Jesu, Charlotte thought. *I'd forgotten.* For a moment, bitter Russian imprecations echoed through her mind, but Captain McDougal called her. "Sister, a number four needle and more catgut for this muscle, and you, George, fetch us the next lad."

Dismissing her failure from her mind, Charlotte turned to work before her.

The Battle of Passchendaele lasted, by official accounts, 86 days. The early days of the contest were enumerated in inches of advance, yards of ground lost, in the numbers of the wounded and the slain. For the men battling over those inches of advance, the minute upon dreary minutes of fear and terror and rage can only be imagined, and inadequately at that.

During the first days of the battle, Charlotte and George, the Doctors Johnson and McDougal, all worked 16 hours at a time, stumbling like drunkards from the CCS tent to smaller tents further from the front, to fall into cots and sleep like the dead, too weary to eat or wash.

Yet, during those long hours in the increasingly shredded CCS tent, to the wounded soldiers who came before them these weary men and that young woman were the very face of God, offering the warriors, if not redemption, then at least another chance. For Charlotte, God seemed very far away. She thought she'd seen terrible sights in the hospital, but now she realized that the most grievously wounded had perished in places like the CCS, or worse, in the tent they called the Moratoriums, where those who were beyond the aid of the physicians were placed to die. Quiet tears were shed by the nurses and orderlies carrying mortally wounded men into that final earthly shelter, but all knew it freed the medical personnel to give their attention to those they might yet save.

And still, the parade of wrecked humanity passed

beneath her hands. It was like working in the forges of Hell, witnessing every cruel result of demonic will exercised upon mere flesh and blood. When the twisted, maimed soldiers began to fade in her consciousness as individual human beings made in a Holy image and began to resemble thrashing, quivering bags of meat, Charlotte forced herself to remember the beauty in the world.

Before she'd come to England, less than seven years ago as a mere girl of twelve, her family had toured the Continent. A stop in Rome included a visit to the Sistine Chapel. Electric lights had only recently been installed in the Chapel, revealing the damage from centuries of candles and torches. A generous donation from her father had allowed the two of them to carefully climb the scaffolding to high above the floor where workmen reverently cleaned decades of soot from Michelangelo's masterpiece. Heedless of ruining her dress and ignoring the castigations of her governess, she lay flat on the wide wooden plank, staring upward in awe at the glorious figures emerging from the darkened grime. After a time her eyes watered. She was unsure if she was weeping or if her eyes teared from straining so hard to see everything that was before her in this moment. She could not credit that something so wondrous had been made by the hands of men.

As she worked and struggled to keep breath and life in the ruined men on the operating table, she was continually reminded how the hands of man could as easily make a hell on earth, even as she used the memory of the Chapel in Rome as a talisman to push away despair. Once or twice, in the scant seconds before she fell asleep, Charlotte remembered the man with the broken arm who had assisted her in those first moments in the CCS tent. Fitzwilliam? Fitz-something. She had heard too many names, and her exhausted brain could not recall what name the man had given. *The Knight,* she thought sleepily. *His hands...his hands had been used to make heaven real, if only for a moment for a single soldier. What had become of her Knight?*

On the thirteenth day of the battle for Passchendaele, a new complement of medical personnel appeared. Charlotte and George were outside at the time, retching. The desperate Germans had once more resorted to using gas, and the vile substance wafted from the wounded, from their hair and clothing. The four members of her team took turns bolting from the blood-drenched operating table, either to empty their stomachs or fill their lungs with relatively untainted air. Although she mentioned it to no one, the frequent trips gave her an excuse to leave the perpetual pain of the CCS tent, to step away for a moment and see something besides suffering. Most of the artillery had fallen silent as commanders on both sides pondered how best to carry on, and she could hear the wind; feel a lingering touch of a fresh breeze on her cheek. She raised her face just after vomiting and in the ringing silence heard a lone bird singing as it soared overhead.

The new team passed her on the way into the tattered CCS tent, and she all but stared at them. In their spotless clothes, their recently-washed faces and hair, their general air of energy and alertness, they might well have been missionaries from a distant land. Charlotte dabbed at her mouth with an unavoidably filthy kerchief and pushed herself upright.

George met her at the entrance to the tent. "We're being relieved. We're leaving!"

"When?" she asked in a thick, rusty voice she did not recognize as her own.

"Within the hour, Sister," George replied happily.

"We must pack," she insisted.

"There's nothing to take. Not even the operating table. Come, Sister, did you not recognize Dr Petersen? Or Matron?"

Charlotte had worked with both those worthies for over a year, yet they had not registered on her dull consciousness when they passed. Angry at her own weakness, she shook her head, forcing herself to concentrate. "Very well, George. I will speak to Matron, you must speak to—"

"Liam," he said, supplying the name of the new orderly, and followed her back into the tent.

Within the tent, the four doctors were conferring while Matron, a plumpish nurse with steel-grey hair many years her senior in knowledge and experience, inventoried and arranged the supplies scattered about the dirty operating table.

Matron raised a frosty eye when Charlotte joined her. Charlotte curtsied. an old habit. "It's been a right dog's breakfast here," Matron observed.

"Yes, mum," Charlotte admitted, wondering how to explain the mess, how to make the older woman understand what it had been like. How the surgical instruments had been cleansed by throwing them into a basin of spirits that was then lighted so it blazed like a plum pudding, how the table had been washed between patients by dashing it with a bucket of the cleanest water they could find, water that Charlotte would have scrupled to give to a thirsty pig.

Matron stretched forth a hand, patted her on the cheek. "Don't fret, Cheri. I served in the Boer War. I know you did what you could."

Charlotte blinked away the sudden tears in her eyes. "Thank you, Mum."

"Now, tell me what to expect."

"We're in a lull, now, Mum. They're bringing in survivors, soldiers they lost for a time between the attacks." Or those who had the strength to crawl back to their lines when the bombardments had ceased, dragging broken limbs behind them.

Matron mused on that as her wrinkled fingers sorted and cleaned. "Poor devils have been out there for days, then, before we see them. A great deal of dehydration and sepsis, I imagine."

"Yes, Mum. And gas gangrene."

"Foul disease." Matron contemplated the operating table before her. "You've done well, Nurse. I thank God that we have young brave women like you."

Charlotte ducked her head again and gave an automatic respectful curtsey again. "Oh, do stop that, girl," Matron said tartly but not unkindly. "I'm not the King. Now, gather your people and go. The ambulance is waiting."

Base Hospital No. 12

The ambulance did not take them directly back to their post at Hospital No. 12. Instead, it transported the four weary veterans of the CCS to an older brick hospital near the coast, at Rouen. All of them had fallen asleep in the rear of the bouncing, jolting ambulance. Charlotte had used bandages to tie herself and George to the stanchions of the vehicle to keep from being tossed like tenpins as it drove. When the rocking ceased, the passengers opened heavy eyes, trying to comprehend their location.

They were each helped out of the ambulance by gentle hands. Two older nurses guided Charlotte to a small room containing a narrow bed and compact chest of drawers.

She stood swaying, staring at the bed. "Here you are, luv," one said to her. "You rest for a while. Would you like a bath?" Charlotte shook her head slowly. She was so weary, she feared she'd relax in the bath, doze, and then drown. As if she were a small sleepy child, the two quiet nurses undressed her with great delicacy and gave her a clean cotton nightdress.

The old nurse sat her on the bed and sponged the Russian girl's grimy arms and hands with a warm cloth before tucking her under the coverlet. "There's always someone in the hall," the old nurse said. "You call if need anything. The loo is just through there," and she pointed at the wooden door in the opposite wall. She leaned closer and lowered her voice. "It's French, so it's not very nice." Then the nurse kissed Charlotte on the forehead. "Sleep now, luv."

And Charlotte did.

She remained in bed for almost two days, rising only to use the lavatory and eat. Nurses fed her a rich, thick soup, and then she would sleep again. The first older nurse seemed to have developed a personal interest in Charlotte's well-being, for on the morning of the second day, the elderly woman was in the room changing the sheets when Charlotte returned from the communal bath, wearing a heavy hospital gown for modesty's sake, with a towel restraining her wet hair. "Tsk, you'll catch your death like that."

Her thoughts slow and languorous, Charlotte was still inclined to agree. For all the kindness of the attending nurses, the old brick building had an echoing, empty feeling, the ceilings high and the bare rooms always chilly.

The older woman gave Charlotte a clean nightdress to wear and helped tug it over her head. "You pop back into bed, missy, there's a good girl." Under the sheets, delicious warmth radiated. Someone, probably the old nurse, had slipped a hot water bottle into the foot of the bunk. Already relaxed from the bath and the luxurious feeling of being completely clean for the first time in over four weeks, as she lay back on the pillow Charlotte's breathing deepened almost immediately. The older nurse took a clean towel and began drying Charlotte's hair. Charlotte was awake just long enough to feel a gentle comb across her scalp and out to the ends of her hair, and then she was aware of nothing.

On their return to Base Hospital No. 12, the members of the CCS team were greeted warmly by their fellows. Kathleen gave her a tremendous hug, sweeping her round. "I missed you!" she brayed in her hearty American accent. She took a closer look at her returned friend. "You look rode hard and put away wet."

Charlotte laughed. "I doubt that's a compliment."

Kathleen chuckled in return, shaking her head. "No, ma'am, it is not." She smothered Charlotte in another hug. "It's good to see you. Alice has been working nights, and that's aces by me. Alice is nice enough, but she's —"

"Reserved?" Charlotte offered.

"Stuck up," Kathleen replied, using another American expression Charlotte had not heard before, but whose meaning she grasped quickly.

Charlotte took the blanket from her own cot. "Maybe she's simply afraid," she said in a moment of charity. She stepped outside the tent and gave the blanket a good shake. Her things inside the tent were dusty and needed cleaning, but she knew that some of the men she'd seen at the CCS, those who'd survived, were inside Hospital, needing trained hands. Cleaning up could wait. There were soldiers to heal.

After a quick breakfast provided by the mysterious Madame, who had enveloped her with sandpapery kisses on either cheek, Charlotte and Kathleen tottered along the duckboards toward Hospital. The rude wooden structure, which may have been horse stables in the time of Henry V, seemed the very model of modernity and order after the chaos of the front and the CCS. The wooden walls and ceiling, firmly planked floor, glassed windows, and electric lights were most welcome.

George was outside with a bucket of red paint, whistling as he walked. Every Base Hospital was easily identified from the air by the presence of two large red crosses in a circle of white on either side of the main buildings. It was almost impossible to not identify a hospital from above. At Base Hospital No. 12, the crosses had been made from piled stones, and it was these that George was painting, freshening up the colour. When he noticed the two nurses, he looked up. There were dark smudges under his eyes, made especially obvious by his pale skin. He gave a cheery wave of the paintbrush and returned to his work.

"Was it very horrible?" Kathleen asked after more carefully considering George's face.

"Yes," Charlotte said simply and spoke no more.

They entered the hospital building by the side door. Most of the patients were still asleep, and thus a peaceful quiet filled the air, with undertones of serious, purposeful movement in the background. Striding through the wards, Charlotte could see at a glance that many of her previous charges were gone, moved on, she hoped, to England or "old Blighty" as some of them called it. Musing on those departures, she stopped in a hallway, peering at a group of the wounded men. Kathleen noticed her lagging behind and turned inquiringly. Charlotte shook her head and caught up with the American girl.

She didn't tell Kathleen of the sorrowful insight that filled her. When walking the wards, she had noticed the changes based on the injuries presented, not because of the individuals in the beds. The first bed had been occupied by a man missing his lower jaw. Now it was used by a boy with burns on his legs. It saddened her to realize she knew her patients by their wounds.

The two young women relieved the night nurses at the bandage station. From further down the hall, Alice saw them, gave them a quick nod, and hurried away as soon as the pass down was complete.

"See?" whispered Kathleen melodramatically at the young nurse's quick departure, but she was only larking about. Charlotte shushed her.

As ever, the quantity of work and the details of the morning quickly consumed the Russian nurse. She found it oddly unsettling to be working in the relative peace of the Hospital, and at a pace that was not entirely a frantic sprint with men's lives hanging in the balance. Not that there was time to dawdle. When she had first arrived at Base Hospital No. 12, she and the others had been expecting a facility with 500 beds. They were greeted by a structure with the capacity for over 2000 wounded. In her section alone, Charlotte was responsible for anywhere from 30 to 40 wounded men during her shift.

She made a quick circuit of her ward, greeting those men who were already awake. The night nurses had left the ward in good condition, clean, and nothing out of place. An old French man, Gustav, was the orderly, and he would assist her during the day. He was a dear fellow, perhaps a bit simple, and some of the other nurses had suggested with a gleam of wickedness in their eyes, that he and Madame were secretly lovers. It was a silly conceit, but not truly malicious, and as it could give a weary nurse a fleeting reason to smile, no one seemed to mind.

Charlotte began her morning by taking the men's temperatures. It gave her a moment to review their charts, and to begin mentally planning the rest of her day. Gustav assisted with face-washing and mouth rinsing. He also aided the men in using their bedpans. Some of them were quite shy about this around the younger nurses, and it was simply easier to have the old gentleman help them. During those private moments, Charlotte would retire to the surgical dressings room to roll bandages or tidy the other stores.

At roughly half-past eight, the ward doctor would

arrive. This morning, Captain McDougal was on duty, appearing a bit more refreshed than when last seen operating on semi-conscious patients in the CCS. Then, even his moustache had drooped as with fatigue. He gave Charlotte a most respectful nod, recognition of their recent shared battle against the shadow and began his rounds with her at his side. As these men were several days post-surgery, the review was brief, mostly to check on the state of their wounds or evaluate them for additional surgical intervention. He made comments or issued new directions for care, which she duly noted in their charts.

His review concluded, the Captain checked his pocket chronometer, said loudly, "Due in Surgery within the hour," and raced off, reminding her a bit of the White Rabbit. Smiling at the image, Charlotte began the real work of the day, which dealt with the dressings.

The wounds had to be tended. Her initial training had shown her how to apply a bandage and cotton padding correctly, that is, not so tightly as to cut off circulation, nor so loosely as to slip free. Rare was the day when her only concern about a bandage was its fit.

No, here, near the front, there were drains to be replaced, shrapnel to be dug out before it was encased in scar tissue, ghastly wounds to be washed and cavities to be repacked with gauze. There were still times she wanted to weep, either at the bravery of some boy who would stoically endure having a brutal bath of antiseptic applied to a gaping fissure in his body, or at the horrors wrought upon their flesh. She would not dishonour these men with tears, not in front of them.

She began by cleaning and rebandaging the most complicated wounds, while her energy was high and her concentration strong, for even a small oversight could bring on infection and then death. Before she knew it, the bell was ringing for soup. Gustav pushed a clattering tray into the ward, and most of the men perked up. She washed her hands and helped him serve the lads. Some of them could feed themselves, others needed assistance. Charlotte stopped by each bed and encouraged them to eat heartily, for she knew their bodies required nourishment to help rebuild themselves. Most of the boys, she knew, would go home, so grievous were their wounds, and she was glad for the ones who would escape the devil's forge.

In later years, she'd remember it was the soup that sent her down the corridor that day.

Gustav found her as she was lifting a spoon to a blind soldier's mouth. "Mademoiselle," he whispered urgently. As he was a bit deaf, his whisper carried clearly across the ward. "We are out of soup!"

"Indeed?" she asked, wiping the blind boy's mouth.

"We are missing at least two bowls, Mademoiselle!" Gustav replied, near tears.

Gustav was a fine gentleman, but he was old. She leaned forward and said to the blind boy in a confiding way, "Can you be a dear, and let Gustav finish feeding you? That way I can fetch the soup. It would be so helpful to me." She had found that the wounded men invariably responded positively if they felt they were being of use. She surmised that it moved them from their role of "invalid" and back toward being individuals capable of action and intention.

The blind boy nodded, turning blank, scarred eyes upon her out of habit, and said, "Of course, Sister."

She handed the bowl to Gustav and strode down the hall. The kitchen was somewhat centrally located, and she was sure she would be able to return to her ward before Gustav finished feeding the blind soldier. She hurried down the main corridor, already thinking of the afternoon to come, mentally scheduling the injections and massages when her steps faltered and she stopped without realizing she had done so.

Charlotte heard her Knight speaking.

"Of course, send him in right in, Miss," her Knight was saying from the ward to her right. "It will be good to see him."

A strange, almost electric flare of feeling ran through her abdomen and up her sternum at the sound of his voice. It was the most peculiar sensation. She found herself thinking again of his hands. Those rough hands that had been so precise and delicate when helping her during that impromptu surgery. How gently that same rough hand had cradled her own when he bent over her in chivalrous homage.

With an almost guilty start, she came back to herself. The memories, the flaring sensation, the odd thoughts; all had raced through her at almost the same time, and what had seemed like minutes of peculiar reverie had likely only been seconds.

"Soup," she said aloud, and a bit sternly. There were two men in her ward who needed their soup. Even as she strode away with a wilfully determined step, she was noting the number of the ward that housed her Knight.

After feeding the soldiers, and after her own hasty meal was complete, Charlotte left the ward in the capable hands of Gustav for a few moments. She felt she must speak to her Knight. She was slightly ashamed she could not recall his name, nor did she think her brief words of gratitude to him in the tent had been adequate. She needed to offer more articulate words of thanks, she thought as she gathered up a bundle of dirty bandages. She would drop those off at the laundry, and then she would properly express her appreciation to the kind gentleman.

She placed the soiled linens on a wheeled cart and pushed it briskly down the hall toward the laundry. She had told no one of the encounter at the front lines. She'd not had the time, really. And she was loath to discuss the horrors of the CCS with the other nurses. It felt unseemly, somehow, almost boastful, for the other nurses saw their own share of unspeakable damage to the human frame and soul.

She passed Kathleen on the way, and, oddly, Charlotte ducked her head and pretended not to notice her tent mate. She and Kathleen were close, as that sort of thing went here, but they'd never shared girlish secrets, and for some reason, Charlotte's desire to see the Knight felt like a selfish indulgence. In a word, she felt guilty about leaving her post, even for these few minutes.

That guilt spurred her feet. She made her way quickly to the laundry, replaced the dirty bandages with freshly washed ones, and instead of retracing her steps, she veered away from the wards. The way back would be twice as long, but, she reasoned, she would not be tempted to stray from her duty by passing the ward that housed that man. She would not think of him again, and certainly not as "Her Knight."

Her roundabout route took her past a nook known to one and all as The Library. It was a mean imitation of a real reading room, but there were morally improving books on shelves and a few battered chairs. Originally intended for use by the staff on their off hours, it was most often used by the more ambulatory patients as they waited for their transport back to the lines or to another hospital. As she approached, determinedly focusing her will upon her responsibilities, she heard his voice and her rebellious feet slowed of their own accord.

"Say that again, will you, Nigel? Oh, sit here, to my right. Seems I've lost a bit of hearing in my left ear."

A very cultured voice, not that of Her Knight, but, she presumed, that of the unseen Nigel said, "Being blown to hell and back will do that to a man's hearing." She heard the sounds of a chair being moved, and Nigel went on, "No soft way to say it, Robert. You're blackballed, old boy. You'll never rise higher than a Lieutenant."

Charlotte blinked. What had Her—what had Robert done? What outrage had he committed? She could not credit any of the usual reasons: cowardice, drunkenness. She chided herself. She knew him not at all. He could easily be the worst kind of man. She drew closer to the Library in spite of herself.

Robert's voice came again, and it was calm and level, even curious. "Why don't they just drum me out?"

"That would be sticky," was Nigel's thoughtful reply. "Enough of your lads know you went out after that Welshman—"

"Do they know his name?" Robert cut in urgently.

"No—as I was saying, your lads know you went out after that Taff. But the asses."

Charlotte wasn't sure she had heard correctly, and even if she had, the words made no sense. Robert said, "I followed the Welshman out, I was trying to bring him back. It was he who wanted to help the donkeys."

Relief surged through her so strongly her fingertips tingled. Her Kn—Robert was neither coward nor criminal nor bounder. He was something else.

"That's well and good, old boy, but it made you look just a touch shy of barking mad." Nigel laughed, but it was a forced sound, mechanical and harsh. His cultured voice now became that of a music hall fop, with effete, exaggerated pronunciation. "His Majesty's Army can endure a bit of eccentricity, Lieutenant Fitzgerald, but not outright lunacy."

"We reserve that for Parliament," Robert offered drily.

Now they both laughed, honestly, if a bit sadly. Charlotte, lost in imagining what Robert—what Mr.

Fitzgerald had done and endured, only vaguely heard the next part. "Besides, Fitz, you were never meant to stay in the Army. Lord Fitzgerald has plans for you. We both know that's why you were not cashiered outright."

"My father? The man most of the House of Lords calls 'That scruffy Irish bastard'? The Army was concerned about his reputation? His honour?" She heard sounds and realized Mr. Fitzgerald was on his feet. Acutely conscious of how close she was to the Library, Charlotte began quietly backing away, praying the wheels on the laundry cart would not squeak and betray her in this ungracious position. She furtively spun the cart and hurried back to her ward.

Gustav and some of the lads were singing in broken French as she entered with the fresh linens. They stopped upon spying her, and from the expressions upon their faces, she suspected the song had been bawdy. Well, she was glad to not be the only guilty person in the hospital.

Stowing the clean linens gave her some time to gather herself together. She forced herself to move with deliberate, focused attention, placing each folded sheet just so on the rude wooden shelves, aligning corners, making sharp-edged fortresses out of the fabric.

That was not enough to drive the aberrant feelings from her mind. She felt nothing short of giddy. In one moment, she felt like laughing out loud, in the next inexplicably she felt as if she might burst into tears. Part of Charlotte wanted to shake herself, part wanted to wrap her arms about her shoulders and dance.

"God's sake," she said angrily to herself. She risked a peek out the door of the storage area. No one seemed to be looking in her direction. Charlotte straightened her uniform, smoothing the pleats, tugging up the thick socks, and re-knotting the laces of her hideous boots. "There," she said with satisfaction.

She would master herself, she thought. Of course, she had been subject to a strange rush of confused thoughts. She did not want her illusions to be shattered about Robert. She naturally did not want her memory of the moment in the CCS tent, when she'd risen above her fears to save the life of that wounded boy, she didn't want the purity of that memory sullied by the knowledge that her strange assistant was some kind of knave. That was all. No more of this nonsense about her Knight Rober—about the patient Fitzgerald. He was not her patient, and the boys out there in the ward needed her full attention.

So saying, she emerged from her place of unintended concealment with steady, dedicatedly serene, ready to attend to her charges. It did not occur to her, not then, that in spite of the heavy responsibilities she shouldered both night and day, in spite of her three years as a nurse and the horrible sights she witnessed each day, in spite of the strength she must show for the wounded that depended on her, and even though at the end of each day she felt tired and old; it did not occur to her that in spite of all that, she was still a nineteen-year-old woman with a heart that was both good and true.

The strange, giddy feeling could not overmaster the combined weight of her long day and the lingering weariness she felt from her tour at the CCS, and thus Charlotte was able to close her eyes without effort late that night. Sleep she did, although she dreamed of donkeys that wandered lost in a broken, fiery world, braying in a piteous way, and it was not a sleep that refreshed.

Her clothes unusually tidy, nurse's hat firmly imprisoning her hair in a way that would have made the most foreboding instructor beam with delight, and an almost severe expression on her face, Charlotte was one of the earliest arrivals at the morning briefing. Then, to her pointed annoyance, she and the other nurses were forced to wait in the central hall for Dr Hartford, the Senior Surgeon. As the older man hurried up, he was plainly no happier to be there than Charlotte was to wait for him.

"Ah, ladies," he said, forcing good cheer into his voice. "Thank you for making time for me in your busy schedule."

"What's the news, Doctor?" Kathleen asked bluntly. "War over yet?"

Her pungent American accent boomed through the hallway, and one or two curious heads emerged from the entrance of their wards. The Senior Surgeon replied soberly, "No, Miss, the War continues. Our American friends have declared for our side, but it may be months before they land on these shores. The final outcome of this contest is in the hands of Higher Authorities." He looked out at the assembled volunteers, smiled warmly and added, "You have done wonderfully, all of you, under the most difficult circumstances. I wanted to let you know we have a new supply officer here at Base Hospital Number 12. It will be his honour to ensure you have everything you need to help the brave lads who pass through our doors."

Dr Hartford looked about vaguely, and for a moment, seemed like a confused elderly man who had gotten lost in a place he'd once known well. Charlotte felt a tiny flush of shame for her impatience with the old gentleman. He was easily threescore years old, and she knew from personal experience the appalling conditions under which he worked, the long hours bent over operating tables in addition to his many administrative duties. He was trying to help them, and she should not be such a shrew as to begrudge his efforts on everyone's behalf.

"Ah, there you are," the Senior Surgeon said and waved someone forward.

Robert Fitzgerald, in a clean but slightly too-large

officer's uniform, with his left arm in a sling, politely made his way through the gathered nurses to stand beside Dr Hartford. Robert was clean-shaven, and she could see a sprinkling of scars along the left side of his face, engraved there, she suspected, by the explosion that had damaged his hearing and cracked his humerus. He was tall, his skin pale, with a premature set of lines around his eyes. His dark hair was combed back in the fashion of several years ago, but it did not lessen the striking blue of his eyes. His face was gaunt, drawing his features into a harsh contrast as if he'd been sketched by a portraitist with charcoal. He was not conventionally handsome—some might have thought his nose a shade too pronounced or the dark hint of beard against his skin too suggestive of a rough nature, but for a long moment, Charlotte was unable to look away from the sight of him. When she did lower her eyes, she told herself it was only the surprise of seeing the man again that had made her so rude as to stare.

"Ladies, allow me to introduce Lieutenant Fitzgerald."

"Robert, if you please," Lieutenant Fitzgerald interjected in a low voice, and some of the nurses tittered. Fitzgerald's countenance maintained a demeanour of disinterested courtesy. He did not smile at the nurses' amusement, nor invite further japery. He addressed them in a pleasant, if impersonal, tone. "I am privileged to have this post, sir, Misses. As a recent recipient of your fine services, I believe I shall have a special appreciation for the work you do. My office is next to the laundry. Please let me know what you need to aid our fine soldiers, and what might ease your burdens, as well. Thank you." He nodded respectfully to the Senior Surgeon, to the assembled nurses, then spun on his heel in a crisp military manner, and strode away.

His departure was abrupt, but somehow not ungracious. A few of the nurses looked about themselves with an air of strangely hungry curiosity. He was a fine specimen of a man —a trifle under-nourished from his time at the front —and clearly well-bred. Even though fraternization between any men and the nurses was expressly forbidden, that would not stop some of the more frivolous girls from wagging idle tongues about the man. It would be a diverting distraction from the incessant pain and death.

Firmly removing any consideration of the clique of gossiping nurses from her mind, Charlotte did remember something she needed. The accursed lice had made a reappearance, as one reminded her by nipping her flank. It would be unladylike to scratch, but she managed a discreet rub of the area with the back of her hand. She walked briskly up to the Senior Surgeon. "Doctor?" she said hopefully.

He turned with a distracted air. "Ah, yes, Miss—?"

"Braninov," Charlotte supplied for the twentieth or thirtieth time. The man had almost a hundred nurses on his staff; he could not remember them all. "Sir, we are finding lice among the patients again, and —" she lowered her voice, for it was shameful to her to admit this, "—among the Sisters as well."

"Damnable things, lice," the old doctor muttered darkly. "Of course, they're coming in with the poor devils from Passchendaele and Messines." The trenches, with their lack of sanitation and the close quarters, were highly congenial places for the lice to take up residence and start pestilential families. They burrowed into the clothing and were one of the many constant small miseries of war. They also carried diseases, a number of them fatal, at which point the misery they inflicted was great and terrible to behold.

"Yes, sir."

"We'll just have to burn the clothing of the wounded before they enter the hospital. They'll have to come in naked as the Lord made them." His voice trailed off. "Let Matron know we'll need to treat the bed clothing of the affected wards. You know the procedure." All the linens and any fabrics would be immersed into kettles of boiling water and brushed with a very dilute solution of carbolic of acid to kill the pestilential invaders. That task, at least, could largely be performed by the laundresses.

"And you nurses…" Dr Hartford mused. While the old gentleman cogitated, Charlotte waited, trying not to glance back down the hall where her ward and her patients awaited.

"Dr Treves taught me this," the Senior Surgeon said after a moment. "Fredrick Treves, remarkable man. Go round the motor pool and gather up the petrol jelly. Rub a thin layer over your skin, and the vile insects won't bite. They can't breathe, I think."

"Yes, sir, I'll try that." She half curtseyed, and headed straight for her boys, thinking *Not bloody likely*. By noon, another eight or ten bites in some especially tender locations gave her reason to reconsider the unlikely remedy.

That night Kathleen scratched at herself, and as she did so uttered sulphurous blasphemies. Charlotte observed her friend's profane fluency with no little respect for the wideness of vocabulary if not the performance itself. Reaching under her bunk, Charlotte offered a jam pot of the gooey substance to the American nurse. "Try this. Dr Fredrick Treves recommends it."

Kathleen scratched and said, "Is that so?" She'd obviously not heard of Dr Treves in the wilds of the West if indeed anyone in America knew of that worthy and humanitarian gentleman.

"I tried it this afternoon. It keeps the damned things from biting."

Kathleen rubbed a bit of the odd jelly on her fingers.

"I'll feel like a greased pig."

Yet another colourful American expression whose exact meaning escaped Charlotte. "Perhaps…but it soothes the bites, too."

By the end of the week, all of the nurses—from the newest like Alice, who blushed at the idea of applying the petroleum jelly everywhere, to the oldest salts like Matron, who several wars ago had lost any maidenly vapours at the varieties of human frailty—were using the jelly to successfully fend off the lice. The clothing of incoming patients was burned, and men treated individually for exposure to the parasite. The louse was effectively evicted from Base Hospital Number 12.

In spite of her determination to avoid Mr. Fitzgerald, Charlotte was in charge of her ward, and the time came later that week when the cupboards in her supply closet were nearly bare. She'd sent Gustav, but his command of English had been inadequate to the task, and he returned with a tin of silver oxide, which was useless in her present circumstances.

At the end of that day, her patients freshly bathed and their bandages replenished with the last of her clean linen, Charlotte took the sturdy wheeled cart in hand and trudged wearily toward the office next to the laundry. Kathleen, just coming off duty, spied her, and fell into step beside her.

"Cheri, you look like you tangled with a badger and lost."

Charlotte had to acknowledge the truth of the sentiment. She was haggard from the end of her shift, her hair was sweaty and her face was probably flushed from the exertion. She knew she looked like a charwoman. "I'm going to fetch supplies," she said, more sharply than she'd planned. "It's not a formal ball."

Unperturbed by Charlotte's tone, Kathleen observed,

"Not the way some of the other gals see it. There's a lot of primping and combing before they stop in to see Lieutenant Fitzgerald."

"I'm just doing the hospital's business," Charlotte persisted stubbornly.

"Yes, ma'am," Kathleen said mildly. "Alice seems to be doing a lot of the hospital's business these days."

Charlotte bit her tongue. The spoiled idiot should be spending time in her wards learning to be a better nurse, not flirting like a schoolgirl with the only young, handsome, respectable man on the staff.

"That is her affair," Charlotte finally said as they strode down the hall.

"Yep," agreed Kathleen, turning toward the exit. "Madame said she's bringing chicken for dinner. I'll save you some."

"Thank you." The chicken would be stringy, no doubt from a lifetime of fleeing wily Frenchwomen like Madame, and the potatoes would be small and pebbly, but it would be a nice change from the rather uninspired hospital soup.

The laundry was running at full speed as she passed, local women and girls plunging bloodied sheets into cauldrons of hot water. It was one of the larger rooms in the hospital, with many windows facing outward. In the summer, it was equatorial with heat and steam, but most congenial in the winter. Large metal boilers at the rear of the room provided an abundance of hot water for the large vats which the laundresses stirred with wooden handles. Tall racks, also of wood, were situated near the boilers to take advantage of the heat thrown off and to speed up the drying of the newly cleaned linens and clothing. The women chatted and laughed among themselves as they worked and sweated.

She continued down the hall, feeling a helpless melancholy spread through her, as of ink dropped into water, slowly spreading to ever so slightly darken what had been clear before. For a moment, she envied the women who toiled in that steamy room. Their country was invaded, at war (as was her own) but for whom did they worry? Loved ones, yes, family, certainly…but there was a finite limit to one's family, and thus a limit to those whom one cared about. She fretted almost constantly about the wounded who passed through her ward…whether they lived or died, how to save them or ease their suffering. Indeed, whether they lived or died in pain and delirium often came down to her efforts. And their numbers were without end.

In another fifty feet, she drew up outside the door of the supply office. To her surprise, the door was open, and Robert Fitzgerald himself sat at the desk where she'd expected to find an orderly. That was the true reason she was coming by so late in the evening—not that it had been any of Kathleen's business whom Charlotte did or did not want to see, nor why.

He glanced up from his ledger, noted the peculiar expression on her face, and said cheerfully, "Just me, I'm afraid. Sent the lad off for some tea. He looked done in. I'm sure I…can…?" His voice trailed off as the Lieutenant truly looked upon her.

He climbed to his feet. His arm was no longer in a sling, she noticed, and he bowed with great respect. "My Lady Sister," he said gravely. "It is most gratifying to see you well."

"And you, Lieutenant Fitzgerald."

He pulled the desk chair around and held it for her. "Please, my Lady Sister, please sit down."

She hesitated and then sat. "Nurse Braninov, sir," she told him, speaking her name very deliberately to save him the discomfiture of mispronouncing it.

"Of course, Nurse Braninov. I am most honoured to

meet you at last."

She found herself wondering why the man was so formal in his speech to her. They were, after all, colleagues, working together in this remote corner of the Pit. "Or Nurse Charlotte, if that is easier. Many of the boys have a problem saying my last name, poor dears." She felt odd, uncomfortable in his presence. The words rushed out of her. "I so want to thank you for assisting me at the CCS, Mr. Fitzgerald. It was most gracious of you." She could not have done it without him, but that felt far too nakedly revealing to say. "You were so helpful and calming, sir."

"What you thought was calm was probably me having a bit of shellshock. It was you saved that soldier's life, Sister. All I did was a bit of lifting and holding. The hard work was done by your hands."

Without realizing it, she gazed at his hands, now not as rough, but still strong. "If you say so, Lieutenant Fitzgerald."

Fitzgerald leaned against the edge of the desk, keeping it between them. "Miss Charlotte, how may I help you?"

"My station is running quite low, sir, on the essentials. We need drains, additional sutures, our retractors have gone missing—"

He held up his left hand, moving it deliberately as if he had to concentrate on willing it into action. "Miss, allow me to tell you a secret." He glanced round, as if for prying eyes, and then said in a comic stage whisper, "I don't know a blasted thing about hospital supplies. I can't tell a suture from a bedpan."

She laughed. "Surely, you're—"

"Oh, no, Miss. This is the Army at its worst." There was the faintest hint of discouragement in his voice that vanished as he went on in a more cheery tone, "The system sees a billet, and the system demands they shove an officer—any officer—into it."

"And you are that hapless officer."

"I am he. Bit of an embarrassment."

Even leaning against the desk, he was taller than she. His height was not intimidating, it was comforting as if she were standing beneath a tall oak on a sunny day, feeling the cool relief offered by the mighty tree. "Well, then, sir, we shall have educate you."

She stood and looked up at him. She had no idea how her eyes glowed in that moment, nor the brightness of the smile that erased the lines and toil of the war years from her face and made her look every inch the young woman she was.

Robert Fitzgerald pushed himself away from the desk and held forth his hands in surrender. "Miss, I am your humble and grateful student."

For over an hour they laboured side by side, arranging the stores, organizing them, labelling the shelves. Fitzgerald listened gravely, repeating the name of each item she showed him, sometimes handling them as if the act of holding the item created a chain in his mind between the name and the object.

"And this is used for what?" he asked incredulously, holding up a shiny bit of metal. "They look like the pliers our coachman used on the tack."

"It's a bullet extractor."

He was abashed. "Dear me." She took the extractor from him and placed it amongst the other surgical instruments.

When the "lad" (a rather gnomish sort of fellow of middle years) returned carrying tea on a tray, Robert asked her to join him.

"Please, Miss, do sit for a moment and eat. You're far too thin."

"Surely, Lieutenant, you'd not ask me to dine while you

do without." Fitzgerald's man instantly turned to leave, with every indication of hurrying out to retrieve another tray.

"I insist," the Lieutenant said, showing her to the lone desk chair. "I shall test how well I have learned what you have taught me by teaching young Orlando here." Orlando, who probably had not been referred to as young since gas lamps had been introduced, drew himself up at that statement, prepared to do his duty. To Charlotte, Fitzgerald added in a conspiratorial tone, "Please do correct me if I make a mistake."

She drank the tea and ate the meal, listening as she did. Fitzgerald had a remarkable memory. He'd forgotten none of the names of the supplies, nor their uses. Orlando was a slower student however, and he repeated the names of the instruments and supplies in a low drone, as if fearful of being overheard.

She was awakened by a gentle touch on the back of her hand. "Miss," said Lieutenant Fitzgerald, "I fear I have abused your kindness by keeping you overlong." She straightened, feeling dampness on her chin. *Good God, had she been drooling in her sleep like a child?* Fitzgerald gallantly busied himself with tidying the teacups and plates while she hastily composed herself.

Orlando waited to one side, drooping a bit himself. Fitzgerald dismissed him, "Good night, Orlando. We'll tackle the rest of this tomorrow."

The orderly saluted and left with dispatch. "Poor fellow. They just assigned him to me." Robert mused. "He's rather old to be up so late."

"I must be going," Charlotte said groggily, her words slurred with fatigue.

"Allow me to escort you to your tent, Nurse."

"There's no need—"

"I cannot allow you to walk unescorted," he said kindly.

He'd been a perfect gentleman, keeping the door open during their entire time together, as propriety demanded. When she came out of the office pushing the laundry cart, now loaded with bandages, linens, ointments, and other necessary kit for the patients, he placed his hands upon the handle of the cart and edged her aside quietly. Neither spoke as he pushed it down the darkened halls, in an unspoken acknowledgement of the men sleeping in the rooms to either side. At her ward, she retrieved the cart from him, whispering, "I'll unload this in the morning. Thank you."

She slipped into the ward and carefully pushed the cart against the wall near her own supply closet. When she stepped out, she expected him to be gone, but the Lieutenant was waiting quietly. He politely gestured with one hand for her to lead the way, and fell into step beside her.

She led him outside, and the coolness of the night air revived her. It was clean, fresh, absent the persistent odours of suppurating wounds, astringents, and the hundred other aromas that told of suffering and pain. Charlotte turned to Lieutenant Fitzgerald, who had stopped on the steps and was looking at the sky.

"It's a beautiful evening, Miss," he observed. "Do the skies in your homeland look like this?"

She lifted her face to see the stars, which seemed to be as waves of diamonds upon the velvet of the night. "No," she said after a moment. "My home is far to the north and the location of the stars differs. Many times in the winter, we'll see the dancing lights in the sky. The colours are marvellous, like curtains waving from a window in Heaven. Have you ever seen them?"

"No, Sister," he said, with what sounded like real regret. "Perhaps someday."

She nodded and climbed down onto the duckboards.

He strode beside her in the mud. "If I may, Miss," he said formally and extended a hand to take her elbow, steadying her.

"Of course, sir," she answered, not willing to think about how strangely warm her elbow felt cradled in his hand. She spoke, somewhat abruptly while remembering to keep her voice low in deference to those exhausted nurses, orderlies, and doctors who slept in the tents around them. "I am so pleased you have recovered from your injuries, Lieutenant Fitzgerald."

"Mostly, Nurse Charlotte," he admitted, his voice as quiet as her own. "My arm is nearly back to normal, but my hearing is still a bit dodgy. I am assured that will return in time."

"Still, sir, I am very pleased at your recovery."

"Yes, Miss. I am much more fortunate than so many others. I pray that I shall never take that for granted."

There was nothing to say to that. She drew to a stop outside her tent. Through small gaps in the door, she could see a dim lantern still burned within. She turned to face him. He stood close, his eyes serious, his head cocked slightly to the right.

"Good night, Lieutenant Fitzgerald."

"Good night, Nurse Braninov. Thank you for a most educational evening." He took her hand, and she tried not to gasp at the flare of heat that she momentarily perceived at the careful, restrained touch of his fingers on her skin. Not appearing to notice, Fitzgerald bent courteously over her hand and backed away into the darkness. She thought she could hear him humming.

Because the Germans had been known to fly night patrols, firing at any stray illumination they saw, she opened the flap of the tent the merest crack to reduce any possible light leakage, and slipped within, tying the flap shut behind her.

"Educational," Kathleen said with a friendly smirk. "Is that what you English kids are calling it these days?"

Charlotte barely heard her, murmuring absently, "Oh, do hush," as she turned back the blankets, readying herself for bed.

Across the tent, Alice sat on her bunk. She glared at Charlotte. The look on the young English girl's face was positively venomous. The depth of feeling radiating from Alice leached the humanity from her features, made them stark, almost reptilian. With a final glare of some indefinable but surely hateful emotion, Alice gathered up her blue coat and swept out of the tent.

Startled, Charlotte glanced at Kathleen, who also seemed taken aback by the other nurse's expression. However, the big American shrugged and held a finger to her lips with a wink, then said to the tent at large, "Lights out, ladies," before extinguishing the lantern.

Removing her boots in the dark and laying her great coat across the foot of her cot, Charlotte gave only a moment of thought to Alice's fit of ill-temper. Robert Fitzgerald filled her consciousness. He seemed so incredibly real to her, more real than her father, or the men at the Czar's court, or even the soldiers she tended each day. He seemed, for these heady moments, like the only real, true, and honest thing in her world. Yet, there had been nothing about him that should have made that impression upon her. He was no teller of riveting tales, no raconteur holding his audience spellbound with amusing anecdotes. His quiet, contained manner had not demanded her attention but invited her as an equal to join him in a few simple moments of satisfaction at a job well-done as they organized the supplies.

She rolled onto her side, facing away from Kathleen and the empty bunk used by Alice, and found herself pressing the pillow against her face and bosom, cradling her cheek in the rumoured softness of the rough fabric. She had seen him, she understood, when he could have been at his worst: the broken arm, the shrapnel in his skin, the deafness in his damaged ear. Yet, in that moment, she'd seen his true self—a man who could rise above his own hurts to ensure that another received aid. And having seen that, when she had spoken to him this evening in the safety of the hospital, she had trusted the truth of the person he presented to her. It was dizzying to have so much knowledge of another human being in such a small space of time.

For the next week, Alice spoke hardly a word to Charlotte, treating her with chilly disdain. It was so wholly irregular, the Russian girl finally turned to Kathleen for an explanation over their morning tea and croissant. Madame was taking her ease, and sat on a corner of the bunk, smoking a small pipe before moving on to her other customers. The smoke from the pipe was white, with a pleasant spiciness that for a time masked the strangely musty odour of the tent canvas.

"What have I done to Alice?" Charlotte asked the American nurse, spreading more jam on her bread. "She's been horrid to me every day this week."

"That girl does have her bloomers in a bunch," Kathleen agreed, wiping crumbs from the corner of her own mouth with a thumb. "I heard Matron giving her holy hell yesterday."

"Whatever for?"

"She didn't want to undress the wounded boys coming in."

Charlotte was shocked. "That's asinine," she blurted. Undressing the soldiers was vital to their health. It removed the lice-ridden clothing from them, and, more importantly, made a thorough inspection of their wounds possible. Early in the war, she'd lost more than one patient whose major wounds had distracted the staff from checking for other, less-obvious but still potentially and ultimately fatal wounds.

"You better believe Matron thought so, too. She told that snotty little Miss so-and-so, 'Girl, you are a nurse now. You save the dying, you suture horrible wounds, and you must remove their uniforms.' And all Alice said was 'It's not proper.'"

In spite of herself, Charlotte snorted at the fatuousness of that, and Kathleen grinned widely. Madame looked up from her pipe inquiringly.

Kathleen said, "Go on, tell her."

Charlotte faced the old woman, and in halting French, recounted the story. Madame pondered it for a second, then removed her pipe and replied in the same language.

The American nurse looked with curiosity at her friend, for the Russian nurse's eyes had gone wide. "What?"

Charlotte was nearly incapable of speech, but she managed to choke out a rough translation. "Madame thinks it odd. She said Alice works with needles all day long…why should she be afraid of a little prick?"

At that, the two young women fairly exploded with laughter, rolling on their cots, tears streaming from their eyes. They tried to stifle the raucous noise by covering their mouths with pillows. After a few minutes, they managed to regain some semblance of self-control only to realize Madame was still in their tent, puffing with great self-possession on her pipe.

The stately French woman gazed upon them serenely and then favoured them with a wink of such suggestive, salacious power the two girls were once more doubled up in fits of near-hysteria. It was only the realization their shift was about to begin that allowed them, giggling, to compose themselves and hurry off to the hospital.

They were almost late to the morning pass down. Faces flushed, a few errant strands of hair poking out from beneath their caps, Charlotte and Kathleen slipped into the main hallway and huddled at the back of the group just as Matron strode up, a frown deepening the lines of her already craggy visage.

"The Huns have bombed another hospital. Let this be your warning, ladies. We must have light discipline at night. Workmen will be installing drapes over the windows —" A few of the younger nurses moaned forlornly. The heavy fabric would restrict the evening breezes, and make the wards more stuffy and soporific for the weary night workers. "Enough of that." Matron snapped at no one in particular. "The drapes will block the light at night…and if we are bombed, they'll capture flying glass. Keep you and your patients from being sliced into chutney."

Matron's surly mood quickly sobered Kathleen and Charlotte. The morning pass down was unusually terse, and the old nurse seemed distracted, if as stern as ever. She dismissed the crowd and then waved to Charlotte and Kathleen. "You there," she called. The two young women stopped, exchanged a quick surprised glance. They had managed to contain their mirth from earlier in the morning and could think of no reason why Matron would require their attention. Dutifully, they composed their faces and approached her.

"I'm moving Nurse Hargreaves from the evening shift to daytime. She needs more hands-on work with the wounded. She shares your tent, does she not?"

Charlotte realized Matron was speaking about Alice. "Yes, Mum," she said while Kathleen kept uncharacteristically, if wisely, silent beside her.

"Very good. She will work in your ward, Miss Braninov." Matron might have been old, but her memory was keen.

Now Kathleen spoke up. "Ma'am, that might not be a good idea."

The older woman slowly turned her head toward the American nurse, as if deeply pondering her own reply. Finally, she asked, "And why might that be?"

Undaunted, Kathleen plunged ahead. "Nurse Alice has a burr under her saddle about Charlotte, ma'am."

Matron almost sniffed but had the good breeding not to do so. "The fool girl can detest you both and your kin for all I care. You, Miss Braninov, are a fine nurse, and I hope Nurse Hargreaves has the sense God gave a goose and will learn from you. That is all."

So dismissed, the two nurses hurried down the corridor to their respective wards. Looking back over her shoulder, Charlotte saw Matron having a quiet word with Alice, who shook her head in a kind of disgusted defiance. Kathleen muttered softly, "She's afraid of a little…"

"Oh, hush," Charlotte told her, a bit more sharply than she intended. The idea of working so closely with this odd English girl, who had, as far as Charlotte could tell, conceived a dislike for her out of the whole cloth, was very vexing indeed. But, she told herself, she would not allow that to interfere with the care of her patients.

That night, a haggard Alice awaited her in their tent, sitting on her bunk with only a tiny lantern for light. "Hullo," Alice said dully, dark smudges beneath her eyes, her hair a bit wild and straggly. As usual, she had changed from her nurse's wear into a nightdress.

The young girl looked so terrible that Charlotte felt a small wave of charity. "Are you well?" she asked, sitting beside her and taking the other's hand.

"Oh, no, I'm grand," Alice replied, her hand resting limply in Charlotte's. "I made myself stay awake. You and I shall have to be on the same schedule now, shan't we?"

Charlotte nodded. "Yes, and you should get into bed.

The morning comes very early, Alice."

"I do hope I won't embarrass myself," Alice said in an airy way. She seemed a touch delirious, as if from a fever. She looked at Charlotte with a face full of naked fear. "I am so frightened of hurting those fellows."

"Hush, now," Charlotte said, pulling back the blanket for the girl. "I know you will be outstanding. Give the boys a cheery smile, no matter what, and they'll forgive you anything."

Alice lay back on the bed, as compliant as a weary child. "Truly?" she asked.

"Truly. They'll be competing with one another to have you learn on them."

The girl curved onto her side, and Charlotte pulled the blanket up over her. "Sleep now," she said as she smoothed Alice's long hair over the girl's shoulders. *There,* she thought. *The poor thing was terrified. As well she should be.*

Charlotte had just reached for her own pillow when a soft knock sounded at the edge of the tent.

"Miss Charlotte?" a low, somehow familiar voice beckoned.

She covered the lantern, filling the interior with a grey gloom, and lifted the tent flap. Orlando, Robert Fitzgerald's aged orderly, stood without. On seeing her face, he said in a quiet tone, "Miss Charlotte, Lieutenant Fitzgerald requests your assistance."

Oh, can't it wait, she thought wearily, but then chided herself. Mr. Fitzgerald had never presumed upon her time and surely must need her help with an important matter.

It was not in the least what she expected.

Robert was crouched down behind the desk when she entered with Orlando. Fitzgerald looked up, gave her a relieved smile, and then spoke down to the floor, with a most wretched accent, *"Observez vous. Mademoiselle...er...*

Soeu...ah, sod it." He stood. "My Lady Sister, I require your services yet again."

For the life of her, she could not imagine what he had been doing on the floor, and so she stepped round his desk to stand beside him. There, in the space normally occupied by the chair, was a pile of dirty rags.

No, that was not it. In a moment, her eyes began to fix on the details of what was before her. It was so unexpected, she had not at first been able to make sense of it. A small child huddled under the desk. A child so begrimed it was hard to tell if the urchin were a boy or a girl. Dark eyes looked out from the dirt-crusted face. Wary eyes. The child cradled something in its arms. Charlotte discovered she was kneeling, not yet certain what was needed here. The child shrank back a bit. Charlotte looked up to Robert, who squatted easily beside her.

"I saw him in the fields. There was a scrum of boys, and he was in the centre of them. They were giving him a good thrashing. For the life of me, I don't know why."

She looked more closely at the boy and his huddled posture. "What does he have there?"

"I don't know." Robert reached out with a slow, steady hand. The boy jerked further under the desk, and the Englishman withdrew his hand.

Charlotte told Fitzgerald, "Your French, if I may say so, sir, is atrocious."

"You may say so, my Lady Sister." Robert turned to her with a look of frank pleading. The need on his face surprised her. "Please speak to the boy for me."

"Of course." She tucked her skirts beneath her, thinking with regret they were going to be streaked with dirt from the floor. As if reading her mind, Fitzgerald unhooked a heavy field coat from a stand, folded it and slid it toward her. She slipped the jacket beneath her legs and then lowered her face until it was level with the frightened child. In a soft voice, her accent making the French somehow more musical, she spoke to the child.

Robert sat back from them, not trying to understand the conversation. Instead, he watched the young woman and the child. *Lord above, Nurse Charlotte is so beautiful,* he thought, and she knew it not, so completely focused was she on the little boy. She was the single pure peal of a church bell that cut through the gabble of unbelief, bringing faith to the lost. And the poor tired child sensed that purity, surrendered to it. Sad, hurting orphan. The boy spoke to her, tersely at first, and then more haltingly as tears begin to bubble up from his eyes.

A look went across Charlotte's face as she listened, and she glanced toward Robert as if hiding her face from the boy. Her expression was fierce and hard and wild, and Fitzgerald, who'd seen battle in all of its awful, mindless horror, thought he would not want that look directed at him.

The expression passed in a moment, and gentle concern returned to her face as the nurse scooted closer to the boy. She was almost under the desk in the chair well with him. She held out her arms, and the little boy wriggled into them.

Cradling the child, Charlotte said softly, "Mr. Fitzgerald, would you be so good as to send Orlando for some soup?"

"Of course." The silent orderly was already stepping into the hall. Robert stopped him, pressed a few coins in his hands. "Try to find some beef, too, will you, old boy, perhaps some milk?" Orlando nodded and vanished.

Charlotte eased herself back from the desk, attempting to stand without relinquishing the child. She felt the Lieutenant's hands on her elbows, lifting both her and the boy easily.

Robert guided her into the desk chair, and as she and the child lowered to sit a strange kind of mewling came from the pair. Fitzgerald glanced down in surprise.

"It's a kitten," she said, stroking the boy's hair, trying to steal a glance at the small animal he was holding. "Ignace—that is what he is called, Ignace—said the other boys were playing a game." Again, that fierce look, gone as quickly as lightning on a summer night. "They were trying to see who could break the kitten's legs without killing it. Ignace ran among them. To stop them, he hoped."

"That explains all of the stomping, I suppose. Is he hurt?"

Charlotte shook her head. "He hasn't said. He's worried about the kitten."

Fitzgerald sat on the floor beside them and addressed the boy. "Let's take a look, shall we?"

Ignace turned his dirty face to Charlotte and said something with a shy glance at the Englishman.

Charlotte replied in a soothing tone before saying to Fitzgerald, "He said you landed among them like a bomb."

"I put my boot to the arse of a few of them. Cowards." He extended his hands to the boy. Ignace looked to Charlotte again for reassurance, and at her nod uncovered the tiny bundle in his arms.

The kitten blinked brilliant blue eyes from its small face. The grey-white fur was dirty, and its ribs showed plainly. Exposed to the light, it gave a long pitiful mew that tugged at the nurse's heart. Both the kitten's front legs were broken below the joint, the flesh over the broken area swollen and abraded.

Looking down at him, Charlotte saw Robert's face grow as still as a stone, although the encouraging smile on his face never faded.

"The evil swine..." Robert breathed, letting his voice trail away as he gazed at the ruined forelegs. He reached forward and scooped the kitten up with hands that were gentle and steady. The wounded kitten gave a yowl of pain until Robert settled it against his chest, cradling and steadying it with one strong arm as he stroked its head with the fingers of his free hand. The encouraging smile never leaving his face, he said quietly in English, "We shall have to put you down, poor puss."

Charlotte had been focusing on the child, murmuring words of patience and encouragement to him as she scanned the hall for Orlando. "Pardon?" she asked, looking over at him.

The smile never left Robert's face, nor did his pleasant demeanour shift, although his eyes were grave. "We shall have to put her down. She would be unable to fend for herself, care for herself. You and I have not the time, not with the wounded continuing to pour in."

Aware of the small boy's anxious gaze on her, trying to match the Lieutenant's easy tone, her arms around Ignace, Charlotte said lightly, replying in English, "Oh, sir, must we? I doubt very much this poor child has anything else in the world but this little cat."

Fitzgerald looked down at the tiny creature in his arms. It panted in anguish, gnawing at his fingers as he stroked the soiled fur. "What if we fail, my Lady Sister? Would it not be more merciful to spare both the boy and this crippled kitten the pain to come?"

"Come, sir…it would be a sin to take away the only thing this boy has to care about. We can do naught but try." Nurse Braninov's striking blue eyes shone when she gazed at him. Their eyes met across the wounded creatures they both held. At that moment, it seemed the most important thing in the world to try to save the baby cat, and perhaps, saving the kitten, save the boy. Life, she observed, her heart taking on a dizzying beat, life is made up of these moments, of these small moments when we choose not for ourselves, but for the well-being of another.

"Very well. Of course, you are correct, my Lady Sister,"

Fitzgerald went on gravely, his eyes still holding her own. "I cannot do it on my own, I have not the skills. I can only do this you ask with your help."

Her heart leapt at Fitzgerald's words. *He does this for me,* she understood in surprise. How foolish she was becoming, she thought. "You have only to ask," she said aloud.

"Will you translate for me? The boy must know what is ahead."

She nodded, and said in French, "Ignace, the gentleman has something important to say to you."

Fitzgerald waited until she had finished before speaking. "Lad, do you love this kitten?"

The boy's fervent affirmative needed no translation.

"The Sister has asked that we do what we can to mend your friend. I want you to know we have no medicine for a creature so small. What we do to save her shall hurt very much. You will have to bear the sight of the one you love in great pain. Can you do that?"

The boy listened to Charlotte's translation with great solemnity. He nodded again, his jaw clenched against tears.

Robert's voice grew gentler. "But you will be there for her; you will be her comfort in her pain, will you not? You must be ready to pledge yourself to her, for you will be the one who keeps her alive…brings her food and water as she heals, cleans her and keeps her warm and safe when she sleeps. Are you prepared to love her that much, lad?"

As she conveyed this to the boy, Charlotte looked away from Robert to hide the tears that trembled and stung on the edges of her lashes, ready to fall.

"Oh, oui, Monsieur!" Ignace declared.

Fitzgerald waited until Orlando returned with a generous tray of food. He set the boy to eat under the watchful eye of the old orderly, and that freed him to work with Charlotte on the kitten.

She might have pilfered a cotton ball of ether from the surgery, but she knew too much could stop the heart and lungs, and she dared not try it with the wee creature, not while the small boy sat a scant five paces from them. Instead, she gathered supplies from the storerooms behind the office, and they cleared a spot on Fitzgerald's desk to use as an operating theatre.

Robert held the tiny kitten immobile with only his hands, pinning its body with one hand and its head with another. She had a moment of fear that those large, strong hands would crush the animal's fragile frame, but he seemed to have amazing control over his grip. It was like he'd wrapped the baby cat in a vise of flesh because although it struggled, it could not escape.

She examined the front limbs, pressing a finger on the joint near the shoulder to keep the leg from thrashing. Speaking half aloud, she said, "At least they are not compound fractures, thank Jesu…"

Fitzgerald only grunted and gave her a nod of encouragement. Working as quickly as she could, Charlotte affixed splints to each front leg, securing them with bandages which she then covered with plaster. She remembered something from her training about setting a limb in a "useful posture." As much as possible, she moulded the plaster so the splints resembled the natural contour of a healthy leg, rather than two straight cylinders. The plaster would pull at the fur, but she reasoned they could cut it off later—better a bald patch than a useless leg.

The frightened kitten yowled pitifully, twisting its head from side to side. Ignace was at the side of the desk, his meal forgotten, watching anxiously.

"Almost done," Charlotte said to them, waving her hands over the cast to set it. She repeated herself in French for Ignace's benefit, and then added, *"Come, wave your hands to help speed the drying of the plaster."* This the boy did with dispatch.

The aged gnome Orlando spoke, surprising her. "The cat will chew on them, she will." He was pointing to the splints. "You'll have to put a collar on her, Miss."

Neither Charlotte nor Fitzgerald followed him. The orderly cupped his hands to demonstrate. "Like the ladies of Elizabeth."

Now she understood. "A ruff." Such as the ones worn by the women of the court in the time of good Queen Elizabeth.

"Yes, Miss. My Da—my father had to put them on the sheep sometimes."

An odd look of amusement crossed Robert's face. "Don't be shy, old boy, step up, step up and lead on."

Orlando *was* shy, she saw, but he came forward. He searched among the cabinets and found a discarded pair of canvas gaiters, the useless boot covers the English wore from time to time. Wielding a pair of scissors like a born tailor, the old man had the vaguely cone-shaped canvas guard round the kitten's neck and held in place with a bootlace in no time.

This last indignity was too much for the poor kitten, which gave a kind of warbling mew of protest and soiled itself.

"Oh!" Charlotte said, looking for a rag.

"No, Nurse Braninov," Robert's voice came to her. "That is for Ignace to do."

The boy was already looking for a towel, which Orlando produced. The urchin tenderly cleaned the animal's hindquarters, then wiped the top of the desk with that same towel before dropping the rag in the bin. Charlotte and Robert's eyes met in amused shared understanding. It was not a cleaning job that would have pleased Matron or a Battalion Sergeant, but it was a start.

Ignace gently lifted the kitten and cradled it. The

exhausted animal leaned against him. Charlotte exhaled, suddenly weary, and smiled up at Fitzgerald just as Orlando said, "Sir, your hands."

Robert slipped his arms behind his back. "Just a scratch, old boy, say no more of it. Orlando, would you be so kind as to escort Nurse Braninov back—"

Charlotte stood in front of him. "You will show me your hands, sir," she said in her sternest voice, the one she used with unreasonable patients.

"I assure you there is no need —"

"Your hands, sir," she demanded in a tone that would have made Matron smile with approval.

Fitzgerald displayed his hands with an embarrassed air as if he'd been caught out at some misdeed. There were a number of scratches and bites covering his palms and fingers, and the blood dripped freely from his skin. The terrified kitten must have rent Robert's flesh in its frantic and misguided struggles to escape.

"Ah, Mr. Fitzgerald," she said. He'd never made a sound. She took him by the wrists and drew his hands over the desktop. The supplies from their tending to the kitten still lay there, and she set right to work.

"Orlando, we must find a place for this lad and his charge."

"I'll find a place for the boy, sir. It will be quietly done."

"Excellent." Charlotte detected the faintest waver in Robert's voice, which was only natural, as she was pouring spirits directly into the wounds on his hands.

"No stitches, I think, sir," Charlotte told him. "But, tush, sir. You must not let such things go…sepsis can set in so quickly." She was vaguely aware she was treating him with much formal courtesy, even as she bandaged his hands. The act of touching him made her oddly lightheaded, and only by speaking to him in such a formal way could she make herself focus. "There," she said. "The worst of it was on the palms. I've tried to keep the bandages small so you can still work."

"Most thoughtful," he said, regarding his hands and admiring them as he would some fine piece of craftsmanship.

Ignace came around the desk to join them, cradling the sleeping kitten with great care in his arms. He spoke to Charlotte, who replied at length before turning to Fitzgerald. "Ignace thanks you very much, Mr. Fitzgerald, and he is sorry about your hands. He would like to return here tomorrow if that is acceptable to you."

Robert nodded, and Orlando interjected, "I'll see to it, sir."

"Lovely," Robert said. "It is late, Nurse Braninov, and you must rise very early. Shall we conclude our charitable mission for the evening?"

"Yes, please," Charlotte told him, suddenly aware of the hour and the weariness that throbbed through her body. She told Ignace to go with Orlando, and the boy nodded in a distracted way, his attention on the tiny creature he held.

For a moment, Robert gazed down at the French waif and his pet. He reached out with a bandaged hand and stroked the little cat softly along the jaw. She heard him say "Beautiful," but it didn't appear that he was looking at the kitten.

The morning came early, and the day was long. Rumours began to drift about the Hospital, whispers of another push in the making at the front.

After a second nurse shared her concerns about the casualties to come, Alice stood frozen at the head of the ward, her hands kneading her smock. "How shall we do it?" she whispered to Charlotte. "We've not the room now."

No one would profit from watching the girl fret,

Charlotte knew. The patients had had their soup and would be napping soon, that is if Alice's jitters did not disturb their peace.

"There are always rumours of another attack, Alice," Charlotte said. She took the blonde girl by the arm and drew her toward the supply cabinets.

Alice looked on the men sleeping on every available bed, and inquired again, "How shall we do it?"

"A step at a time," Charlotte said calmly. "A bandage at a time. A stitch at a time, if we must."

Charlotte opened the cabinets, revealing the half-empty, disordered shelves. "And if it comes, we must be ready."

She kept them working past the end of their shift until the shelves were tidy and fairly bulging with supplies. She reasoned that if Alice were working, and perhaps even a bit resentful for having to do so, the girl could not dwell on her own fear. Charlotte had felt that fear, but it had come and gone an age ago. One could not simply talk it away. A nurse would either find that fortress within her that allowed her to shut out the screams and pleas while still listening for the vital information that she needed to do the difficult work, or she would not be a nurse for long.

It was nearly 8 o'clock when Charlotte dismissed Alice. The other girl's eyes drooped. She barely acknowledged Charlotte as she trudged away to her tent.

Charlotte, too, felt the weight of her own fatigue. But she knew sleep and rest would elude her until she had checked on her newest, tiniest patient.

Mr. Fitzgerald sat at his desk working when she knocked hesitantly at the door. *Did the man ever rest?* she wondered, eyeing the profusion of ledgers and correspondence that lay in drifts about him.

He looked up at her, confusion on his face, as he moved his awareness from the record-keeping under his pen to the person standing before him. Then a smile briefly lit his face, before it was replaced with a much more business-like expression of cordiality.

"Nurse Braninov," he said by way of greeting, standing politely. "How marvellous to see you this evening. Please do come in."

She took a single step inside the room. "I do not wish to intrude upon you, sir, but I was hoping you could tell me how Ignace and his kitten are."

Robert gestured at the far corner, to the distant side of the door to the storeroom. "Ask him yourself. I think he's fairly bursting to tell someone, but I can't make out a thing he's trying to say."

A figure rose from the corner and approached her, excitedly chattering in French. It was, of course, Ignace, but the change in the boy was so remarkable that she had to stop and take a long look. The boy was clean, for one thing, his hair loose and careless in the manner of the freshly washed. He wore new—well, newer clothes, with proper buttons and a belt that held the too-large pants around his waist.

The boy raced over to her, threw his arms around her waist in greeting, then took her by the hand and pulled her toward the corner. She looked back at Robert.

"Yes, I know. I think old Orlando scrubbed the boy like one of his Da's prize lambs. Not sure where the old fellow found those clothes. Thought it better not to ask."

Ignace dragged her to a pallet of blankets in the corner. It was a neatly made rectangle of thick quilts, and beside it, in a carton that had once held condensed milk, was a similar, if smaller pallet, upon which the kitten was sleeping, her small face hidden by the ruff. Ignace proudly began telling her, in excruciating detail, of the many services he had rendered the kitten today.

Charlotte turned to speak to Robert. He was walking

toward her, carrying the desk chair. "Please, Sister, do sit. I know you've been on your feet most of the day."

She gratefully accepted the chair, saying, "Sir, you must hear this."

He leaned against the wall beside her. "Do tell, Miss."

She translated for Robert, occasionally holding out a restraining hand to Ignace to slow the progress of his story. Robert listened with great patience to the long recitation. He even submitted to being pulled closer to the kitten and asked to confirm her cleanliness, to the extent of the boy lifting the tail proudly to display the relatively pristine hindquarters of the mortified baby cat.

At some point during Ignace's retelling, Orlando appeared with a tray, from which he dispensed tea, as well as soup and milk for the boy and even a broth of stewed meat for the kitten. Sipping the tea, luxuriating in the delicious warmth that spread through her, Charlotte heard the clink of coins as Orlando turned away.

"Oh, sir, you must not," she said, suddenly realizing that Fitzgerald had surely paid for all this that the boy now had. "You must let me—"

"Think nothing of it, my Lady Sister," Fitzgerald said with a gentle dismissive wave of his teacup. "One has so little opportunity to be of true good here, it is the least I can do." He inclined his head respectfully, "Unlike yourself. You are the soul of assistance. I have positively abused your good nature, and I regret I must impose upon you again."

Ducking her face behind her cup at this unmerited praise, she replied, "You have but to ask, sir."

"We need to tell the boy to exercise the kitten. If she lies about, her limbs will atrophy."

This thought had occurred to her earlier in the day but had escaped her until Fitzgerald mentioned it. "You are correct, sir." She relayed this to Ignace, who replied with a puzzled air.

"Ignace asks if you can show him how. He's unsure."

Robert glanced about as if confounded. Charlotte returned his gaze with equanimity. It was his idea, after all, and she found she was impishly curious as to what he proposed the treatment be. Robert pushed himself off the wall. He knelt beside the smaller pallet, reaching out to lift the limp kitten. She opened her eyes, her ears flickering about in peaceful curiosity. "There, there, puss," Robert crooned.

"Nell," Charlotte offered. "He calls the kitten Nell."

Watched avidly by the boy and the nurse, Fitzgerald cupped the kitten's torso in one hand, suspending her so her legs touched the ground. "Well, I suppose it would be something like this." On his knees and one hand, with the other guiding the kitten, he crawled across the floor, keeping the splinted legs of the baby cat in contact with the ground, in effect walking her. He spoke encouragingly to the small patient in a soft voice. "Good Nell, there's a good puss."

It was a sight so comical that Charlotte had to repress a smile. Mr. Fitzgerald was large, compared to the tiny cat, and he was working as hard as any mother to care for the wee beast. Charlotte said, for Ignace, "He wants to try."

She watched Robert carefully transfer the kitten to both of Ignace's smaller hands. He supervised closely, slowing the boy, raising his hands a bit. "Now," he said, stepping back, slapping the dirt from his trousers, "you must do this four times a day. At least two circuits of the office each time."

Upon hearing the translation, Ignace nodded in agreement. He soberly set off upon his first lap, the bewildered kitten looking around for an explanation of this foolishness.

From outside came the bugler, calling lights out.

Charlotte said, "Oh, I must run."

"Of course, Sister. Can you tell him one other thing?"

"Certainly, sir," she replied as she placed her cup on the tray.

"Tell him it will work better if he makes it a game for the kitten."

Charlotte quickly relayed this to Ignace.

"Will you come again tomorrow?" the boy asked her from his circuit with the kitten.

"Yes," she agreed without thinking.

Orlando was off on some mysterious errand, and Robert escorted her back to the tent. He walked beside her, his hands clasped behind his back. He was so determinedly a gentleman, she almost felt as if she were walking with one of the young priests as she had when a child in the rolling hills near their estates in Galitzna, outside of Saint Petersburg. As it was night, the darkness hiding much of the mud and unavoidable disorder about the camp, the illusion was very hard to dismiss.

He was making some neutral comment about the weather when she thought to ask him in a low voice, "How did you know to have Ignace exercise the kitten?"

"I bunged up my leg riding when I was a boy. Had a plaster on my leg for weeks, and the stableman was the one who told my father to have me walk on it as much as possible. The good man probably kept me from being lame."

She could not help thinking, *Lame, you would have not been in the war, and I'd never have met you,* but no sooner had the sentiment passed through her mind than she attempted to persuade herself that it had never occurred to her.

"Peculiar," he went on, peering again at the stars, "odd, really, how help comes to us, when we need it if we but only have the eyes to see. As you came to us, my Lady Sister."

She could not stop herself from giving him a doubtful look.

"I do not exaggerate, Miss," he insisted. "When I arrived this morning, the lad was already there. Orlando's work, I'm sure. Ignace had swept the office and emptied the bins. And the lad chattered to me the entire day, and I had no idea what he was saying. He was sad at first, but then cheered up and kindly overlooked my ignorance. Without you, that poor boy and his little cat would be lost. You're an angel of both mercy and translation."

"You truly have no French?" she asked.

"I wasn't the best student, I dare say," he admitted, looking a bit chagrined. "I confess, I have almost no French."

She heard herself saying, "Then, I shall have to teach you, sir."

So it began.

Later in her life, when she looked back on that time, she could remember how it seemed to have been months, but she knew it could only have been a matter of weeks.

As the war went on around her, as the wounded came into her care, and some lived and some died, there was an oasis that awaited her at the end of each day. A small room of peace, and laughter, and hope. Strangely, it became more real to her than the suffering and pain she witnessed each day.

No matter the hour, at the end of her shift, she would wash her face and make the walk to the supply office. There she would sit in the desk chair, often with the kitten upon her lap, and attempt to teach the basics of French to Robert Fitzgerald.

He was, it was true, an abominable student of the language, mangling and mispronouncing the simplest words and phrases, to the great amusement of Ignace.

Even Orlando allowed a smile to crease his face from time to time.

Often Robert served them tea himself, ordering Orlando to sit and be still, which caused the older man no end of discomfort. She had discovered the gnomish fellow was not a mere orderly, but, in fact, a batman, a kind of military servant assigned to officers in the British Army. It was a peculiar arrangement, but not the first odd thing she had encountered in His Majesty's service.

It mattered not. There in the room, with Ignace learning English with great ease, even as Robert struggled to learn Francais, she began to feel the strange elasticity of time. The minutes of the days in the wards seemed endless, yet those same minutes spent in the congenial company of Fitzgerald and the others slipped away from her, evaporating like spilled ether before her eyes. Perhaps it was the mundane normality of a little boy, his kitten, a servant, and tea on a tray, in contrast to the daily brutal horrors found in the wards—a difference so stark that like ether, those precious, seemingly intangible minutes left her dizzy.

The middle of the second week of the language lessons she found Matron waiting just up the hall from the supply office as Charlotte approached happily at the end of her shift.

"Let us walk together," Matron said. Charlotte ducked her head respectfully and fell into step beside the older nurse who said without preamble, "Word has reached my ears that you are spending time alone with Lieutenant Fitzgerald."

A hot indignation blossomed in Charlotte's chest. She kept her voice level and controlled. "Mum, respectfully, that is incorrect."

"You are familiar with the regulations, Nurse Braninov. The Sisters are forbidden from fraternizing with the men.

It would be a scandal, and we cannot have that." Matron stopped and faced her. The door to the office was just beyond, and Charlotte could hear Robert laughing. It was a happy sound, but in light of Matron's concerns, an unfortunate one. "Cheri, when I applied to Miss Nightingale a mere twenty years after the Crimean War, I was but a little older than you. Do you know what proper society thought of women nurses then?"

Charlotte, distracted by another full-throated laugh from Robert, shook her head. Her superior went on, "They whispered that we were but one step above prostitutes and actresses." Charlotte did not hide her shock at Matron's blunt speech. Matron concluded forcefully, "I will not have my girls spoken of that way."

"Mum, please come with me. You will see it is not so." Charlotte opened the door to the supply room without knocking.

Inside, a most unmilitary air prevailed. Robert pushed Ignace about in a wheeled desk chair. Ignace held a length of ribbon in his hand, while Nell the kitten tottered after the fluttering bit of silk, stilt-like on plaster-casted legs. Orlando watched from the corner as he arranged the tea tray, and Fitzgerald laughed with delight at the frantic antics of the kitten swatting clumsily at the ribbon.

Robert looked up at them. "My dear Matron," he called out with every indication of real welcome, "Do come in! We need a referee, as this young scamp..."—here he playfully cuffed Ignace on the head—"claims, as best I can tell, that he is a better playmate for Nell than I, obviously the superior choice."

An inscrutable expression passed over Matron's face. "Lieutenant, I would hate to interrupt—"

He pushed the chair over to them, as the galumphing kitten followed. "Nonsense, I must insist." He took her apron in one hand and jovially tugged the fierce old nurse into the room.

In the end, Matron took her turn in the chair, with Ignace on her lap as Robert gamely pushed them about the room to the delight of both boy and cat. By then, the poor kitten was almost done in. While tea was served, Ignace and the kitten took up residence on Matron's lap. Matron had no difficulties with French, and Ignace regaled her with the lengthy tale of the kitten's rescue and the events that had followed. Charlotte, who could follow their conversation, was able to tell that Matron was rather subtly interrogating the boy about what transpired in the room when they were all together.

Oh, please, she found herself thinking, *please do not find wickedness in our time together.* For she knew in her heart that nothing untoward had occurred, either here or on their walks to her tent, even though those quiet moments in the dark, walking beside Fitzgerald, were somehow transcendent to her, moments that filled her heart with peace and longing at the same time.

All too soon, it was time to go. Ignace and the kitten had retired unselfconsciously to their pallets, the urchin insisting that Matron kiss the kitten good night, a kiss which had been delivered with graceful good nature. The tea things had been cleared away. Matron caught Charlotte's eye, and they walked to the door of the office with Robert. Matron had a touch of colour in her cheeks, and her eyes were bright in an unusual way. She drew herself erect and looked Robert straight in the eye. "This is a most peculiar situation, Lieutenant Fitzgerald."

"Of that, I agree, ma'am," he answered seriously.

"You are being very kind to that boy, sir," she went on. "And Nurse Braninov, as well, teaching him to speak the King's English. The kitten is delightful," she added, without seeming to want to admit it. "It is very irregular. While I find no actual impropriety in what you are doing—

although I suspect the Senior Surgeon might frown on the boy's presence, but that is not my concern—however, I fear the appearance of impropriety is here, and that would be too easy a target for idle tongues in the hospital. I must forbid Nurse Braninov to continue her visits."

Charlotte felt the pulse in her neck give a lurch at these words.

Robert gazed gravely upon Matron. "Then, perhaps," he offered, "you would be so kind as to join us? I observe you have excellent command of French, Matron. It would be a shame to deny the lad an opportunity to improve himself."

Charlotte almost held her breath. "Perhaps," Matron finally said. "It would depend upon my other duties."

"Of course," Robert agreed. "I am very grateful for your consideration. Now, allow me to escort you both to your tents."

Robert chatted amiably with the two of them as they walked. He steadied Matron across the duckboards, and Charlotte found herself learning more about the stern old woman than she ever thought she might. Matron hailed from London, from a family of distinction which had been shocked nearly to apoplexy by her decision to become a nurse. "I had to help the suffering," Matron declared stoutly. "I could not be a nun, nor was I going to marry some fool of a baron or other member of the nobility, so it was the nursing service for me."

Robert stopped outside Charlotte's tent. As always, he stood back with his hands clasped behind him. Charlotte curtseyed to Matron, who nodded in return. "Good night, Mum. Good night, sir."

She slipped inside her tent and put her eye to the tent flap to watch them walk away. Lit by the three-quarters moon, Matron walked beside Fitzgerald, and Charlotte thought she heard a chuckle escape from the old nurse.

In the darkness of the tent, Kathleen asked, "What was that about?" Charlotte could just see her, reclining on one arm on her cot. The cot creaked as Kathleen dropped onto her back. "I didn't know the old gal made house calls."

"It was nothing," Charlotte said, striving to keep the bitterness out of her voice. "Someone reported me to Matron. She feared I might be behaving improperly after hours."

Kathleen snorted. "I wonder who gave her that idea?"

Her inference was clear. Kathleen had been speaking in her normal, rather loud voice, and it was already dark in the tent, thus she and Alice were already abed. The new nurse's silence at their conversation was odd and remarkable. Sick at heart at the thought of not seeing Ignace, of being denied the antics of the kitten, of not sharing tea with Mr. Fitzgerald, Charlotte walked dejectedly over to her cot. She stumbled on something large and very hard in the dark, and a venomous Russian curse burst from her lips before she snarled, "Who?!"

Alice peeped, "Sorry." A scramble in the dark, and the offending trunk was dragged aside.

Charlotte attempted to quell her own ill-temper and strove to speak calmly. "You must keep the centre of the tent clear, Alice. We've told you that."

Again, the peep from the darkness. "Yes. Sorry."

Charlotte strode to her cot, peeled back her blanket, and lay down. She felt so sad, suddenly, and then she felt cross with herself. She was being childish, she told herself. Do shut up and go to sleep.

She eventually fell asleep, but her pillow was damp by then.

The next day, Alice did not join her in the ward. A notice from the senior nurse on duty indicated Alice had been transferred to another ward, for "additional training."

Just as well, Charlotte sighed. The girl was a wretched nurse, clumsy with the men and capable of inflicting additional pain on them when she should be simply cleaning their wounds and changing their bandages.

As evening drew near, Charlotte bade her patients good night with forced cheerfulness. The blind boy in her ward would be going home soon, and some of his mates wanted to send him off in style. She told them she would see if it were possible. Straightening her apron, she was already thinking of how she would approach Madame for some special pastries when she noticed Matron in the hall outside. Charlotte squared her shoulders and walked up. "Good evening, Mum," she said. She had nothing of which to be ashamed, and she would not hide herself away like some guilty miscreant.

"Good evening, Nurse Braninov," the older woman replied in a cool, neutral way. "Come; do take the air with me."

"Yes, Mum," Charlotte answered obediently, falling into step beside her.

"How did you like England?" Matron asked, surprising her.

"I like it very much, Mum," Charlotte admitted as they walked through the halls of the hospital.

"That is good, Sister. I should hope you would consider staying on in our country after the war. You are a gifted nurse."

"Thank you, mum. I...I don't know." She had not heard from her parents in months. The rumours of revolution had been bad before, and now with the worker's riots and the rise of the Bolsheviks, she could not honestly say. In Russia, she had no true occupation or calling; she imagined that like Matron, she was expected to marry another member of the aristocracy, a future that seemed dismal at best. Yet, Russia was her home, or, it had been.

"Do think on it, Nurse. I should be pleased to have you work on my staff someday."

"Thank you, Mum." Charlotte was perplexed by this unexpected interest in her future. "Mum, do you think the war will be ending soon?"

The older woman shook her head, dislodging a stray strand of hair, which was quickly captured and returned to its proper location under the nurse's cap. "Nay, I have no inkling. I know this. No war lasts forever. It only seems as if they do."

They stopped. Their ramble had taken them the long way round to the hallway outside the Supply Office. "My goodness, look where we are," Matron said in a completely unconvincing show of surprise. "I suppose we had best inspect Mr. Fitzgerald and his two charges, see how he is keeping them. Men, you know," she went on in a confidential tone. "They think they rule the world, but they need a woman's touch to keep from driving everything aground."

Mutely, Charlotte followed her. She feared to speak, feared she might break the brief spell of insanity that had obviously overtaken Matron. She feared, too, the joy in her heart might cause her voice to tremble.

Matron knocked loudly on the office door. "Open up, Mr. Fitzgerald! You cannot keep us out."

The door was opened by Robert himself. He bowed low, ushering them into the dingy office with a sweep of his hand. "My dear ladies, how lovely to see you both."

At the time, Charlotte did not puzzle over Matron's actions. She merely felt great gratitude toward the stern old woman. Later, when Charlotte had ample opportunity to ponder much in her life, she realized that Matron had as great a need for those carefree hours in the Supply Office as she; perhaps even a greater need. For Matron had no children, and, Charlotte believed, she had no one to love. She could little afford to exhibit great softness with the nursing staff, but everyone, Charlotte felt with all her heart, everyone needed to love something outside themselves. And Matron could give her love to Ignace and the healing kitten.

Thereafter, Charlotte could depend up running into Matron at the end of her shift, and being asked by Matron to take the air with her. As if by the veriest of magic, they would arrive at the Supply Office and Matron would express her surprise at their location before recommending they check in on that "odd Mr. Fitzgerald and his menagerie."

There in the office, Ignace would happily demonstrate the kitten's growing strength, and then practice his English upon them all, while Robert, the slower student, would stumble along behind, mumbling phrases in broken French. For an hour or more, Matron would listen happily to the boy, not missing the opportunity to wash his face and comb his hair or to instruct him in the proper way to clean his hands and person. She seemed to take as great a delight in Ignace's love of the kitten as she did in the boy.

In her heart, Charlotte thanked Matron for each of the few minutes. For while she did not spend a great deal of time speaking to Fitzgerald, simply being near him refreshed something in her. His blue eyes that could smile at her without his mouth moving, as if they had a wholesome, humorous secret between them; the calmness within him as he moved about the room serving tea or playing with Ignace; the respectful, yet not subservient deference he extended to Matron.

Each evening, the time would come when Matron would announce it was time for Ignace and Nell to be off to bed. The kitten would be offered all around to receive her goodnight kiss (and Charlotte had to stifle an impolite, startled laugh the first time she saw Orlando wrinkle up his gnomish face into something strangely beautiful as he solemnly bussed the kitten), Ignace would collect a hug from the men, kiss the two women on the cheek, and then climb happily onto his pallet, cradling Nell.

Robert would escort the two women back to Charlotte's tent in the darkness, and there, her spirit filled with a private joy she could not explain, she would bid them goodnight. She thought Matron returned to her own tent after that, but Robert had told her he walked the older nurse back to the wards, where she made a final, thorough inspection of them before retiring. "I accompanied her that first night," he'd admitted in a quiet voice as they prepared the tea things one evening. "But the old girl nearly walked my legs off."

The idyll could not last, she knew this. It was becoming clearer every day that the Americans would finally send a true army to validate their declaration of war against Germany. The Axis powers would redouble their efforts, and then the wards would run with the blood of the wounded. Once more, she would work until she could not stand, and she would fall into exhausted sleep still wearing clothing that reeked of the lives that had expired under her helpless hands.

She did not expect it to end so soon.

Some sound awoke her. She had only been asleep for an hour or so, she was certain. Nearly a month had passed since Matron had started to accompany Charlotte to the supply office. They had spent the evening teaching Ignace to sing "God Save the King," with everyone taking a turn. The singing had distressed the kitten, and when Robert began to lustily bellow his verse, Nell raced over and nipped him on the thigh before galloping back awkwardly on splinted legs to hide beside Ignace; neither of the two young creatures understanding why the adults were laughing so heartily, Robert the loudest of them all. Whatever his other virtues, music was not one of them, and this he knew.

It had been a lovely evening, and Charlotte had fallen asleep with a small smile on her face. She had by now started to ignore Alice's strange fits of pique. She remained civil to the moody English girl, but nothing more, and the girl's presence rarely intruded on her awareness.

However, this noise...Charlotte had become fully conscious on perceiving it. A hum, that's what it was. Then she shook her head, realizing she was far more groggy than she had imagined. The sound did not emanate from the canvas or the rope tie-downs vibrating in the evening breeze. It was from high overhead, a hum that was almost a buzz, rising and falling.

She realized the source of the sound. The engine of an aeroplane flying high overhead, not in the orderly pattern of a routine patrol, but in the questing, random manner of a predator seeking a target. She was stepping toward Kathleen's cot when the first bomb fell on the far side of the camp. The sound and a ripple of moving air reached her first, followed almost immediately by a rumble she felt through her socked feet.

Kathleen leaped from her cot. "Air raid?" she asked, her voice wild. Outside, beams of intense white light stabbed into the night, bouncing off low clouds as searchlights burst to life around the Hospital grounds.

"Yes," Charlotte said. She was closest to Alice's cot. She turned, but before she could speak, she heard Kathleen tumble to the ground.

"Damn it!" the American swore heatedly. "We've told you to keep your blasted trunk out of the centre of the tent."

"Sorry," came the voice from Alice's cot. A sweeping

beam briefly illuminated their tent, showing Alice sitting up in her useless nightdress, blanket clutched to her slender chest. "I was putting away my things."

"Horseshit!" Kathleen replied, hurling the trunk aside. "You were dolling yourself up all night!"

As darkness fell on the tent again, another explosion came, closer this time. Charlotte could hear Kathleen's hands scrabbling at the floor of the tent. Charlotte said calmly, "Come, Alice, come with me."

Outside were the sounds of shouting men, boots pounding over the duckboards. Alice sat rigidly on her cot, hands wrapped in a rictus of fear around her blanket. "No, I want to stay here."

Yet another blast, and this time the canvas of the tent flexed. "Come on, girl," Kathleen barked. "Get your carcass over here."

There was someone at the tent flap. Charlotte turned, thinking it was one of the senior nurses, come to impress them into emergency duty. Robert Fitzgerald stood at the entrance to their tent, breathing hard, outlined by the sweeping searchlights.

"I had to see…that you were unharmed," he said, between gasps, looking first within the tent, then up to the sky.

"Yes, I'm fine," Alice said before anyone could speak.

A new explosion rocked the ground beneath them, and debris sprinkled down upon their tent. An anti-aircraft gun began firing, with a heavy chug-chug that seemed lost and purposeless.

Robert glanced in Alice's direction with a perplexed expression. Dismissing her, he stepped into the tent until he could see Charlotte. "Nurse Braninov, are you perfectly well?"

"Yes, Mr. Fitzgerald."

"We must get you to a bunker—all of you."

Kathleen started to answer, "We have—" when Alice leapt from her cot and hurtled out of the tent. She ran into the Lieutenant, rebounded off him, and sprinted into the dark.

Fitzgerald sprawled backward at the girl's impact, tumbling off the duckboards and into the mud. "Christ!" he grunted.

"Are you all right?" Charlotte asked him, kneeling and scrabbling under her cot for her boots.

He pulled free of the grasping mud. "Yes, grand." He saw her lacing the boots and held out a restraining hand. "I will get her. You must get to the bunker."

"We're protected here." By the searchlights, Robert could see where Kathleen knelt in the centre of the tent, the floorboard levered up onto one side. "But please, hurry." Charlotte pointed toward the rear of the camp. "She ran that way."

For a scant fraction of a heartbeat, he seemed about to speak, but instead turned and disappeared into the night.

She had never felt as alone in her life. She knew Kathleen hunkered in the dirt behind her, but Charlotte's consciousness was out in the dark, questing with Robert. She stood, enveloped by the blackness. The night would be slashed by the searchlights, the blinding pillars scoring the sky, seeking the faceless enemy that attacked them in violation of all rules of war.

Fear coursed in her, but it was not fear for her own safety. When Robert, muddy as a dog from a field, had risen and dashed off into the night on a fool's errand of mercy, some part of her had surrendered the last of her resistance and she silently gave her heart to this man, her Knight Robert Fitzgerald, whom she might never again see in this world. The helplessness nearly drove her mad as she crouched in the illusory protection of the canvas tent. She had never been so unable to assist someone, so completely powerless to aid the suffering or to protect the fallen.

She could hear her pulse pounding in her ears. Explosions near and far sent blossoms of flame into the sky, as if light were pressing against the armour of the darkness, forcing its way through the seams. Kathleen was saying something, pulling at her arm. Charlotte shook her off. She would wait for Robert; wait until death if that were required.

Robert emerged from the darkness before her, carrying Alice over one shoulder like a rolled up rug. *Oh, thank you, merciful Father,* Charlotte thought in gratitude. *Thank you for this gift.* "Take her!" Robert shouted, slinging the limp girl into Charlotte's arms. His eyes were stark in the illumination of the lights. "Get under cover!"

Charlotte collected Alice, who stirred in feeble protest. "Sir, you must hide—"

"No," he shouted again, and she realized the explosions must have deafened him. "I must help dig out the bunker!" He reached out, and squeezed her hand, too hard, but she did not notice the bruises until later, and he was gone into the night.

Charlotte turned to Alice, trying to shove her toward Kathleen. Outside, there was a flash, and then some great force hurled Charlotte across the tent where she crashed into her cot.

She was only stunned for a moment and found herself reflexively rolling out of the debris-covered cot to land lightly on the fingers of her hands and the balls of her feet, reminding herself of her mother's languid cat. Alice—it could only be her—Alice was screaming.

Charlotte understood the girl wasn't hurt. The screaming contained too many breaths, too many attempts to form sentences about novel emotions the terrified nurse did not currently have the vocabulary to express. The screaming of the truly wounded surrounded Charlotte many times each day. That sound had an entirely different diabolical music to it; more animal wails of pain, often interspersed with pleas to divinity for release. It was only when the men screamed for their mothers that she truly feared for them, for that was when the wounded knew they were dying. Rising to her knees, Charlotte patted her own face and head, then repeated the action rapidly down as much of her body as she could reach. She was dusty and gritty, but not wet. She decided she'd not been cut by anything.

That would change, she knew, if the German pilot decided to take another pass at this area. "Alice," she snapped, crawling forward to where the silly screaming girl stood clutching her pigtails, one in each hand. "Get down! *Rapidement, vous dupez!*" She lapsed into French without thinking. Another shell strike, closer, the rolling rumble through the earth coming more rapidly upon the sound of the impact. Debris pattered down on the canvas tent overhead, bits of it dribbling through new rents in the thick fabric.

The fool girl commenced to shrieking more wildly. Charlotte, who had been the only daughter amongst seven brothers, abandoned lady-like behaviour (an act which her grandmother, *Requiescat in Pace*, would have deplored), launched herself across the wooden floor and tackled the English girl.

Alice's most recent cry of terror was cut off with a click as her teeth slammed together, and she and Charlotte tumbled to the dirty wooden floor on the far side of the tent. Charlotte took Alice's face in both her hands and shouted in her face. "Listen to me! You must stay down!"

Then came another explosion, this one close enough to thunder with physical pain against their eardrums, followed immediately by a hail of debris and metal, some of which tore through the canvas like deadly grease through a goose. Kathleen knelt by the levered up wooden planking in the centre of the tent, waiting for her friend; stout, strong as a bull and steady as a granite statue. Charlotte wrapped her arms around Alice and, with the struggling girl on her chest, began wriggling backward toward the small pits that had been dug into the dirt under the wooden floor. Outside, the beams swivelled, casting blades of light as they passed, illuminating Kathleen through the torn fabric as she crouched in the shallow trench beneath their tent. Another trench was beside it.

At the sight of the frankly grave-like depressions in the ground, Alice began struggling with a strength born of utter terror. "No," the young girl wailed. "We'll be buried alive! Don't make me go in there!!"

Stolid Kathleen knelt in the dirt, holding the iron-plate section of the floor braced against her back. A high-pitched shriek, this one from overhead. No time for discussion. Charlotte wrapped her arms around Alice, clamped her knees against the outside of the girl's thighs, and rolled them both into the nearest pit. Kathleen dropped prone, and the heavy cover slammed down over them.

For a time, Alice fought and keened. Then she wept. Charlotte kept her arms around the girl, for she knew the nightdress would not keep Alice warm in the chilly embrace of the French soil. After a time, the younger woman fell silent, and Charlotte thought they might be able to sleep until the barrage had stopped. Between the blasts of bombs and the coughing report of the anti-aircraft gun, she could hear Kathleen's snoring echoing off the iron sheeting one of the soldiers had nailed to the wooden floor to protect them from ricocheting bits of wreckage.

In the darkness, Alice's voice was close to her ear. The girl's voice was tight; it seemed to be hissing steam escaping from a broken pipe about to burst. "How can you stand this? Why do you do it?"

Poor girl, Charlotte thought. She has no idea what terrible really is. She will find out if she stays. "If not us, then who?" Charlotte responded with deliberate gentle care. "We are not permitted to go into battle. If they are willing to die for us, then I am willing to be here."

Alice was silent for a long time. When she spoke again, her voice was even tighter, and her breath against Charlotte's ear seemed to scald the skin. "I'll never forget what you did to me. I'll never forgive you."

The vehemence in the girl's voice was shocking, and for a minute Charlotte trembled on the edge of scrambling from their shelter to the safety of the storm outside. She had the strongest sense she'd rather endure the uncontrollable fury of the bombardment rather than face this girl who'd become unhinged with terror. The fancy passed. She gently chided herself. What was the tiny wrath of this child compared to what the men in the trenches were experiencing, or what Robert might at this very moment be confronting?

Charlotte calmed herself and began to pet the girl's hair, the way she'd stroke the mane of one of her father's horses, speaking in a low, gentle voice. "It will pass soon, Alice." She continued to murmur, the words not as important as the soft sounds and the reassuring, calm touch. Alice still trembled but spoke no further.

The heat of the two living bodies in the earthen crypt began to warm them, and in time, they slept, exhausted, one from fear, and the other from toil.

The silence awoke her this time. Some part of her mind realized the bombing had ceased, the blasts of sound and the shaking of the earth had paused. Her arms still around the young nurse, Charlotte called loudly, "Kathleen?" Alice awoke with a cry and began trembling anew like a rabbit staring at a fox.

"Here, Cheri!" the American girl answered.

"I think it's over."

"Yep." There was a clang of boots on the metal, and then the cover was thrust from them.

Charlotte could sense that dawn was nearly upon them. She clambered out of the pits. Much of the tent hung in rags that dipped downward in the stillness of the morning. There were gaping holes in their trunks and belongings, gouged there by flying shrapnel.

"That was a bad one," Kathleen observed.

"Then they will need us," Charlotte said, brushing the dirt from her clothes with her hands. She didn't bother to look for her nurse's cap. There was no time. "Kathleen, take Alice to Hospital. Some of the patients may have been hit. I'll go and see if there are any wounded in the camp."

Alice spoke in a low, flat, ugly voice, one that seemed aged with resentment and hatred beyond her years. "You're going to look for him, aren't you?"

Charlotte continued as if Alice had never spoken. "Check the men closest to the windows first."

"Right," Kathleen said. She glanced over at Alice, whose nightdress was dark with dirt. "Throw on your jacket, we have work to do."

Alice, her pale face almost alabaster, looked about the ruined tent and then outside, where the first rays of the sun revealed smoke rising from craters. She backed away from them and sat on her cot, hands in her lap, muttering something.

Kathleen found her own boots, shook several unidentifiable chunks out of them, and started to pull them on. "What did you say?" she asked, lacing up her boots without looking at Alice.

"I can't do it," Alice said in the bitterest tone of

acquiescence that Charlotte had ever heard. Without looking up from her clasped hands, she said distinctly. "I cannot go out there."

They spared no time to scold her into action. Those seconds wasted might mean the loss of another life. Kathleen and Charlotte exchanged a look of resignation and plunged out of the tent to do what they could.

Charlotte moved toward raised voices, leaping off the duckboard path to struggle through the muck toward a knot of soldiers pawing at a shredded tent. Mud had fountained up from a crater just outside the back of the tent, covering the inhabitants and their belongings in a layer nearly a foot thick. The soldiers, some of them plainly wounded themselves, dug without organization, yanking at whatever shattered limb presented itself.

"Uncover their faces first!" Charlotte barked sharply. Her clear statement gave the men a direction for their energies. They dug into the mud with their hands, feeling along like blind men scrying the outlines of an elephant, until they found a head. One short man lay full length on the mud, his arms acting as reference stakes for the others to dig around. Lads near him clawed at the mud with their bare hands until the face was revealed. Two other soldiers in the tent were performing similar searches.

Of the three victims, all nurses, two were saved by clearing the mud from their mouths and nostrils, and then forcing air into their lungs. The third, a thin woman with grey hair that Charlotte had only seen from a distance, had been struck by some misshapen piece of metal in the chest and had likely died instantly.

Charlotte directed four of the soldiers to bear the other two nurses to the hospital and moved on. She passed men with bloody faces, and limping nurses. She quickly examined each one for critical injuries and sent them on to the hospital with others.

But she did not see Robert. Fear began to burn in her chest; she could taste it in the back of her throat. Yet, she could not tarry. It was clear that the personnel tents had not been the real targets of the raid. Looking at the hospital, she could see several sections that had collapsed and were burning. Soldiers worked around them with buckets or dug in the rubble. They would need her there.

She climbed from the mud back onto the duckboard path and began an unsteady trot toward the building. The rising sun began to burn off the mists of the night, and more of the damage became visible. She could only spare the wreckage about her a glance as she moved, until she passed something so perplexing that she slowed to a stop, incredulous, to look again.

A pair of human legs hung from a telegraph line overhead. For a heartbeat, her brain was unable to make sense of what her eyes perceived, but after a moment the details resolved. The boots (men's, she thought), the heavy woollen trousers, and then nothing above the thighs. It was, she guessed, all that remained of some poor soul who had been in the direct path of a blast.

"Father, have mercy," she whispered, and continued, for there was nothing she could do here. Somewhere, there were people she could help.

Other nurses were coming forward from the tents, many of them dishevelled and unkempt. Some came quickly; others stumbled along on sheer will. They each had a look of fierce determination, moving to answer the call of service that pulsed in them like their very blood.

Charlotte met those other nurses at the entrance to the hospital. She looked hopefully for Matron, but she did not appear. The nurses, young and old, stout, thin, pale or swarthy, looked up at her, as she happened to be the person standing before them. The Russian girl recognized the folly of waiting for anyone who might give them direction.

She moved up to the top of the steps and faced them. "Pair up quickly. Each pair to a ward. Inspect the soundness of the building. Check the patients. If they are further injured, assess, and send one nurse back here with a report on the status of both." Charlotte could hear the faint accent in her voice become more pronounced, but ignored it. She pointed to a girl she knew slightly, who had limped up to the group. "Virginia, you will stay here and collect the reports. Can you find something to write on?"

Virginia nodded. "Aye."

"For now, these steps will be our HQ, understood?"

The other nurses murmured assent, yet remained immobile, continuing to stare up at her. "Go on now," she ordered them. "This is the duty to which we have been called."

A voice asked, "What are you going to do?"

"I'm going to break into the bloody supply closet. We're going to need everything I can find."

She ran through the halls. Patients cried out from their wards or were dazedly wandering the halls. She could only give them a brief explanation. "We're coming for you, fellows! Get back into your beds, help your mates! It's over!"

Cabinets lay overturned from explosions, in places glass tinkled and crackled beneath her feet. The electric lights in the hallways were on intermittently, and thus she moved in alternating areas of darkness and mere dimness.

She was imagining ways to force the door of the Supply Office as she ran, but there was no need. The office door was open, and Orlando was within.

"Miss Braninov," he said as she burst in. He gestured at the chaotic pile of blankets. "I cannot find the bairns or

Master Robert!"

Ah, *merde*, there was no time. "Leave them in Heaven's care for now, Orlando. You must help me distribute these supplies. Can you do that?"

The little man nodded vigorously. "Yes, Miss."

"Good fellow," she told him. "Open the supply closet."

He fumbled with the keys, and on his second try unlocked the door at the rear of the office. When he pushed, the door squealed and only opened to the width of a foot before stopping. The bombing must have thrown it out of true. She leaned her weight into the door beside Orlando, forcing it open another 6 inches.

The little man's face contorted with anger. He no longer seemed gnomish to her, his aspect was that of a dwarven warrior of the Old Norse tales. "Damned Frog workmanship!" he swore. He wedged himself into the gap, his back against the door with his feet against the jam, and shoved. With a loud crack, the door gave way, dumping the man onto the floor.

She pulled him to his feet before slipping past him. Several carts stood against the front wall. She pushed one toward Orlando. "Come with me, sir!"

She quickly piled the most necessary supplies onto each cart: bandages, ointments for burns, extra scissors and scalpels, splint materials, needles, catgut. As they dragged the loads outside, she told him, "You go east, and I shall go west. Stop at each ward. Leave the closet open, someone may need something from within." And to hell with the inventory, she added silently.

"Yes, Miss," he said and set off straight away.

She turned and pushed the cart before her, going as fast as she dared without risking overturning the entire cargo.

In the wards that had not been directly struck, the injuries were slight...men had hurt themselves hurling to the ground or had reopened wounds as they attempted to hide themselves or their fellows.

Five of twelve wards had suffered damage. Three were burning. Outside the first burning ward, Charlotte passed her cart to a very young-looking but determined orderly and sent him to complete her rounds.

The fire was at the rear of the ward, thank the Lord, burning at the edges of the ragged gap blown into the outside wall. Through the gap, she could see daylight and a mass of men—doctors, assistants, orderlies, soldiers—at work fighting the fire. Some were aiming feeble hoses at the flames as others of them worked with shovels and rakes hauling away the ashes and flaming wreckage, while still more used grapples to pull down the burning debris from the edges of the building.

Inside the ward, the ambulatory patients had banded together to aid their own. Blind men were being led out by those who could see, others were being pushed in chairs away from the flames. She saw two men, amputees, each with only one remaining arm, carefully place a boy with no legs on a mattress, each grasp an edge with their only limb and drag the fellow from the ward and to safety in the hall. "Good lads," she told them as they passed her.

"Aye, Sister, bloody Huns!" one replied.

She had to search for other survivors. Charlotte moved as close as she dared to the burning gap in the wall. Three hospital beds lay in pieces amid the rubble, shattered bodies nearby. She quickly examined each of the broken forms and saw there was nothing she could do for them.

"Come away, Sister," a sooty silhouette told her. "The men are out. We must clear the room."

"All the men?" she asked, even as she scanned the floors and beneath the beds.

"Yes," she was told.

"Get those boys outside," she said, pointing to the still, fallen forms. "We will not leave them to burn." She ran to the next ward.

In the future, she would never speak much of her experiences during the Great War. Not the horror, for that was all around her. Not the grotesqueries she saw, for after a time it all became a matter of degree. The Great War and its events were too important, too deeply real to her to be reduced to the sophistry of wondering which kind of death or crippling injury would be preferable to another, in the manner of college boys arguing about questions of history that had been settled by fate centuries before.

When she was asked by the callow or uninformed, those who had not been smote by the hand of Mars, she would speak of the honour to be found there in the foundries of Hell. Of the decency. Of the kindnesses she witnessed. She would speak of men like Orlando, of women like Matron. Of human beings living in a way to bear witness to the beauty to be found within their souls in the very worst of moments.

By 10 o'clock that morning, the fires were out. Matron had appeared just after sunrise, her nurse's uniform blackened by smoke and grimed with blood. She'd been briefed on Charlotte's makeshift recovery plans, nodded approvingly, and then moved on to oversee the reapportionment of the surviving patients to serviceable wards.

By nine, Charlotte had been impressed into service in the surgery. Outside, there were, blessedly, only fourteen dead, most of them soldiers or orderlies, although two nurses had perished. There were at least two score more injured, some suffering merely from mild cases of concussion to others with broken bones or internal injuries. And these were in addition to the patients who had re-injured themselves, some of whom would require surgery, as well as the unending stream of wounded from the front. Captain McDougal from her tour at the CCS, he of the walrus moustache and bluff manner that hid a good heart, had requested her steady presence to help him.

At 3 pm, Matron pulled her out of the surgery. Charlotte was swaying, having been up since before dawn, with neither rest nor food, and having only snatched a few gulps of cold tea. "I can stay," she protested.

"Not likely," Matron replied woodenly, guiding her out of the surgery as another nurse took her place beside Captain McDougal. "We will need you in the wards tomorrow, Nurse Braninov."

Outside, the sun struck her eyes with force…she'd been under the electric lights of the surgery, and was not prepared for the brilliance of the afternoon. She shielded her streaming eyes. "I can find my way to my tent, Mum," she insisted.

Matron sniffed. "Your tent was turned in a sieve. You'll be staying in a new one, near the stables."

"Yes, Mum." Charlotte blinked, trying to clear the water from her eyes. She could not make herself remain silent any longer and dared to ask, "Mum, have you seen Mr. Fitzgerald?"

In a voice that she hardly recognized as coming from the old nurse, Charlotte was told, "No, lass. I would have you follow me, Nurse Braninov."

She led Charlotte toward the far side of the hospital, and to the dreaded Moratorium tents. There, on the ground in a silent row covered by blankets, were laid the dead. Many of the shapes beneath the simple grey wool were horribly awry or strangely foreshortened.

Toward the end of the row, there was to be found one shape that was small in size, but whose outlines did not speak of any deformity or loss of limbs. Matron stopped solemnly beside this shape and glanced at Charlotte. The younger woman slowly lowered herself to both knees beside the shape, almost in an attitude of prayer, and with a steady hand gently folded back the thick blanket, parts of which were stiff with dried blood.

Charlotte beheld the form of Ignace. At first glance, he might have appeared to be sleeping, but he lay there in the wholly unnatural stillness of death. There was dried blood on the corner of his mouth, and at the base of one ear. Something lay on his chest.

She made out the motionless, tiny form of the infant cat. "Poor Nell," she breathed without realizing she had spoken aloud.

"He was found with the wee kitten in his arms." Matron's voice was unsteady.

"Shell-shock?" Charlotte asked, her voice flat. She knew already, from the fluids leaking from his mouth and ear. A bomb had landed near the boy, and the concussive force of the expanding gases from the chemical action of the explosive had killed him, perhaps ripping his brain loose from his spine, perhaps in some other equally vile way. The details of it mattered not. The urchin and the little cat he'd fought so hard to save were now resting in their Father's arms.

Matron stood, one hand reaching toward the boy's supine body as if to demand an answer of him, a reply that Ignace could never make. Charlotte carefully replaced the blanket over the boy's still face, then rocked back on her feet and levered herself upright, wiping the dirt from the front of her skirt.

After taking in Matron's face, which was suddenly all lines and wattles under her chin, Charlotte said, "I shall tidy him up, Mum."

"That would be most...kind of you, Charlotte," Matron replied absently.

"Let me fetch some clean wash clothes," Charlotte told

her.

"Will you be very long?"

The soft appeal in Matron's voice shocked her as much as the suddenly aged appearance of the Head Nurse. Charlotte had no idea that her own face had gone starkly pale, giving her the appearance of a marble death mask. "No, Mum, I will return swiftly," she assured the old nurse.

Matron lowered herself beside the blanket-covered form. "Then I shall wait here with them both." Without seeming to be aware of it, Matron reached over to stroke the tiny shape of the dead kitten.

Charlotte curtsied deeply. "Of course, Mum."

Mechanically, moving with as much thought or care as one of the damned lumbering tanks she'd seen at the front, Charlotte turned and strode toward the front of the Hospital. She'd beg or steal the first set of clean towels and basin of water she came upon.

She was aware in only the most abstract way of those she passed: soldiers raking out smoking debris, quartermasters dragging forth new tents, carpenters replacing shattered duckboards and rebuilding the paths between various buildings and the living quarters. She might have been a ghost wandering among the living, so little did she heed those around her. Or perhaps they were ghosts on errands unknowable to her, moving around her, passing through her without knowing she breathed still.

So much death she had seen, yet this one—these two, these two deaths had struck her numb. Was it the unfairness of it? Was it that she knew the boy, had held him and his beloved kitten on her lap? Was it that she saw, too clearly, the life that might have been: the kind-hearted little boy who might have grown into a fine, kind, loving man? Now, that would never be. Would never be.

The nearest entrance to the hospital was within her sight. She was dully aware of men to her right, tamping out the embers of the last fire at the edge of one ward. One of the dim ghosts approached her. "Nurse Braninov?"

She continued to walk and only slowed when she faintly perceived her name being spoken again.

The ghost came closer. Dark, it was, and tall, its burial clothing torn and dirty. She continued to walk, the entrance to the hospital was not far now.

"Nurse Braninov?" Robert Fitzgerald took her hand and pulled her to a stop. She was forced to turn. "Miss Braninov, are you very well?"

She could see him now, tall, soot across his face and forehead. Burns...he had burns on his forearms. His uniform was ripped in many places. He was real. He was alive.

He was alive.

She threw her arms around his neck and wept.

Robert had helped her clean the body, while Orlando had raised Matron to her feet and assisted her back to her tent.

They buried Ignace that evening. The boy lay with the kitten curled in his arms. Orlando had fetched the small pallets upon which they had slept and cushioned the rude coffin with them.

Matron joined them for the short funeral. Her face was once more composed, her uniform spotless and proper in every respect. She stood at the head of the grave with her hands clasped before her. Orlando, biting his lip, tears leaking from his eyes without making a sound, attended to her right.

Charlotte and Robert were side by side, watching the small, hastily constructed coffin lower into the cold earth. Robert had scrubbed his own face and Charlotte had wrapped bandages round his forearms. His shirtsleeves were rolled up past the wrappings, and he gazed straight ahead while a chaplain said words that gave no comfort to any standing there.

By unspoken accord, the witnesses turned away as the first shovelfuls of dirt began to drift down into the grave. The sun was setting, and darkness quickly began to fill the world. Robert stepped up beside Matron, who strode along with flinty determination. "Ma'am, may I escort you to your tent?"

"No, you may not, sir," was her sharp reply. Robert checked his step, and realizing her tone, Matron went on more neutrally, "You will escort Nurse Braninov to her tent. I declare she has done more for the hospital and our patients than any of us today." She fixed him with a steely gaze as if daring him to contradict her.

"As you wish, ma'am," Robert assented.

She turned her attention on Charlotte. "And, you, Nurse Braninov, you are to go directly to bed. I need you fresh tomorrow, do you hear me? The lads in their wards need you, as well." She leaned a little closer and added, "If you must have a spot of rum to help you sleep, take it."

"Yes, Mum."

Robert waved Orlando forward, and the good fellow hurried closer, wiping tears from his cheeks with the back of his wrists. "My man will see you to your tent, Matron."

"Thank you, sir," Matron said nodding at Robert, then at Orlando. "Thank you, Mr. Pyle."

"Of course, Mum," Orlando said, offering her his arm. The dignified old nurse took it without slowing and they marched away.

Robert faced Charlotte. "Well, Miss. We have our orders."

They turned toward the nurses' tents. Already, most of the damage had been repaired, and except for the smoke drifting from the burned wards that could just be seen in the last of the fading light, it was difficult to believe the bombing had ever happened.

One nurse had been in a tent that was near a bomb, and now she lay dead while Charlotte lived on, to grieve the lost and to keen in her heart—especially for the lost boy and his baby cat. It was odd, she mused, how proximity had created destiny. *What a horrible thought.* Truly, if that were all, that one's fate was decided by the random events that could literally explode around one, tumbling a person about like a tenpin, then what would be the reason to bother with any of the mess and inconvenience of life at all? The idea had an ugly, gripping fascination. Had Charlotte not been at the CCS, she'd not have met Mr. Fitzgerald. Oh, he might have come to Base Hospital No. 12, but he would simply be another of the official staff whom she largely ignored when she was not tolerating their ineptitude.

Yet, because she had been there in that hell-hole, she'd met Robert, the very person whose quiet steady presence gave her such comfort on this awful day. What would she be doing now, had she not met him?

She could not allow herself to believe the world was so harshly made. Surely her Father in Heaven was not so cruel as to allow His children to suffer for nothing. There had to be a reason.

"God, how peculiar," she blurted, looking out over the camp, striving to shake the black mood that threatened to swallow her. "It's like they were never here."

"Who, Miss?"

"The Germans. Ignace. Those other poor chaps who were also killed."

Robert agreed with great deliberation, "Yes, Miss. It was a terrible thing. Heart-breaking about the boy, Nurse Braninov. He was very fond of you." He paused, and then went on, speaking with great earnestness. "Nurse Braninov, I am so pleased you were not injured."

They were alone on the path in the darkness of the early evening, but she didn't realize it. The yawning emptiness of the death all around roused her, infuriated her. She faced him and said fiercely, "Is that all I am to you, Mr. Fitzgerald? Am I just Miss? Am I just Nurse Braninov? Just the Sister?"

Robert stopped, transfixed by the intensity of her question. "No, Charlotte," he replied, his voice raspy from the day's smoke, yet filled with a growing wonder. "You are most dear to me. You are the dearest person I have ever known." He took her hand, raised it to his lips, and kissed the palm gently as if he feared breaking her.

She thought *Propriety be damned,* and stood up on her toes as she pressed her lips to his. She wanted him to feel the love that burned within her, to know it in every kiss she rained upon his face and mouth.

His arms pulled her close, and she felt the beating of his heart against her breasts, felt the warmth of his body radiating into her own. "I love you most hopelessly, my dear Charlotte," he said, his face buried in her hair, his breath against her ear.

She pulled back from him, took his face in both her hands. He saw upon her face that same feral expression he'd seen when she was listening to poor Ignace tell of rescuing the kitten. But now, her countenance was softened by something else. Indeed, he thought, he could gaze forever at the wild beauty blazing in her blue eyes.

Charlotte spoke to him in Russian. *"You are my own, Robert Fitzgerald. I will have no other."* She uttered these words with all the savage fervour of her ancestors of the Steppe, who fought wolf and winter for centuries to survive and triumph.

Robert enveloped her in his arms for a moment before reluctantly releasing her. "Miss Charlotte, there is work for us to do."

He extended his arm to her with great gravity. There was something of a vow in the motion, in the deliberate movement of his forearm toward the young woman. With equal solemnity, Charlotte took his arm and allowed him to lead her, in the utmost respectability, back to her tent.

They walked in the silence of their own thoughts for a time, until Charlotte turned to him. "I shall never forget what you have said to me, Mr. Fitzgerald."

"Nor I what you have conveyed to me with more than words, dearest Miss. Although...I would someday like to know the meaning of what you said in that foreign tongue."

"One day, I shall gladly tell you, my dearest sir."

She curtseyed playfully. He leaned down swiftly and gave her the most of chaste of kisses, although she felt the fire of his mouth on hers for a long time after.

And that was the beginning of the end of their war.

In time, she dared to ask him what had brought him to the hospital, had brought him into her life.

In time he told her everything.

And she loved him the more for it.

A Trench in Passchendaele

Robert Fitzgerald was dreaming.

Not of home —not for years—nor did he allow himself to think of England when he was awake.

He dreamed of December 25, 1914. "Over By Christmas" had been revealed to be as much of a fantasy as Saint Nicholas and his eternal bag of toys. Missing were the bright and cheerful chaps from his officer corps at Eton, just barely older than boys, drilling with rifles on their shoulders, wearing gentlemanly frock coats and top hats. Scattered were the smiling French citizens who'd cheered the Infantry as they marched smartly along the farm roads, showering them with cheers and food and sloppy, garlicky kisses. Gone was all the early and childishly naive optimism.

That morning was clear, the night having swept away the smoke from the German's deadly machine guns and the British artillery. To his left, in the dream or the dreaming memory, he could not be sure what it was, but to his left, one of the Chums risked a peek over the crumbling edge of the English trench. The boy was part of a cadre of schoolmates, the Chums, created by a former headmaster in the belief that men who'd grown up side-by-side would make superior soldiers. His dreaming self wanted to warn the boy, "Don't forget where you are, you cretin. They'll paint the back of the trench with your brains if you look up like that." The game of snipers waiting patiently as a hungry cat by a mouse hole for the sight of a careless forehead above the enemy's trench works, that deadly game would only be played later, when this celebration of the Day of Our Lord's Birth had passed, and both sides had demonstrated how much of His teachings they had forgotten.

The youth turned to Fitzgerald in his dream, as the boy had done that morning, face still bright and unmarked enough to see how terribly young the fellow was. "Here, sir. Listen!"

Robert surely hadn't heard the singing that morning as clearly as it now came to him in the dream. The words were German, floating across the churned mud as if carried by the last of the dawn's mist.

"*Stille Nacht, heilige Nacht,*
"*Alles schläft; einsam wacht*"

The English Lieutenant had known the tune. Silent Night. The singer's voice had a gentleness, a sweetness that made Fitzgerald's throat tighten as his eyes moistened. Further down the German trench, someone took up the song in a fine tenor. More voices joined in, from both sides. Beside him, the lad lowered his Enfield rifle to add his voice to the chorus.

At the conclusion of the song, the voices trailed off, leaving a heavy stillness. A Captain not much older than Robert was walking down the line, crouched low with his hands behind his back. "No fraternizing, lads," he said mechanically. Fitzgerald could see the shame in his superior's eyes. The Captain walked on without looking back, droning on to forbid them to consort with the enemy, doing his duty to the letter of military law, if not the spirit.

"Ho, English!" a voice called from between the trenches.

That morning, the figures had been gauzy with the mist, but in the dream he could see them as clearly as they appeared to him later. Men. Men with moustaches and dirty faces, any one of whom could have been the driver of the hansom cab that had taken him to Victoria Station. Without speech, the only thing that marked them as German were the helmets and the uniforms.

The lad beside Robert hoisted himself up onto the lip of the trench and took a cautious step toward the Germans. *"Guten Morgen!"* he called out in an atrocious accent.

The dream Fitzgerald stared at the small lad advancing on the enemy with no weapon in his hands. The dream Fitzgerald bestirred himself into action, telling himself it was his duty to look out for this boy. The sleeping Fitzgerald knew better. He knew that he'd climbed up beside the lad, hoping for release. Hoping this was all a ruse, a trap. Hoping for the bullet that would free him from the constant fear, the fear that ever gnawed at him as the rats gnawed on the dead men that were scattered across the ground.

There was no deception. There was, for those few hours and on those few square meters of churned dirt and blasted heath, peace on earth. In the centre of the deadly bog between the trenches, a huge bear of a man extended a hand to Fitzgerald, and rumbled in accented English, "Merry Christmas, my friend." Numbly, Robert took the man's hand and wrung it with great solemnity.

"And to you, Herr."

At that, the burly German grinned widely and pulled Fitzgerald into a hearty embrace. When Robert wriggled free, unsteady on the broken ground of no man's land, the German shoved a bottle at him.

Fitzgerald couldn't help smiling in his sleep. Good God, it had been peppermint schnapps, sweet and harsh and landing like a fiery meteor atop the paltry breakfast of beans and hard bread sitting leadenly in his stomach.

Robert had some cigarettes in his pocket. He offered them round, for more soldiers were standing with them, out in the open, upright, standing like men, not bent and twisted like beasts.

Additional bottles were pressed on him. A tin of biscuits passed from hand to hand. One of the Scots returned to his trench for a set of pipes, and he played favourite hymns, with the ragged voices accompanying the melancholy wailing of the pipes. A German showed up with a banjo, of all things, and plinked along with more determination than skill.

Like men, they talked and gestured and laughed. They spoke of their families. Folded photographs were taken with care from wallets. Serious-faced children were praised, wives respectfully complimented, sweethearts shown properly deferential appreciation. They complained about the cold, the wet. They grumbled about superior officers who weren't fit to pour piss from a boot. They described homes and farms, and the celebrations that were even now taking place.

They did not speak of the war, or the reason they were standing together on this Flanders field. Small trinkets changed hands. Pipes were exchanged, pocket knives, the odd Jew's harp or harmonica. A sausage appeared from somewhere. As it moved from grubby hand to grubby hand, the men bit off small parsimonious chunks with loud exclamations at the fineness of its quality.

Sleeping Fitzgerald squirmed, knowing what was coming. He wanted it to go on, the hymns and laughter and singing. He wanted to stay there, in that moment of goodwill toward men, but the time eclipsed suddenly, and his dream-self heard the deliberate cough behind him. *No, don't look back,* his rational-self cried out, but Robert turned as he had in life, at that moment, and saw the heads of the senior officers there the edge of the British trench, beckoning them back.

All of them out in the field, in the mud that was as yet that day unsoiled by fresh blood, they looked round like schoolboys caught out on an illicit lark. The German officers in their trenches, fierce moustaches and those strange helmets with spikes, furiously waved recall at their own troops.

The moment hung there, the men—for they were all just men out on a cold, wet morning, far from home and those who loved them—the men looking ruefully at one another across the dirt.

The burly German found Fitzgerald and held out his hand once more. *"Auf Wiedersehen,"* he said with profound ceremony.

Robert could think of no similarly pithy sentiment in English. A loving phrase from his Irish nanny came to mind, and he said, *"Slán go fóill."* The German raised his eyebrows. "Goodbye for now," Robert translated, wondering if the big German had enough English to understand. The man nodded, gave Robert's hand a squeeze, then turned and strode back toward his trench.

In his dream, as the men moved apart, all of them, English and German alike, became gauzy and insubstantial as they shuffled toward the gouges in the earth that were their homes. He understood they were becoming as shadows in his dream because most of the men who'd stood on that briefly hallowed ground on Christmas Day, 1914, were dead.

He knew they were dead because he'd killed some of them himself.

Robert Fitzgerald, Duke of Lesser Devonshire, hereditary Lord to a small estate near Hendon, awoke on a July evening in 1917 with a hand on his boot. An orderly was shaking him awake and shoving a hot cup of thin tea into his hand. "Here you go, guv." Fitzgerald forced apart gummy eyes and pushed himself upright. His uniform and great coat creaked with accumulated, impacted filth.

As always, his first impression on waking was how weary he still felt. He could not believe it possible, but in this dusk, he felt even more fatigued. How could that be? Every day at the front he felt the weight of his exhaustion pressing down on him like the stones that had been laid on the chests of the medieval accused to make them confess. The weariness compressed him, squeezing the life and animation and spark out of him, leaving behind only this numbing misery of fogged thought, halting movement, and vague aches everywhere. The aches themselves were worse than usual this evening.

The second thing that pressed itself upon his consciousness was the startled, ever new awareness of the horrible, Stygian stench of the trenches. The odour of corruption, human waste, rotting refuse, decay; it smote him yet again.

Fitzgerald had been sleeping in a dugout along the back wall of the trench; a small box hacked out of the earth, just barely large enough to sit in upright. It was an officer's privilege to sleep in one the dugouts, which put them off the wood-plank highway that was the centre of the trench. In theory, it might give one the illusion of a restful sleep, since one was less likely to be trod on in the night by a tramping patrol. In reality, it was far too much like a tomb. And the rats were often emboldened by the deeper darkness in which the officers lay.

Fitzgerald crawled awkwardly out of the pit, one hand cradling the steaming mug. He stretched each limb carefully and risked standing upright. With no lights behind him to outline his head and the moon not yet risen, he gambled that no sniper could see him.

It would be his watch in a few minutes. He groggily walked north, toward the current headquarters. Supposedly, by now, the trench system ran from the English Channel to the Black Sea. He dully fancied he could simply keep walking north and then swim home.

His mouth tasted especially foul. He swilled a mouthful of tea and discharged it at the duckboards, where it was possibly the least noxious substance upon them. Ahead, two infantrymen were peering at their rifles. They noticed Robert and started to stand to attention. He waved them off.

"Mud?" he asked, unnecessarily.

"Aye, sir," one replied. "Can ye lend us a hand?"

The other soldier was already unbuttoning his fly. Robert held the tin mug in his teeth and fumbled with the buttons on his trousers. As he began urinating on the weapons to clear the mud that clogged the barrels, he thought *This would make mother so proud.* For a moment, he actually grinned, recalling those geologic ages ago during his induction physical; what an embarrassed boy he'd been when the examining Medical Officer had told him to disrobe.

"Thank you, sir," the soldiers said as he strode away to the Command Post, fastening his trousers.

The CP was crowded. Weary men looked anxious to be on their way, to whatever small crumbs of peace they might find before the battles started again in the morning. There were some grunted greetings at the sight of him. Captain Wallace noted his presence. "Ah, Fitzgerald, good man."

Robert saluted. "Sir." He took another surreptitious sip of the tea.

Wallace addressed them all. "As you know, we laid a new line of barbed wire last night."

A voice offered from the darkness, "Which means the bastards will be out trying to cut it tonight."

"Indeed." Wallace's face crinkled, the face of a patient teacher with intelligent if mischievous students. "We'll want some patrols along the line, listening."

Robert spoke up. "Sir, should we move the firing steps? The Bosch will have their location noted by now." That was part of the game. Each side's snipers had sighted in on the firing steps, so shuffling them up and down the trenches was one way of preserving one's forces. Although even that was ultimately futile, as once you fired at night, the muzzle flash from your weapon gave away the new position.

"Take care of it, if you please."

"Sir, I'll make the rounds, and move the lads as I do."

"Very good."

Robert saluted, drained the last of the tea, and handed the mug to an orderly as he left the CP.

Volunteering for the first evening patrol had nothing to do with duty to King and Country. Rather, he'd found that when moving, the infernal stench of the trenches was lessened. Moving about in the mud changed the nature of the stench, made it seem less an oppressive punishment from a querulous god, to something more of this world. Robert felt the stench as a physical presence, as one of the now disproved and discarded miasmas, those evil humours or bad airs that in the century past had been thought to be the cause of disease.

In the trenches, with the bloated dead floating unburied atop in the mud, with the sickening loss of sanitation and basic cleanliness, he could believe that a miasma clung to his skin and coated him with its noxious touch. He said nothing to anyone about this belief, rightly suspecting that he'd sound a bit mad. Strangely, that suspicion comforted him as few thoughts could these days. As long as he could see the lunacy of his thoughts, then he'd not succumbed to the insanity he feared.

"Evening, sir." Robert looked up. It was one of the infantrymen, saluting him. Robert absently returned the salute. He couldn't immediately place the soldier. It was hard enough to recognize the ones you knew through the coats of mud and the red pinpricks of lice bites, without having to recall the faces of the new replacements or those who had simply washed up in your company when their own had been shot to rags. Not one of Robert's crop of callow youths, surely this lad had seen some thirty years of life before this tour in the underworld. The infantryman looked at him with a strange good humour. "Off to your nightly prayers, sir?"

That was not exactly what the man had said. His Welsh accent was thick, rolling and lilting, nearer singing than speech, about as far from English as could be and not be considered a foreign language. Three years—three!—had trained Robert's ear, and the young Lieutenant translated the rising and falling sounds that fell from the man's lips into something Fitzgerald understood as clearly as if King George himself had been addressing him.

The Welsh soldier's grin was infectious, and it invited a response in kind from Robert. "Surely, you've heard it said there are no atheists in the trenches."

"Aye, sir," the Welsh soldier answered, shifting his various belts into a more comfortable arrangement, and taking out a bayonet to sharpen. He gave Robert a wink, leaning over as if imparting a secret of great weight. "In truth, the atheists disappear once the machine guns open up. Or the damned Fokkers begin strafing us like we're rabbits trapped in a culvert."

"And afterwards?"

The infantryman pulled a whetstone from a pocket, spit on it with admirable accuracy and economy, and began sharpening his sticker with the concentration of a concert pianist. The comparison was no idle one; Robert had seen some of the best in his father's parlour, and the level of focus and intensity was the same. "Afterwards, ah, then, sir, one begins to question."

"Indeed. Please, excuse me."

The infantryman stood and saluted. "Of course, sir. God keep you."

Robert saluted again, and moved away, his briefly buoyant spirits deflating under that last. *God keep him?* He shuddered at the thought. Here, slipping on the duckboards clotted with scabs composed equally of mud and blood, passing the still, misshapen forms of men who were sleeping or dead, and envying them either state, the Welshman's blessing had fallen on his ears like a sentence from the Highest Court.

God keep him here, God throw him down here where men were scourged by machine gun and grenades wielded by the faceless, anonymous wraiths that surrounded them. Beaten, chewed, and clawed at until there was naught left that was human.

Unconsciously, Fitzgerald began striding through the trench faster, his feet skittering over debris atop the duckboards; spent shells, cooking utensils, items that normally would have required a disciplining word to the troops, but he was being carried by his thoughts, and they threatened to break and run like terrified horses.

Where was God when they crouched in the trench, rain running down into their clothes, affixing the bayonets, and waiting for the shrieking blast of the whistle held in the old Sergeant's mouth? Where was He when they hurled themselves from the dank safety of the living graves whence they hid to the open land of what should have been the living, suddenly revealed in their fragile weakness before His pitiless eye? Did He walk among them as both sides raced toward each other, the shambling stumbling shapes nearly identical except for their helmets? Did He smile while the bullets arced and tracers sizzled, observing with delight His children's clever handiwork when blood ribboned out, bones splintered, brains flew through the air?

"Lieutenant Fitzgerald!"

Robert drew himself up sharply. He was standing near the Officers dugout. He'd covered nearly a quarter of a mile, insensible to his surroundings. A man's hand was grasping his shoulder. It was Captain Wallace.

"Sir," Robert said weakly, saluting.

In the light of the shrouded lantern, he could see that

Wallace's face was webbed with fatigue and dirt. "Are you well, Lieutenant?"

Robert felt a strange, floating lightness as if the bonds that held him tethered to the world were slowly slipping from their moorings. He took a deep breath, attempted to will himself back to earth. Good Christ, how close had he come to running madly through the trench, eyes stark and mouth open in terror? What would his father say? For his father, that would not do. "Aye. Yes, sir, most excellent."

Wallace grunted. "So you say." He gestured behind him off-handedly. A private stepped forward. "Report," the Captain ordered.

The lad saluted. Robert blinked, trying to force himself to concentrate. He focused intently on the lad's face. The boy had pits on his face, signs of the pox. That, more than the boy's lowly rank, let him know the lad had come up from the slums of Manchester or Southwark...with the war gnawing its way through the finer and usually fitter men of the Empire, more and more of the soldiers pouring into the front were slight, undernourished, and marked by the signs of old disease.

This lad may have been marked, but his eyes were sharp and his manner precise. "Isakson, sir. Forward listening post."

Robert felt his heart begin to speed up as Isakson went on. "Heard 'em digging, sir. Scrape of the shovels and all. They're digging hard."

Wallace added, "This was not five minutes ago."

"Then we may have time to stop them," Robert said, his voice sounding far away to him. The Germans had lately taken to digging under their opponent's trenches and blowing them up. Sapping them, it was called, for no reason Robert could discern.

"Get a squad," Wallace told Robert. "I've called in the coordinates." Wallace said it proudly. He had a new telephone line strung back to the rear, as yet unbroken. After the evening's bombardment, it would be severed again, and more of the lads would risk life and limb to splice the wire and return it to service. Still, while whole, maybe it would save a few British lives. "The artillery boys will begin in…"—a quick consultation of his pocket watch—"seven minutes. They'll shell for three minutes. The pounding may collapse their tunnel. If not, get over there and roll some grenades down on them."

"Sir," Robert replied, saluting, no longer even conscious of the fact he'd just agreed to take part in entombing men, trapping them underground to a slow, suffocating death, or, if that failed, to throw explosives at them until they were shredded, quivering heaps of bloody rags.

He turned away, the sudden movement making him unsteady on his feet. There was a hand upon his arm again. This time, it was Isakson. "I'll lead you and your lads back, sir."

It felt as though Robert had cotton stuffed into his ears. "Yes, fine," he said sharply. There was no time to gather his own squadron. The bloody Huns could detonate the trench under their feet at any moment. He lowered his voice to a hoarse whisper, pointing north. "Grab the first five men you see. Rifles, bayonets, and grenades only. I'll get five myself. Move."

Isakson took off without even saluting. He, too, must have been imagining the industrious Germans beneath their feet.

Forcing himself to take deep focusing breaths, Robert crouched near three sleeping forms and shook their feet roughly. He didn't dare take them by the shoulders…many soldiers slept with knives in their hands and awoke swinging. Two of the men sat upright, eyes wide and white under the mask of grime. The third man didn't move. Robert checked again. The third man was dead, had apparently died in his sleep. No wounds, and no time to ask how. Fitzgerald gave the men their orders. As the two men quickly shrugged out of their harnesses and began gathering their gear, Robert stood to find two others.

As he rose upright, the brown and black world spun around him. He kept himself from falling only by throwing both arms out to catch the sandbagged back wall of the trench.

"Here, now," a musical, accented voice said to him, applying a steadying hand to him. "Are ye well, sir?"

Robert shook off the hand and managed to stand on his own, although he swayed a bit. It was his philosophical Welshman, looking at him with concern in his dark eyes. "Come along," Robert ordered, turning north. With the other two soldiers, the group shuffled as quietly as they could, crouching to ensure their heads would not be seen above the lip of the trench.

Isakson was waiting, and without a word, he took the lead, Robert and the rest falling in behind him. Robert stole a glance at the luminous dial of his wristwatch. Good God, three minutes until the shelling would begin.

The young Isakson took a sharp left into a narrow, pitch black trench. The listening post, as dangerous a place as any along the line, projecting twenty feet out from the main trench. No duckboards, the better to silence their footfalls, but there was little one could do to silence the squelch of boots in the mud. The small boy held up a hand, and they all stopped.

Ten men huddled in the listening post made for tight quarters. Robert waved the soldiers close, and they leaned in, while Isakson applied his eye to the periscope mounted at the terminus of the trench. Robert tapped his watch and held up three fingers. The men nodded their heads gently, fearing to even make their helmets rustle or clink. Robert clenched his other fist, dropped it down sharply, raising three fingers again. His soldiers signed understanding. Three minutes of bombardment.

Fitzgerald motioned with his hands, parting them. The men separated into two lines, leaning against the two sides of the listening post. Robert pointed to the second man on his left, and the third man on his right, and pointed at the ground. Undisguised relief flooded each man's face. Lacking a firing step or ladders, those two would be the living stairs the others would step on to climb out of the access trench. Robert had just bestowed the gift of life upon them. They would not be expected to leave the trench, but to stay behind to provide covering fire for the return of Robert and the remaining men.

The cotton in his ears and his unsteadiness had faded. The fear swallowing it up, he supposed idly, stepping up beside Isakson. He nudged the boy and pointed to the ground. The little soldier's eyes widened and he shook his head in defiance. Robert took him by the front of the jacket and gave him a hard jerk. He would not send this boy out to his death. Isakson would be the young Lieutenant's step when he led the men out. Robert took the crude wooden periscope from Isakson. It enabled the listening post to look out on No-Man's land without risking a bullet in the skull.

Robert peered into the eyepiece. In the darkness, it was almost worthless, but he had to use what tools he had if he wanted to live. Swivelling it across the field of no-man's land made his head swim, and for a moment, he feared he might vomit. Clamping his jaws and closing his eyes, he mastered himself. He opened his eyes and moved the periscope in a slow arc. Something glinted to his right. He lowered the periscope. Were the sappers out already?

He thumped Isakson hard on the shoulder. Held up both hands, the fingers curled into semi-circles. Isakson handed him a leather case and then dropped to all fours. Robert shook the binoculars free of the case, and gently stepped up onto Isakson's back, trying to keep his weight on the young man's shoulders and hips. Very slowly, Fitzgerald raised his head above the level of the trench. No doubt, the snipers already had the listening post sighted. Sudden movement would catch their eye if there were any light at all. A leisurely dark patch didn't have the same effect.

Cautiously, Robert raised the binoculars to his eye. Again, the smallest thing could give him away. An errant flash of light off the lens, even something as insignificant as a stray romantic moonbeam would be enough of a target to send a bullet crashing through the binoculars, through his eye, and into his brain. But…he must know what was out there. It might mean their lives.

Cupping the front lens of the glasses with his left hand, Robert scanned the field to the north. He looked for a moment and then swore soundlessly before slipping back down into the trench. Isakson stood, wiping mud from his hands and knees, and shot him a silent question. Robert shook his head, not important.

He'd seen a loaded cart out there, pulled by two donkeys. There were barrels in the back. He guessed from the casks that someone was bringing water to the Germans in the trenches opposite, foolishly taking a shortcut across no man's land.

Another quick glance at his wristwatch. He struck out, left and right, at the men leaning against the trench. They, in turn, nudged the men next to them, and so on until all of them were looking at Robert. He held his hand up, and near his eyes, and then snapped the fingers down, closing his eyes as he did.

The men hunkered down, screwing their eyes shut. Some threw their arms over their faces. Every one of them pressed harder into the crumbling walls of the trench.

Then came the faintest of whistling shrieks that quickly increased until it was like the scream of the damned, and the bombardment began. There was a terrific flash of white light which Robert, even with his face pressed against into the dirt, could perceive, and then almost simultaneous with that, the booming blast that shook the ground. It was something they'd never experienced before the war—sound that had physical force. It was an experience they grew to hate, and to fear.

They'd covered their eyes to protect their night vision. Perhaps the first blast had caught some of the Hun unaware, but any experienced soldier would have heard the tell-tale whistle of the incoming round and immediately scrabbled for cover. The effort to save their night vision might have been an illusion, but in the chaos and random death of combat, illusions were often the only thing a man possessed to get him to his feet.

The first explosion was followed by another, and another, blasts that began to merge, shaking the ground, hurling waves of dirt and war debris over them. Silence was no longer required, and through his ringing ears, Robert could hear men unsheathing their bayonets behind him, could sense the metallic snick as they locked into place on the ends of the barrels of their Enfield rifles.

He pulled his own bayonet and fitted it over his rifle by touch alone. There was a rumble from beneath the earth and a belching kind of sound. Dirt trickled down the sides of the trench. Perhaps one of the barrages had set off the charge underground. He couldn't hazard a breakthrough in the line on a "perhaps." They would still have to go out and confirm the destruction of the sapper's tunnel.

Fitzgerald risked a glance at his watch. One more minute. Impossible. They'd been shelling for hours. For his entire life, his whole existence, he'd been crouched here in the mud, mouth dry, rifle clenched in sweating hands, while the fires of Hell erupted only feet from his head.

Palm flat, he gestured sharply down. The two step men jammed their bayoneted rifles down into the mud, where they quivered upright. The men lowered themselves to the ground. Isakson was slow to drop. Robert leaned in. "You stay in this trench, do you hear me, lad?"

The boy nodded sullenly, which suddenly, improbably, struck Robert as funny. He was trying to save the fellow's life, and the little bugger resented him for it. As he stepped up on the boy's back, crouching, all humour left the world.

In front of them, the ground was obscured by dirty white smoke from the shells. Yet, in the smoke, light flashed, and from within came booms and other horrible noises that defied identification. A Bible story from Genesis came to mind. God wanted to meet the Israelites on Mount Sinai, but the mountaintop had been wreathed in mists and flame and lightning. Upon seeing the fiery storm, the refugees decided that perhaps Moses was better suited to speak to The Most High and had sent him there alone.

A final glance at his watch. By the dial, three minutes had passed. Robert counted to ten…and no additional bombs fell.

In the silence, the smoke drifted toward them and the lights within continued to dance and glow. Robert Fitzgerald shifted his rifle, straightened up, and charged forward to meet his Lord.

He slowly became aware of himself sitting slumped in a trench, his back against sandbags, his knees bent. It was still night, how could it be otherwise? Filthy water sloshed around his waist and legs, the cold soaking into his trembling muscles. He was gasping, his breathing ragged, broken, harsh, but as hard as he drew in on the fetid air, it seemed as thin as if he were on a towering mountaintop. His ears rang from the bombardment and mucus trickled from one nostril. His eyes burned as well, familiar burning from the acrid smoke of gunpowder and high explosives. His mouth was dry, sand dry in spite of the foul water all around him.

He turned his head from side to side. Nothing in this

section of trench looked familiar. He knew he'd scrabbled back into British territory. That was obvious to him by the disorder and crumbling walls. The damned Bosch had been in France before the English arrived and thus had the leisure to choose their ground. And they usually choose well. German trenches were often constructed with care, employing sturdy walls and drainage, even small hospitals and cafeterias. No, the God-cursed mud, the debris, and the fact no one was trying to eviscerate him with a rusty piece of metal told him clearly on whose side he'd landed, but not where.

Fitzgerald began shivering now, and the weariness he'd known less than an hour before was as nothing to the bone-deep fatigue that seemed to seep from his very marrow. He must find his troops, what remained of them. What would his father say? It would not do, no, sir, it would not do.

He tried to stand, and only then noticed the rifle clutched in his hands. It was of German make, and a ruin. Barrel clogged with mud, wooden stock broken and split lengthwise, the splintered oak clotted with gore. Robert had an impression of himself swinging it like a club.

Using the ruined rifle as a staff, Robert struggled to his feet, clawing at the sandbags to pull himself upright. Now other recollections came to him; images that made him wince away as if he were in the midst of them again.

Isakson, the fool boy, running beside them, nimble and light with youth.

The distance to the Germans stretching ahead of them, fear compressing his vision and making the tens of feet into miles of open land.

Gaping shell holes, pits filled with water and mud, where dead men floated silently like obscene lily pads.

The bitter, deadly bug's flit of bullets starting to fly past them.

The smoking crater of the sapper's tunnel, wires spewed out of it like a man's entrails, along with the glistening guts of the poor devils who'd been in the tunnel when it had exploded.

Grenades. Tossed left and right into the tunnel.

Then men coming at them. German curses, grunts, clang of bayonet against rifle barrel. Thud of fists, screams.

Sharp pop of small arms at close range. A pistol in his hand, smoking, a silhouette falling away from him with the utter limpness of death.

Job done, sappers stopped. Fall back, retreat, scramble back into their earthen tombs like Lazarus fleeing the truth of his return to life.

So few. Where was Isakson?

The Welshman—what the bloody hell was the man's name?—the Welshman grabbing Robert, shoving him forward, bellowing "The boy's dead, sir, move!"

Fitzgerald was upright now. Standing helped, gave him the illusion of being once more in control. To his left, he perceived three of the squad huddled, also gasping for air. Three. Had he only brought three back?

Dear God, he thought suddenly, what was that sound?

Only now was he hearing it, only now had it pierced through the noise of his own ragged breathing and drove like burning wire into his ringing ears. A terrible wailing shriek.

"It's the donkeys, poor things," a lilting voice said behind him.

Had Robert spoken his thoughts aloud? He turned to find

the Welshman only an arm's length away, covered in mud and blood, struggling to his feet. The man took a long deep breath, then, with a careful twist, removed the bayonet from his Enfield rifle. He slid his helmet off, placed it over the barrel of the weapon, and leaned it carefully against the back wall of the trench. "T'will keep the mud out," he said by way of explanation.

The Welshman slid the bayonet into a sheath at his hip and stepped over to the front edge of the trench. There was low place there, a dip, no doubt where he and Robert had slid down during their retreat. He turned and nodded at Robert companionably, saying, "Sir," and began to climb.

"Where the blazes are you going?" Robert managed to croak.

The other soldier looked over his shoulder, and there was compassion in his eyes. "They're the only innocent creatures on this field, sir." Robert suddenly understood the compassion was as much for his Lieutenant, for his blindness to their anguish, as it was for the injured donkeys. The sounds echoing in the night were truly terrible, pitiable, almost human. "You'd not leave them to suffer, sir."

The Welshman scrambled up the side of the trench and was gone.

Words and thought failed Robert for a moment. The Welshman was going back out there…without a weapon? Without a team?

Rifles cracked in the night. Fitzgerald and his remaining soldiers threw themselves against the front wall of the trench. Robert risked a quick glance over the edge, just enough to see the thrashing shapes of the wounded animals and the Welshman creeping toward them. The infernal Huns were sniping at the Welshman. God blast them, he thought.

Robert turned to last of his squad. Again, the vertigo, the dizziness. He forced it away, stumbled closer to the three infantrymen. He pointed them toward the German lines. "Lay down suppressing fire as needed. And for God's sake, don't shoot us." He dropped the useless rifle. Checked his pistol. Four rounds remained. "Grenades?" he asked, holding out a hand. He took two from the befuddled soldiers, shoved them into the pockets of his soiled great coat, moved several feet to his right, and risked another glance over the edge at the mad Welshman.

The man must have been part mole; he had burrowed so deeply in the mud he was almost swimming across the field. Small eruptions all around him showed the sniping fire. Sickened, Robert knew the Germans were treating it as sport, as a diversion from the tedium and terror of regular fighting. He witnessed his own men doing the same thing on other occasions.

A shot hit the Welshman low on the leg, and something went flying. Robert could hear cheers from the German trenches. *Bastards*, he thought with a flare of white-hot hate. Without thinking, he freed a grenade, twisted it, and threw it hard toward the Huns. Even as it arced across No Man's land, Robert dove out of the trench and landed on his belly in the pestilential mud.

It was a good throw. He'd possessed a strong arm at Eton, and he'd not lost much in range. The hollow boom and hurling mud stopped the Hun's laughter. The fact it was not followed by another grenade or more rifle fire seemed to confuse the enemy. He could hear muttered, questioning voices from the other side.

Slithering like a snake, Robert elbowed his way toward the Welshman, cursing him in a low voice. "You barmy fool, I'll have your Taff arse nailed to the door of regimental headquarters."

The Welshman forged steadily ahead, seeming to pay no mind to either the Germans or Robert's increasingly blasphemous imprecations behind him. Ahead, the two donkeys thrashed amid the ruins of their cart, further tangling themselves in their leather traces. "No need to worry, sir," the Welshman said in a soothing voice, never slowing. "I'll just nip over and take care of these bairns. Never you mind, sir, go back to the lads, there's a good gentleman."

By God, Robert thought, anger lending him focus and speed as he wriggled across the filthy mud. *I'll have the man court martialled.* The sounds from the wounded animals were ghastly, boring into his ears. He'd seen men struck down, seen a savage blow or rifle shot turn them in an instant from rational if terrified beings into an incoherent collection of wails and pleas for help. The groans of the donkeys were not that much different from those of horribly-stricken men. *We have that in common,* a part of Robert observed even as he ploughed after the Welshman. A colder part of Robert answered, *But we men knew what we were facing. How could the donkeys conceive of such a thing?*

It was such a damning insight that for a moment, Robert slowed his serpent-like progress in the darkness. His men did know, like it or not, and they'd been driven by duty or love of country, even of fear being seen a coward or of the gaol if they had not complied. The poor animals knew not what was being asked of them, nor what could happen to them. *Christ, that's an ugly thing,* he thought as shame laid a clammy hand round his heart.

Ahead, the Welshman stopped. Robert dug his elbows into the dirt and pulled himself beside the madman. The Welshman turned on his side, and a hand clutched to his thigh.

"Are you hit?" Robert hissed, looking round. They were only feet from the thrashing animals, surrounded by ruins of casks of water and shards of cart.

The other man glanced down at his own foot for some reason. "No, sir, they just snatched away my boot heel."

Robert had been referring to the man's hand clutching at his thigh, thinking that was where the snipers had shot him.

He realized the man was digging in his trouser pocket. The Welshman said, "Ah," and pulled out a roll of bandages. He then crawled away to his left, away from the donkeys.

The man's insane, Robert thought, following him. *I'll have to club him with my pistol and try to drag him back to the lines.*

Just beyond the debris of the cart, someone lay in the mud, moaning. It was a German soldier, the cart driver, Robert surmised. The Welshman called out to the German, who pointed at something on the ground. It was a rifle. Reaching over, the Welshman flung the weapon clear before tossing the driver the roll of bandages. He patted the German on the foot and turned back to the wounded animals.

His irritation growing, squirming on his belly, Robert followed the Welshman, beginning to imagine himself a lost puppy following a kindly stranger. That fancy vanished as the Welshman drew nearer the donkeys. The animals grew quieter as the man approached them, their eyes wide and white in the fuzzy, comical faces, muscles twitching, still giving involuntary groans of pain.

The Welshman crooned at them as he moved closer, his voice taking on an even more musical, soothing tone. "Ah, thee's a good lad," he sang, crawling up beside the first donkey.

Robert slowed, not wanting to startle the animals. The Welshman waved him forward, continuing that gentle singing. "Thee's a good strong lad," he said, reaching out to lay a gentle hand on the donkey's neck.

No one is firing on us, Fitzgerald realized with surprise. Whether out of sympathy or apathy, the guns were silent for now. Coming abreast of the mad Welshman, for the first time Robert could clearly see the extent of the animal's wounds. The first donkey's legs had been shattered, and they flopped weakly, limply, with the animal's pained thrashing. The other donkey lay on its chest, intestines coiled on the ground, hindquarters dragging uselessly behind it. It neighed in a feeble parody of greeting.

Something ignited in Robert's chest, flooded up his throat and his eyes. To his surprise, tears trickled down his cheeks. It amazed him that he could weep when so outraged that raw murder thudded in his brain. Yet he knew he wept for pity, too. The Welshman stroked the donkey's neck, keeping low to the ground, supporting its head against his chest. "T'art a poor silly thing, you are," he said, gesturing Robert closer. In same musical tones, he said, "I can't reach my bayonet, sir, can you lend us a hand?"

Lying as flat as possible, blinking away the tears that smeared the hellish vision in front of him to a blurred tableau, Fitzgerald found the sheath pinned beneath the Welshman's leg. He scraped a gap in the mud, creating a space between leg and ground, then pulled the blade free. The Welshman continued crooning to the wounded animal as if comforting a child. "Ah, ye've done a grand job, lad. Thou art a fine boy, thou art."

Still crooning, he extended the arm that was over the donkey's neck, and rotated his palm upward. Robert passed the bayonet to him, handle first. "Pat his muzzle, sir, there's a good gentleman," the Welshman crooned, turning the blade in his hand.

Fitzgerald reached out and gently brushed the sturdy forehead. He stroked the soft, warm nose, from whence blood trickled. Fresh tears stung Robert's eyes at the pressure of the donkey pressing its head gratefully against his hand.

"Yes, thou art small and pathetic, but a brave lad," the Welshman sang, the blade moving a little at the donkey's throat. The donkey's head jerked, just a fraction. "Keep petting him, if you would, sir." Robert could feel warmth around his knees, the donkey's blood draining out, the heat shocking in contrast to the chill of the charnel house mud where he crouched. The animal's wounds were so great, the razor-sharp bite of the bayonet against the artery must have been hardly noticed. "Good boy, brave boy," the Welshman whispered, cradling the donkey as it died.

Robert's hand remained on the donkey's muzzle. He only moved it when the Welshman squirmed out from beside the dead animal's body, the darkly glistening blade in his hand.

Three things happened in such rapid succession, Robert only experienced them as one continuous event.

Small flame crack puff.

Small flame from the barrel of the German cart driver's rifle
Crack of the gunpowder sending the bullet on its way.
Puff of air as the bullet passed Fitzgerald and drilled into the Welshman.

The Welshman said, most unmusically, "Bugger me," as he tumbled back.

Robert spun. The wounded German cart driver was up on one knee, levering the bolt on his rifle for another shot. The pistol cleared Robert's holster and he put three rounds into the German's chest.

When the German fell, so did the rain of hellfire.

From the British trenches, Robert's three soldiers began to belatedly fire at the fallen German driver. Across the way, the Huns fired back at Robert's men. Who would finally shoot and kill Robert and the Welshman was strictly academic. Out here, trapped between the fury of the two sides, they were dead men.

Pressing himself ever deeper in the mud, Robert snaked an arm across the Welshman's chest, and dragged them both through the freshly blooded mud close to the first, now-dead donkey, using its body as a breastworks. He prayed God his soldiers had paid attention during their training, and would shoot over them. He doubted the Huns would take such care.

The corpse of the donkey rocked at the impact of German bullets. The remaining wounded donkey began to cry out in terror and pain as it was struck anew. Robert flattened himself even further.

"Have you any shells left in your pistol, sir?" a weak voice breathed in Robert's ear. Fitzgerald turned, dragging his face through the mud but unwilling to raise his head any higher. The Welshman still lived, skin parchment white, eyes bright and blazing into Robert's own, a red bubble on his lips. Surely lung-shot and dying.

The Welshman held out a trembling hand. The wounded donkey shrieked again.

Tracers sizzled overhead. Robert twisted and unholstered his pistol. Holding it close to his eyes, he could see a single round left in the chamber. He found the Welshman's extended hand, slipped the grip into the man's fingers.

The Welshman's hand quivered and dropped into the mud, just barely keeping the barrel out clear of the clogging dirt. He looked up at Robert. "Please, sir."

Higher pitched whistling sounds overhead. Mortars, falling on each side's trenches. "Good Lord, man, I can't shoot you."

Though warm and strangely kind, the Welshman's grin was ghastly to see, with blood staining his teeth and filming his lips. "Not I, sir. The poor thing over there." The man's head moved slightly, slowly, gesturing at the other donkey, who continued to add the shrill sounds of its torment to the continuing symphony of death that whirled all about them. "It would be a kindness, sir."

In weary desperation, Robert told him, "It'll be over soon…" but the look on the dying man's face robbed him of any excuse. The Welshman couldn't lift his hand, but instead shoved it and the pistol across the mud at Robert.

Fitzgerald snatched his pistol back, now in a rage. *God damn the Huns, God damn the Austrians, God damn the bomb-throwing dribbling arsehole anarchist Serbian who'd started this God damned war, God damn this insane Welshman, and God damn these damned donkeys.*

More whistling noises overhead, booms, mud rippling from the impacts behind and in front of him. Less gunfire, almost none now that the mortars were falling, men from either side scrambling like terrified squirrels into whatever bolt holes they could find lest the mortars tear them apart. The donkey, almost keening now. The sounds all around him were nothing short of diabolical.

Fitzgerald risked a look over the neck of the dead donkey. The other donkey was not five feet from them, just off to his right. He struck the pistol against the heel of his left hand to clear the barrel. When he lifted his head again, bringing the pistol up to rest on the shoulder of the dead animal as he did, he could see a German soldier within twenty feet of them, a potato masher grenade in his hand.

The still-living donkey lifted its head with great effort, foam around its nostrils and mouth. The large limpid eyes in the dirt-streaked, comically sad face gazed directly at him. Robert didn't know why. Perhaps it was simply because Fitzgerald was so close; a human, and the little animal had come to look to humans for what was good in a donkey's mind: food, warmth, relief from toil and pain.

Robert's glance tracked back to the German soldier. The Hun's arm was going back, the fuse on the grenade hissing. At twenty feet, Robert would have no problem dropping the soldier before he could release the grenade.

Fitzgerald's eyes went back to the donkey. Its front legs tried to pull it toward Robert but lacked the strength. The small creature neighed again, forlorn and questioning.

It didn't know why it was dying. It didn't know why it was being tortured.

Robert's arm snapped out and he pulled the pistol's trigger.

The bullet caught the donkey squarely in the forehead, knocking it as flat and still as if it had been driven down by

God's own hammer.

It was the only innocent creature on the field.

Robert found himself flying upward, and wondered for a moment if he were dead and Heaven-bound. In that same moment, he knew that was not true, for no just God would accept such as he into the Presence. Then he was descending, and it passed through Fitzgerald's mind that perhaps he was *dead. He* was *certainly heading in the proper direction.*

Flames blazed up to receive him.

It was cool. Yet, there was brightness above him; he could vaguely sense it through his closed eyes. He was so tired. He'd been hot before, now he was comfortable. In the absence of the searing heat, the only sensations that came made him guess he was at ease since nothing hurt for now. In this lack of pain, this lack of effort that passed for ease, he could rest.

He was hit in the face by something. It wasn't a blow, no, half his head was draped in something wet, clinging. It interfered with his breathing. His easy, slow, barely noticeable breathing. Then he had to decide, but even that began to resemble effort far too much. He had to decide if he were going to lift his arm to brush away whatever covered his mouth and part of his nose.

It was the taste that pushed him to action. Whatever was draped over his mouth was vile beyond belief. *Push it away,* he thought, and then he could retreat into cool, soft restful lack of pain.

An arm moved, not the one he'd thought to extend.

Above him, Robert heard a frightened gasp. "Jesus jumpin' Christ. This poor bastard is still alive."

That terrified voice brought Fitzgerald back into the present. Rough hands wiped his face and eyes, and Robert could see.

When he perceived his immediate place in the world, he wanted to close his eyes again. He was in a shell-hole half filled with mud, submerged roughly to the chest. The hole, blasted out of the earth, was irregular, with crumbling edges. His arms floated on the gelatinous surface of the dark earth and water mixture that entombed him. The presence and pressure of the batter-like mud all around him was overwhelming to his senses, to his ability to perceive anything except that which encased him. Fitzgerald had no idea if he even existed below the chest. He knew, from ugly, brutal first-hand witness, it was entirely possible to live, for a few stunned minutes, as half a man.

Someone leaned over the edge of the shell hole. Robert focused on that person. The man, with his spade, was as clearly a chap who shovelled dirt over the dead as if he'd been on stage with the Prince of Denmark juggling poor Yorrick's infinitely jesting skull. Fitzgerald wanted to only look at him and didn't care to know who or what pieces of whom might have been slung into the shell hole with him. Shell holes were natural sites for burial of the dead and discarded. The gravedigger, head shaved against the lice as so many were, had huge tufts of black eyebrows, like capering caterpillars above his eyes. Another man was braced behind him, holding the bald gravedigger's harness to keep the man from toppling into the mud as the other offered a tin cup of water to their newest discovery.

"Get the mud out, lad," the gravedigger said harshly. The man holding onto the other's leather strapping was covered in mud as bark covers a tree. "Sip and spit. Ye don't want to swallow that muck."

Robert did as he was ordered. Glancing down, he could see that his coat was gone, along with his insignia. Shredded, no doubt, in the final blast that had sent him Heavenward before delivering him to this earthen perdition. The tufty eyebrowed man refilled the tin cup and held it so the young Lieutenant could drink now. The gravedigger was stretched out almost full length, supporting his weight on his straightened legs and abdominal muscles. The strain must have been terrific. "Y' hold on, lad. I've sent a couple of the boyos to get some planks and lashing. We'll get you out, never you worry."

For the moment, there was no room in Robert's mind for worry. The water was a blessing of cool silver flowing down his parched throat. He drank, forgetting to breathe, until he was forced to draw in a breath, and coughed.

The grave-digger pulled back the cup. "Easy, now."

Still keeping his eyes on the strikingly harsh, yet kind face of the gravedigger, Robert asked, "The Welshman?"

The man shook his head, then looked over his shoulder for confirmation at the mud-barked assistant behind him before answering, "Naught but you here, lad."

"And some pieces of a poor sodding donkey," the mud-barked man uttered in a tone that could only be described as grave.

Gone as if he'd never existed, Fitzgerald thought. A direct hit, he speculated. If the Welshman had still been alive when the mortar hit—and with that lung shot, there was no certainty of the man living more than minutes—then he'd have not felt a thing, nor even had enough time to know additional terror at the fate screaming toward him.

"How long have I been here?"

The gravedigger shook his head again. "Only God knows, lad. We'd no idea we'd find anyone living out here. We've attacked Passchendaele again; can you no' hear the artillery?"

Robert closed his eyes. Suddenly, the very act of living felt like a burden to him, the work of drawing each breath more effort than it was worth. He wanted to lean back, return to the cool embrace of the foul mud, and slip beneath the surface. He'd go under like a plum vanishing into a pudding, and like the plum, he would know nothing of pain or fear or failure ever again.

" 'ere now," the gravedigger was saying as he manipulated a thick leather strap beneath Robert's armpits, around his back, and across his chest. Fitzgerald turned his face away. He would have turned his entire body away from them all, save for the relentless grasp of the mud on his torso. "Easy, lads," their leader cautioned, then said, "Slowly, now."

The straps tightened around Robert's body. He opened his eyes at the new sensation, hating the weight of it, the solid reality of the stained leather straps and metal buckles running cross his body as it pulled him away from the cool dark oblivion he craved and back into the harsh world.

The straps ran from under his arms to a stout beam that stretched across the shell hole. Four men crouched under the wood, legs bent, beam resting on their shoulders. The gravedigger and his solemn mud-covered assistant to the left, two other men from the graves battalion to his right. To a guttural chant, they straightened their legs in unison, and slowly began to prise Robert from the cold, deadly embrace of the shell hole.

At first, Robert tried to ignore them, tried to will himself back into oblivion, but as he emerged from the mud, midwifed by the gravedigger and his brethren, his arms began to droop as they cleared the surface. Another moment and his upper body was clear of the mud. His left arm dangled free. Pain, hot and bright as lightning, arced through him. An animal noise of agony hissed from between his lips as he snatched with his right arm to cradle the wounded left. Even that protective touch made him gasp, but he clamped his hand hard on his opposite forearm. It was superstitious or insane, but he had the irrational sense that he was keeping the pain from flooding through him by the strength of his grip.

A shout from the gravedigger halted his upward progress. "Are ye—?"

"Just my arm," Fitzgerald gasped, his voice clotted and thick. "Keep moving, damn your eyes!"

Accustomed to such talk from the wounded, the tufty eye-browed gravedigger resumed his chant. Another four count and Robert's body was free of the mud, save his feet. His saviours moved in unison, walking the beam toward solid ground and towed him out of the shell hole to lay him on the broken earth of the field.

The gravedigger bent over the young Lieutenant while one of the other men dragged a wooden stretcher toward him. "We'll get you to Hospital now, lad. They'll tend your arm."

Releasing his wounded arm seemed to inundate his left side with agony, but Robert reached up with his right hand

and clutched the gravedigger's shoulder. "Thank you. Pray, excuse my language."

In reply, the good fellow patted Robert's hand and moved it back to his wounded arm. "Hold on, if it makes ye feel better." He turned and bawled, "Where are them bloody stretchers?"

The solemn mud-man loomed over them, his mournful face concerned. "Not so loud, Henry," he scolded. "The heathen Huns will start shootin' agin."

Robert felt as if he were staring up at two characters from a Kipling story. Kipling knew his army men, his enlisted especially, Robert had realized early on in his unchosen military career. But the mournful mud-man had a point. "What time…" Fitzgerald managed to croak.

"Just a tick past 7 am," Henry of the caterpillar eyebrows answered. "Every one of God's children"—here he spared a meaningful glance at the mud man—"has agreed to let Christian charity rule until nine of the clock so as to collect the wounded."

"And bury the dead," the mud-man added, apparently to ensure his presence at this farce was sufficiently explained. "We thought they'd got all what was wounded. That's why we didn't have no stretchers."

Henry patted Robert with surprising gentleness, considering the huge, broken-knuckled workman's hands he was laying on the wounded soldier. "What's your name and rank, lad?" Henry asked.

He belatedly recognized the man was checking him for further injury. He couldn't feel any wounds beyond the fire that seemed to burn in his upper left arm. "Fitzgerald, Robert," he said, and added in an apologetic tone, "Lieutenant." He thought it better they knew. He'd seen other officers who became nearly apoplectic when the proper forms of address were not adhered to under all conditions. "Nothing else seems to be out of order," he continued. That wasn't entirely accurate. His left ear was ringing. He was about to mention it when he began to shiver.

"Aye, sir," Henry responded absently, then turned to bawl again, "Where's them—" only stopping when he saw the mud-man right behind them.

"Here, now," said the mud-man, breathing hard, a stretcher balanced on his head. He lowered it to the ground beside Robert.

"This may hurt a bit, sir," Henry said cheerfully.

Another wave of shivering took Robert. He clenched his teeth to keep them from chattering, and merely nodded. Henry grasped Robert by the shoulders and hip, and rolled him onto his right side, allowing the stretcher to be slide beneath him. He did it with such skill that Robert only groaned once as his wounded arm settled on the wood pole that ran the length of both sides of the stretcher.

The canvas was bitingly cold against Robert's back and scalp. He shivered with such force it looked like a convulsion. Henry called out, "Let's have your jackets here, lads," as he stood and peeled off his own mud-caked greatcoat.

Robert shook his head, attempting to refuse, unable to speak through his clenched teeth. Henry blithely ignored his mute protests and draped his jacket lovingly over Robert's chest. Other jackets were passed to the gravedigger, and he wrapped them around the patient as gently as a mother tucking in her child. "These boyos will be working up a sweat soon enough, sir, never you mind about us. Rest now, Lieutenant."

The shivering racked him again. He had to close his eyes...looking about at the mud, the men's breath steaming in the morning air, the macabre, melancholy sight of the heap of men and donkeys' limbs in the shell hole...it all seemed to wrap him in a winding sheet of ice.

The gravedigger began his guttural chant once more. Robert felt himself lifted into the air and the burial detail began to move jerkily away from the front line and the place that had almost been his tomb. Swaying in the air, for a moment he thought he might vomit, but Robert refused to do that to the men who'd worked so hard to save him. He clutched his wounded arm harder, breathed forcibly through his nose. The focused attention kept him from being sick. He finally began to warm under the jackets. God alone knew what novel kinds of lice lived there, but he'd had lice before. Slowly the shivering left him.

His eyes closed, borne aloft, Fitzgerald could not see his progress, but he'd assisted in enough evacuations of the wounded that he knew intimately what the gravedigger and his lads were experiencing. The weight of a normal man on the shoulders of four strong men would normally not be more than an inconvenience. But add the weight of the mud in which he had been drenched, and the additional mass of the heavy jackets, and now it was as if they were carrying two men. Further, each step was a battle against the gelatinous earth which sucked at their boots, even stripping them off their feet at times. The effort of fighting forward with the weight on their shoulders and the greedily clutching ground under and around their feet was tremendous. After twenty steps, the men would be winded, and probably have to stop to breathe.

If they could make it into the trench proper, it might be slightly easier. There might be duckboards on which to walk…unless the pumps had failed and the trench floor was flooded. And they'd have to stand aside for hurrying men or supplies being moved or step over men dead asleep. Somewhere, they'd locate a communication trench, which ran at right angles to the main trench, and then the going would be easier. One hundred or so feet to the Regimental Aid Post set in a shell hole or abandoned trench, and there the gravedigger and team could lay down their burden and the medical staff would take over. If he lived, he'd go to the Casualty

Clearing Station.

Robert felt consciousness slipping away. He was warmer, but this was not drowsiness. He thought he should tell someone, but blackness overtook him.

The End of Their War

It was clear the War must end. While the Americans declared against the Axis powers in April of 1917, they had not yet grappled with the enemy, as the Yankees first had to transport their soldiers and stores to France. The spectre of the American Army's strength of men and material frightened the German generals. Spurred to new heights of slaughter, the desperate Hun fought ever harder, as if to destroy as many lives as possible before they themselves fell under the weight of history and the fury of their opponents.

In consequence, during the winter of 1917 and the spring of 1918, Charlotte and Kathleen spent ever more time in the operating rooms, their experience and calm a tonic to the sweating doctors and the bleeding soldiers. Younger, less seasoned nurses were assigned to the wards, although like as not the Russian nurse and her brawny American friend would drop by in the evening to see patients, sometimes to even dispense a forbidden treat of chocolate or some other sweet.

Alice was no longer serving as a nurse at Base Hospital No. 12. The morning after the bombing, Matron had come to the new tent where the nurses were now quartered and asked Alice to step outside with her. Charlotte moved past quietly, wishing to give the girl her dignity. Neither Charlotte nor Kathleen heard what was said, but as they left, Alice looked defiantly at the ground while Matron spoke in a low voice. Matron's mien was firm, but not harsh.

In a way, it was not Alice's fault she had run mad the night before. She simply lacked the mental armour to be a nurse, the ability to be both compassionate and hardened, the skill to be indifferent to immediate suffering in the pursuit of healing while at the same time being able to extend a woman's kindness to those who were in pain. Nor did Alice understand how to face the dangers attendant to being here, in this place where her natural constitution was tried beyond her ability to cope.

Charlotte knew not from where her own ability sprang. She didn't think of it as courage…rather, there were simply tasks to be done. She was thinking of this as she hurried toward the surgery. She had become a favourite of Doctor McDougall, who, all-in-all, regarded her with a fond, hearty paternal eye.

One of the new nurses, just a slip of a girl in an as yet unstained uniform stiff with newness, passed her in the hall and automatically dipped her knees and lifted the edges of her skirt the tiniest bit.

Ever since the bombing, the nurses who had been present that morning had taken to giving Charlotte a subtle, half-curtsey when they greeted her. The new crop of nurses soon began to follow suit. The Russian girl was deeply embarrassed by the gesture, but Kathleen bade her allow it. "Missy, they're grateful you took the bull by the horns when the rest of them were running around like a chicken without a head. They can't salute you, Cheri," she added, "but they damn well want to. Let 'em do it."

Thus, Charlotte accepted each of their respectful homages with a slightly forced smile and nod of her head in acknowledgement. Strangely, Matron's hawk-like powers of observation were blind to this breach of hospital protocol.

The bombing and the death that followed had changed so much in Nurse Braninov's life. In the evening, at the end of her shift, it was common for Orlando to appear with an invitation from Matron for tea. In the good lady's tent, she would find Robert Fitzgerald, sometimes reading aloud to the elderly nurse, sometimes playing a hand of whist. Charlotte would join them, gratefully accepting a cup of tea from the attentive Orlando, and basking in the quiet companionship of the group.

Matron had aged since the attack. The lines in her face were more pronounced, and it seemed that her hands on occasion trembled the slightest bit. She had lost none of her steel, however, and her eyes could glint when the occasion demanded.

The sharpness of the older nurse's vision did seem to come and go at will. Sitting in her tent with the young Russian girl and the two men, Matron did not appear to notice if Robert's hand lingered softly atop Charlotte's, nor did she seem aware of the kisses that from time to time landed upon the young nurse's lips when Matron's back was conveniently turned away.

For now, the Russian nurse was at peace. In the musty tent with the kerosene stove lit for warmth in the cool evenings, her brave dwarfish warrior Orlando at one side and the solid presence of Robert to the other, Matron's gently beaming face opposite; during those quiet moments so lacking in drama yet so full of contentment, Charlotte felt as if she had finally come to the home she had always desired but never known.

As the spring passed into summer, the American Expeditionary Force closed with the enemy in June of 1918, staggering the proud Prussians, and the beginning of the end was clearly at hand. The only question was how much useless slaughter would occur before reason asserted itself and Germany sued for terms of peace.

About that time, the hospital became the destination of a number of unexpected visitors: civil servants, elderly inspectors from charitable organizations and others who, in the words of one jittery specimen, "fairly quivered to improve the lot of our brave boys." Worst of all, government representatives began to flow into the wards more and more often. Many of the visitors were accompanied by Alice, who was now fulfilling some clerical function in the personnel department of the hospital, even from time to time by Mr. Fitzgerald, his dress rather formal and his face professionally pleasant.

"They're a damned nuisance," Kathleen grumbled, watching yet another delegation tromp through the wards, tracking dirt upon the floor that dear Gustav would hurl himself upon to clean as soon as they had left.

"They are a necessary nuisance," Matron said drily behind them.

The nurses turned. "Yes, ma'am," Kathleen agreed unconvincingly.

"They help arrange funding, girls," Matron told them, her eyes following the delegation frostily. She, too, had noticed the dirt. "They also work to aid the lads when they're mustered out. Some of these poor fellows…"

Charlotte and Kathleen nodded in understanding. Many of these men would live with the marks of war upon them but could hope for a normal life. Some, though, were nothing less than pitiful. The men without lower jaws or noses, only gaping spaces upon their faces. Those missing their limbs, or, most awful for them, their genitals. She'd wept for these men. How could they know a normal life or love? It was possible, surely, but how difficult it would be for them.

Dismissing the visitors by turning to face her two nurses, Matron said, "There is one good thing. When we begin to see more government men emerge from their offices, then you know the end of the war is near. But they are damned nuisances. Nurse Braninov, would you care to join me for tea this evening?" She favoured Kathleen with a smile. "Nurse Williams, your presence would be most welcome as well."

"Thank you, Mum," Charlotte replied, while the American girl declined the invitation, explaining that a warm cot with a blanket over her head was the only company she desired tonight.

As was his custom, Robert walked Charlotte to her tent when their tea was finished. Matron had looked tired, and so they had concluded their fellowship early. The moon was just rising, and a distinct chill was in the air. As she walked, Charlotte tugged her thick blue cape jacket more tightly about her, and then let her arm fall to her side, where, by some wonderful alchemy of pace and rhythm, Robert's fingertips happened to gently brush the back of her hand.

They paused outside her tent, and she pivoted to face him.

"Thank you, sir," she said with mock gravity, her blue

eyes teasing in the moonlight.

"It was my privilege, Miss Charlotte." She could not help herself, and she shivered in the cold. "Ah, Miss, I cannot selfishly keep you out here."

"You are not selfish if it is my wish to stand here with you."

He smiled, and it warmed her, yet made her shiver anew, not with the cold. His face grew serious. "Nurse Braninov, there is a question I must put to you."

"Of course, Mr. Fitzgerald." What on earth could he want? Was there some horrible bit of hospital business that he'd suddenly remembered they needed to discuss? "What may I do for you, sir?" she replied in an equally staid tone.

"Nurse Braninov. Miss Charlotte. I was wondering—hoping, really—that you would do me the honour of being my wife."

Charlotte looked up at him, stunned, her mouth open in a most common manner. She had thought about it, had possibly daydreamed for a moment or two, but she'd never allowed herself to seriously consider the possibility. The world was at war, for pity's sake. He was an English Lordling of some kind, she was a foreign girl thousands of miles from home.

Concern crept into Robert's eyes. He took a step back, fearing he had imposed upon her, had submitted her to the embarrassment of having to refuse him.

Still afraid to believe what he had said was so, Charlotte looked into Robert's eyes. "Truly, sir?"

"Truly, my dear Charlotte."

From inside the tent came Kathleen's exasperated voice. "Say 'yes' and kiss him, you idiot!"

"Yes, Robert, with all my heart, yes!" She threw her arms around his neck and pulled his face down to hers.

She could not stop smiling as she went about her days. Nor could she share her secret with anyone, as fraternization was most strictly forbidden. Kathleen, she knew, would keep her silence. However, Matron stopped by her ward the next evening, clipboard in hand. As she frowned and made notes about the condition of the beds and furnishings, without taking her eyes off the clipboard she said in an off-hand manner, "Nurse Braninov, should a certain happy event come to pass, might an old nurse be as bold as to invite herself to attend?"

Her heart bursting with joy, Charlotte managed to reply in almost as casual a voice, "A young nurse would be most distressed if a deeply respected and admired dear friend should miss such a happy event."

Matron nodded and dabbed at her eyes before making a final note on the board. "I see dust under those beds, Nurse Braninov. Do have it removed by end of shift."

The surge of wounded slowed the next day. At week's end, Charlotte volunteered to scrub the primary surgery. The room had seen so much use in the weeks past, there had only been time for the most rudimentary of cleaning. Strangely, she itched to attack the grime and ground-in blood stains as if they were her personal enemies. The medical procedures for the day—planned, non-emergency actions—could be shunted to a smaller surgery, permitting free reign to Charlotte and a crew of less-enthusiastic nurses.

Nurse Braninov had determined to begin early. If they worked with a will, she hoped to release the nurses just after lunch to a rare few hours of free time. She knew that most would spend their free time sewing or catching up on their correspondence. She herself had mending to do (and she meant to stitch some buttons back onto Mr.

Fitzgerald's dress shirts) as well as letters of her own to write—she'd yet to risk sending a letter to Petrograd to tell her parents about Robert. She knew well that her parents had plans for their youngest daughter, but after her years of being trapped in England by the war, and her service with the Nursing Staff, Mother Russia seemed a small part of her life, if not another life entirely.

The young nurses—well, young in experience, not age, better to call them "new"—the new nurses huddled together inside the entrance to the surgery. Many of them were older than she, some with faces already careworn before they'd seen their first tours of the CCS. All were wearing, as instructed, their plain student uniforms.

Charlotte greeted them with a smile. Everything made her smile these days, and why not? She carried Robert Fitzgerald's love in her bosom and knew he cradled her within his heart as well. "Good morning, Ladies," she said, in a loud voice, with more energy and cheer than they expected at 5 of the clock in the morning. "Thank you for joining me."

A few showed signs of life, at least to the extent of looking doubtful. One girl gave a sardonic grin. "Yes, Mum," she said cheekily.

"Just 'Charlotte' will do," the Russian girl told them. "I know it's miserably early. But I have a surprise for all of you. Allow me to introduce Madame."

That worthy Frenchwoman swept forward in her tattered clothes, pushing a laundry cart as regally as you please. "Madame, for those who do not know, supplies breakfast for some of us. She's very dependable, and her prices are quite reasonable."

Madame wiped a cover off the cart with a flourish. Contained within were all manner of rude pastries, a jug of cream, and a cask of black coffee. "My treat, girls, as a way of thanking you for volunteering."

"We didn't—" someone said, and was hushed as the nurses moved forward, none wanting to appear greedy. They hesitated until the cheeky nurse snared a croissant and took a vigorous bite.

"Oh, Lord," she enthused. "That's bloody marvellous."

The nurses descended upon the cart and soon made short work of the provisions as Madame looked on, beaming. Charlotte was not above touting Madame's wares as the women sang the praises of their meal. "She brings breakfast round for a few pence a morning. She has a map of the camp…show her where you sleep."

It was a markedly more jolly group that faced her as Madame rolled the cart away. "Ladies," Charlotte told them, a mock frown upon her face. "This surgery is a disgrace."

"Yes, Mum!" the cheeky girl replied.

"I should be embarrassed to have one of our brave soldiers brought into such a sty. It's not fit for a dog."

Now she was answered by several of the grinning nurses, led by the cheeky one. "Yes, Mum!" they said loudly.

"Well, then," she said, pointing to the cleaning supplies in the corner left by the dependable Gustav. "Let's turn this sty back into a surgery, shall we?"

Laughing, they roared back at her, "Yes, MUM!!"

She had planned to do her fair share of the work herself but found her energies diverted to overseeing. The nurses worked with a will, chattering among themselves, and relying on Charlotte to direct them to the areas they were most needed. After everything higher than the floor had been scrubbed until it was glistening, she turned to her still-energetic group of young and youngish women saying,

"The deck, ladies. There is nothing for it but our hands and knees."

This work was much harder and more uncomfortable. She lined everyone up against the far wall, and rags in hand, scuttling around on their knees, they hurled themselves at the floor, backing up as they went.

She could tell the nurses were tiring, as was she. Where the impulse arose, she could not say, but she began to sing as she scrubbed the floor.

"What's that, Miss?" Bethany, the cheeky one, asked her.

Charlotte paused to wipe at her forehead with the back of her wrist. "Something my governess sang to me. The…" she searched for a translation from the Russian for an English word for serfs. "The field hands would sing it, too, at the end of the day, when the last of the wheat was picked up by the harvesters, and the hands were waiting for the wagon to pick them up and take them home."

Bethany returned to scrubbing the deck. "It's very pretty," she said.

Charlotte bent down with her, rag in both her hands, rocking her whole body as she ground the dirt from the floor. "It's a happy song, about going back to one's home and—" she lowered her voice to a music-hall's theatrical whisper—"to the lover that waits for her with open arms."

The nurses chuckled. "Go on, Miss," Bethany urged her. "Sing some more."

The song had a comforting, even energetic feel to it, so Charlotte began again. As she sang the chorus, some of the girls sang along, mangling the Russian, but mangling it with gusto.

When Charlotte finished the song, another girl began singing in a pronounced Irish accent. "Oh, Danny boy…" but was drowned out by cheerful boos and hoots of "No sad songs!" Gamely, the nurse switched to another song, something about a rooster and his love for a duck which seemed to have ribald undertones that made the older nurses smile knowingly.

The nurses joined in on the easy parts of the chorus, and it amused Charlotte to note that unconsciously, the women's arms began to move across the floor in unison. What a jolly story this would make to tell Robert and Matron this evening. And Orlando. She would serve Mr. Pyle this evening, she thought with a hint of wickedness. The poor old soul would be beside himself at being waited upon, and she would insist on knowing more about the brave little man.

The cleaning of the floor fairly flew by between the singing and the laughter. They were nearly to the entrance to the surgery when the door opened and the day's bureaucratic delegation was led into the room by Robert and another Englishman, with Alice at the rear of the group shepherding them.

"My goodness," Robert said in surprise, as the nurses' singing trailed off. "I did not know." He turned to the odd group of men that had accompanied him and spoke with a slightly exaggerated cadence. "Our good nurses are being so kind as to clean our surgery. We are fortunate to not need it today."

Charlotte was thinking how equally fortunate she and the other nurses were not to have had the visitors approach from the other hall; the newcomers would have been confronted by the site of the nurses' bottoms wriggling in the air as they scrubbed and sang. Imagining Robert's face at such a sight made her giggle.

She ceased giggling when the Englishman beside Robert said, in accented but perfectly understandable Russian, *"The nurses have volunteered to clean the surgery today. We are very fortunate to have them working for us."*

"Thank you, Nigel," Robert said, then gave a slight bow toward the nurses, who had halted their cleaning. *Nigel*, Charlotte thought. She'd heard the name and now recognized his voice. *Robert's friend from the Army.* Her Lieutenant went on, "Ladies, I apologize for the interruption. Please excuse—"

Alice suddenly spoke up. "Perhaps the Russian gentleman has some questions for Nurse Braninov. She is from that land, after all."

Nigel, a good-looking man with a thin face and hair that was already receding on either side of his forehead, translated, addressing the question to a thick-set man amid the other delegates. *"Mr. Sverdlov, one of our nurses is from your country. Is there anything you would care to ask her?"*

Charlotte climbed to her feet, flashing a look of mock martyrdom at the nurses around her. "Keep on working, my girls. We're almost done."

Sverdlov stepped forward, edging the other delegates aside. *"'Comrade Sverdlov,' if you please,"* he said brusquely. *"'Mister' is a term used by the bourgeoisie to identify themselves as being of a higher station than the proletariat."*

Inwardly, Charlotte sighed. Sverdlov was a Bolshevik. She'd known things were going badly back home, but his presence here as a delegate suggested that there had been some kind of official recognition of Lenin and his murderous rabble. This did not bode well for her country or her family.

"Bugger insists on being called 'comrade'," Nigel said to Fitzgerald in an aside. Robert's friend had apparently heard his share of revolutionary rhetoric, for he went on smoothly, *"Comrade Sverdlov is there anything you would like to ask to Nurse Braninov?"* He put just the slightest stress on the word "Comrade."

The two Russians faced one another. Charlotte gazed up at the man. His clothes were plain, sturdy workman's clothing, stained with food and travel. A ring of grime circled his neck, his fingernails were nearly black with dirt, while his hair hung in thick clumps that seemed both matted and greasy. He was, she decided, the filthiest human being she had ever seen. Perhaps he and his kind considered regular bathing a bourgeoisie affectation. The thought of this vile and unhygienic person in the newly cleaned surgery turned her stomach. She wanted him out of their hospital as fast as possible. She would answer whatever inane questions he might have and send him on his merry revolutionary way.

Robert watched with interest. He could not mistake the moue of distaste that faintly coloured Charlotte's expression. It was a distaste he shared, having spent the last two days with the man. Sverdlov was a buffoon and a bully, who wielded his "rights as a member of the workers' revolution" like a club. His rights, oddly, seemed to somehow provide him with the best breakfast, preferred seating on the tram taking them round the hospitals, and a supply of His Majesty's rum, all before ten in the morning.

Sverdlov looked Charlotte over, as if examining a side of beef for purchase. Outright disgust showed on his face, and he uttered something harshly in their shared language.

Charlotte blinked as if she had been slapped without warning, and color drained from her face. She took a half step backward.

For the rest of his life, Nigel relished telling the story.

"I nearly swallowed my tongue," he would say. "That Russian fellow had cheek. I think he only dared say it because he thought no one would understand him—or that I was too 'bourgeoisie' to repeat what he said."

Here, usually, the story was interrupted by a sip or two of a malt whiskey, his preferred conversational libation. "And poor Charlotte, I doubt she'd ever been addressed so."

Another sip. "Robert though surprised me. He stepped up and grasped my arm, asking, 'What did he say?' I had no idea, you see, how he felt about Nurse Charlotte. Robert had been most discreet. I attempted to defuse the moment, said something about how their politics differed. Robert was having none of it. *None* of it, I assure you. His hand ground into my arm, and it was frankly painful. I don't think he was even aware he was doing it. 'What did that biscuit-arsed barking spider say?'

"It was then I knew Robert was serious, even more than the grip on my arm. One rarely heard Robert speak of someone so, it was very similar to the way you Americans would say 'that dirty son-of-a-bitch' or some such."

Another judicious sip, a thoughtful pause. Truly, Nigel had honed this story to high art. He would then go on. "And he frightened me, I must admit. I don't think I'd ever seen his face like that. We were never in battle together, you see, and thus I had no idea what he looked like in the middle of one. And, given all that, I told him."

What, the listeners would usually ask, *what did Sverdlov say?*

Nigel turned to Robert. "Fitz, old boy, it's just a political squabble." Nigel didn't look at Charlotte as he said this. Robert's eyes bore into those of his friend. Those eyes would have nothing but the truth.

"He said..." Nigel lowered his voice, "he said 'So, Comrade Braninov, you have abandoned Mother Russia to become a whore for the English Imperialists.'"

There was a gasp from the nurses kneeling nearby.

Nigel's voice had not been as quiet as he supposed.

Robert burst into action faster than Nigel had ever seen him move, even on the rugby field. He slammed a forearm under Sverdlov's chin while simultaneously pistoning his hand into the Russian's crotch and lifting him bodily off the ground from both points of contact. As the delegate gave a strange, high-pitched squeal and a few of the nurses shrieked in surprise, Fitzgerald drove the Russian into the wall with such force the entire surgery shook.

For all the fury on his face, Robert spoke in an even, level voice. "In His Majesty's Hospital, we do not speak to our dedicated and hard-working nurses in such a manner." He appeared to apply additional pressure with his forearm, and another strangled noise leaked from the Russian delegate. Nigel translated out of habit. When Nigel had finished speaking, Robert went on. "And you shall never again speak to Nurse Braninov using such unmannerly terms. Or I will kill you where you stand."

Fitzgerald waited for this last to be translated. Sverdlov's eyes were bulging; whether from the arm blocking his windpipe or the threat was difficult to determine. His arms quivering from the effort, Robert lifted Sverdlov even higher up the wall. His voice remained level, all the more frightening for its strange calmness. "Do we have an understanding, Comrade?"

Nigel translated again, and then added in English, "Robert, you must let the man down. He can't breathe, much less speak."

Robert allowed Sverdlov to drop to the ground. The English Lieutenant brushed off his uniform and batted at something on his neck before turning to the shocked nurses and stunned delegates. "I do apologize for this unpleasantness," he said, a slight quaver in his voice as he mastered his emotions. "Most discourteous. Pray, forgive me."

Alice was staring at him, as was Charlotte and everyone else in the room. Alice managed to croak out, "We are due in the rehabilitation ward next."

"Well, then, let us hurry along." Robert said, pulling the shaky Sverdlov to his feet and steering him toward the door. Nigel had the impression that Fitzgerald would have applied the toes of his boot to help the Russian diplomat along, had they been alone. Robert gave the nurses a cheerful wave as they departed. "Sorry to have interrupted you, ladies. It looks lovely in here."

Silence hung in the air after the door closed behind the delegates. Then the nurses turned to Charlotte, and the questions flew at her.

"Did you know that awful man?"

"Lord, he was dirty, are all Russian men like that?"

"He's a Bolshie, isn't he?"

Charlotte held up her hands. "Let us finish in here first, girls. We have done so well today, let us not be distracted now when we are so close to being done." She dropped to her knees and examined the floor, striving to pay no heed to the whispers around her. There was a crust of soap from the interrupted scrubbing that she would now have to work harder to remove. As she reached for her discarded rag, she noticed her hand was trembling.

Bethany spoke up, as Charlotte had known she would. "Mr. Robert certainly taught that ponce how to speak to a lady."

Rocking on her knees, grinding the rag into the floor, just wanting to be out of this place, Charlotte replied, "Lieutenant Fitzgerald is a gentleman in the best sense of the word. Any other gentleman would have responded exactly the same."

And she would speak no more of the incident. When

the surgery was sparkling, just before lunch, she dismissed the nurses with her thanks. They, in turn, paid their respects in their usual, private fashion with a half-curtsey before happily departing for their tents.

She did not see Robert that night. Orlando escorted her to Matron's tent, as usual, but made his apologies for Robert's regrettable absence due to duty. Nonetheless, Charlotte and Matron passed an enjoyable evening in quiet companionship. Charlotte carefully stitched up the sleeves on Robert's work uniform…they had been torn fighting the fires from the bombing, and she had coerced Orlando into bringing the offending garment to her. Matron pored over the schedules for the month to come. At first, Charlotte was tense, but Matron made no comment about the day's events, confining her conversation to observations about the hospital, the course of the war, and such.

As she lay down in her cot that night, the first night in several months when the touch of Robert's mouth was not upon her lips, Kathleen spoke from the darkness. "Do you think he would have done it?"

Charlotte had not been expecting her to speak. "What?"

"Do you think your beau really would have gutted that fella who called you a whore?"

An automatic *No, don't be silly,* almost leapt from Charlotte, but then the memory of that moment came to her. She could not see Robert's expression, as his back was to her and the rest of the watchers. But she had seen Sverdlov. He was looking directly into Lieutenant Fitzgerald's face, and what he saw there brought naked fear into his eyes.

Instead, she said, more honestly, "I'm not sure. I don't think so."

Kathleen grunted, unconvinced. "You don't know your Mr. Fitzgerald as well as you think, then, missy."

Robert was unavailable the next night, as well. Matron's previous equanimity shifted a bit, and she directed a tart inquiry at Orlando. "Mister Pyle, is Lieutenant Fitzgerald so constrained by his duties that he cannot take some tea with two ladies of his acquaintance?"

Orlando looked at some middle space between them, not exactly meeting the gaze of either woman. "Mum, Miss, Master Robert…that is, Lieutenant Fitzgerald…well, he's terribly busy."

The little man appeared positively shifty. There might have been a slight dappling of sweat on his upper lip. Charlotte was moved to pity for the old fellow…whatever was keeping Robert, Orlando had obviously been compelled to silence.

She took the mended uniform shirt from her sewing basket and placed it in the orderly's hands. "Do tell him his company is sorely missed," she said with a gentle smile.

"Yes, Mum…yes, Nurse." With a curt bob of his head, Orlando fled the tent.

Staring after the orderly, Matron said in a thoughtful tone, "I suspect your Robert upset a few members of His Majesty's government yesterday."

Choosing not to comment on "your Robert," Charlotte contented herself with saying, rather stupidly, "Pardon, Mum?"

"There are some in the government who think the Bolsheviks have the right idea. Tear down everything and start over." Matron sighed. "They would not be happy to hear that Lieutenant Fitzgerald swatted their fool around like he was a wicked child. No matter how much the imbecile deserved it."

Thus dismissing the subject, Matron settled into her camp chair. She had her own sewing to do. Charlotte noticed the senior nurse was taking in one of her uniform skirts. "I seem to be less than I was," Matron confessed as she pinned the fabric into place.

Indeed, she was. Now made aware, Charlotte could see that Matron's face had noticeably thinned in the past weeks, and there was greyness to her skin that Charlotte had not perceived previously. *Of course not*, she thought in reproach. *You've been too busy swanning about over Robert to have noticed a zebra if it had walked in front of you.*

"Mum," she said casually, "may I get you some tea? I could find some sandwiches in the mess kitchen, I'm sure…"

Bent over her tailoring, Matron didn't look up. "Tea would be lovely, my dear. But I'm not really hungry at this moment."

Undeterred, Charlotte fetched sandwiches from the kitchen and filched an orange while she was there. True to her word, Matron had only tea, and Charlotte gave the uneaten food to a pair of grateful nurses on night watch.

She missed Robert. She had become so accustomed to his nearness. His sheer physicality within her life. She realized just the awareness of him, simply knowing that Robert was in the world, that he existed, anchored her. Like a ship riding out a storm, she had a point of continuity, of stability that helped her to survive the roiling seas and lashing winds.

She did happen to see Orlando that next morning, on his way to perform some mysterious errand. She had stepped out of the surgery for a breath of air and to take a bit of soup. "Orlando," she called after him. The little man jerked his head nervously. "Did Mr. Fitzgerald like his shirt? Was it mended to his satisfaction?"

Curious emotions played across his face...first relief, to be quickly replaced by a fretful contemplation. After a strange interval, he finally said, "Yes, Miss Braninov. He liked it very much. He donned it straight away."

Trying to keep the hopefulness out of her voice, she asked, "Shall we see him this evening for tea?"

Again, the odd flurry of emotions on the orderly's face, before he settled on saying, "Yes, Miss, I know he wants to be there."

"Do tell him I asked after him," she asked, while her eyes cried out, *Tell him I miss the sound of his voice and touch of his hand, and the stolen kisses and that I love him more than I know how to say.*

Alas, for although a good man, Orlando appeared to lack the particular poetry of soul required to translate the true message that poured from her, and thus merely nodded before disappearing down the hall and out of her sight.

At the end of her shift, Charlotte did not long linger in the wards. "Her" patients had moved on to old Blighty, and the current patients did not know her. They had already grown attached to the new nurses. She stood in the main hallway, apart from them all, noticing her aching feet and confirming with an alarmed sniff that she was in need of a bath. Even so, she tarried a while in the main building, lingering in the rear to watch the new nurses.

Charlotte had to smile. The new nurses were doing fine, gently teasing the soldiers, quietly rebuking the one or two who whinged about their medication or bandages, encouraging others in their recovery. The new girls were doing fine, as well as Charlotte and Kathleen could have done.

It was late. There was no sign of either Orlando or

Robert. Taking a deep breath against the stab of passing sadness at his absence for yet another evening, she decided to stop by Matron's tent for just a moment to pay her respects, and then, she resolved, she would take a thorough sponge bath and go to bed.

Good Orlando caught her just as she reached Matron's tent. "Miss Charlotte, Mum…" he said helplessly.

Charlotte turned. She'd been deep in thought, feeling slightly opiated with fatigue, and had not heard him approaching in the night. Before the young nurse could speak, Matron was at the entrance of the tent in a proper dressing gown, spectacles on her nose. "What is it, sir?" she asked in her usual voice of command.

"Please come right away. Mr. Fitzgerald is not well, Mum."

Matron instantly stepped out, pulling the gown more tightly about her waist. Orlando looked aghast. "Mum, you must—"

In her most icy voice, Matron replied as she pushed past him, "Is Mr. Fitzgerald in need of our assistance or not?"

Charlotte and Orlando sped along in the older woman's wake. There was nothing grey-faced or diminished in Matron's swift movement.

"He's not himself," Orlando explained to Charlotte as Matron ploughed ahead, then added, "He was confined to quarters for speaking harshly to that Russian gentleman. That is why he's not been round to see you, Miss. But the past days—"

"Symptoms, man," Matron barked. "What symptoms?"

"He was laughing, ma'am. Not at anything that one might call amusing."

That seemed, well, it seemed a small thing to Charlotte. Perhaps Robert and Nigel had shared a dram or two of whiskey. Orlando went on, "He had me put out the light, for it hurt his head dreadfully."

Those symptoms sounded familiar...yet they could be anything.

"Where is he now?" Matron demanded.

"In his office, ma'am. He would not leave the desk. He was working, you see —"

Matron stopped the torrent of useless exposition with a curt gesture. "Nurse Braninov, you will not wish to see this. Take Orlando —"

Charlotte said firmly, "I must go with you, Mum."

Defying Matron's directives was uncommon in the extreme. Matron paused, taking in the firm set of Charlotte's jaw, the rigid outline of her shoulders. "Indeed," she finally admitted. "Mr. Pyle, fetch the night nurse, Nurse Hynes. Do you know her? Good. Tell her to come quickly but neither of you is to enter the office. Do you understand?"

"Yes, ma'am!"

"Then fly!"

Orlando fairly sprinted down the hall. A terrifying thought began to blossom in Charlotte's mind. "Mum, you do not think..."

"We do not know anything," Matron said crisply. "All we know is that a man is taken ill. We are nurses, and we shall aid him as best we can."

Charlotte wanted to run, but she forced herself to emulate Matron's swift, steady stride. It was purposeful, it was direct, but it would not cause fear or comment. To any who saw them, they were two nurses hurrying to an important assignment. That is, if one happened to overlook the unique sight of Matron out of uniform. Yet as the older nurse strode beside her, Charlotte could not help but admire the way that good woman wore the dressing gown with as much dignity and gravitas as a judge in his robes and wig. Her character came from the way she lived her life, not the clothing she happened to wear. Something about that realization calmed Charlotte's fears a bit and allowed her to breathe more normally.

If Robert were taken ill, then who better than this pair of dedicated nurses to aid him? If he were tipsy, then she would have to speak to him, assuming Matron did not bring him to see the error of his ways first. Men could be allowed their foolishness, but not to the extent of humiliating themselves in front of their servants.

Matron drew up outside the door to the Supply Office. No light burned within. She rapped her knuckle sharply on the frame.

"Mr. Fitzgerald. It is I, Matron. May I come in?"

The voice that reached their ears was faint, weak. "Ma'am, I am in no fit condition for your company."

Matron put her hand upon the door handle, and turned. The door clicked open and she eased it wide enough for the two nurses to slip inside. A wedge of light fell through the crack and across the floor.

There was a kind of shuddering gasp from the desk. "The light, please. It stabs like hellfire."

Charlotte shut the door firmly, and all was dimness within the office again.

Matron moved cautiously toward the desk. "Mr. Fitzgerald, do let us examine you, sir."

"I would not trouble you, ma'am." His voice was barely audible, tremulous, yet, unaccountably, a long hearty laugh burst from him. "I seem to have caught a most ferocious cold. What an inconvenient thing to have happen at this time of the year."

In the dark, Matron's hand found Charlotte's shoulder and held her there. The message was unmistakable. *Come no closer.*

Charlotte stood where she was, fear growing within her with renewed ferocity.

"Let me cover your eyes, Lieutenant Fitzgerald, so we may examine you."

"I hate to trouble you," he replied and uttered again that strange laugh.

"It is no trouble, Lieutenant," Matron told him in a kind voice. "And it would ease Charlotte's mind if we may be of some comfort to you."

"Dearest Charlotte," he said in a dreamy voice, and she almost wept to hear him speak so. "Would be wrong of me to worry her…"

Matron moved to the cabinet. She knew where the clean rags were stored from their time spent with the lamented Ignace and his kitten. She took one, and in the dimness, Charlotte saw her raise it to her nose. Apparently, it was clean enough, for she said, "Now, Lieutenant, I shall place this over your eyes. It should block the light."

"All right," he said diffidently. "Is Charlotte here?"

"I am here, Robert," Charlotte told him in a slow, clear voice.

"Could you hold my hand?" he asked. "I seem to be floating away…I don't want to drift past you."

Without waiting for Matron's leave, Charlotte stepped forward to take his hand in hers. At the clasp of his fingers around hers, she looked up at Matron in alarm. His flesh was dry, almost papery, but burning hot. Matron nodded. She had surely felt the same heat when tying the rag around his head.

"The light, if you please, Nurse Braninov," Matron requested in a cool, professional tone.

Robert released her hand with reluctance and she found the wall plate. She pressed the button inward, and watery yellow light filled the room.

The Russian girl instantly wanted to plunge the room back into darkness, for surely the man she beheld was not Robert. He was unshaven, from perhaps the last time she had seen him. His face was strangely puffy, yet he appeared to have lost weight and his complexion was sallow. He was wearing the uniform shirt she had mended for him, and it hung loosely across his chest. A wave of shivering rolled across him as they watched.

He turned his face toward her. "Charlotte? I am floating in the darkness…" and then he folded up, collapsing onto the desk as soundlessly as a suit of clothes dropped to the floor.

Matron would allow no one into the room besides herself and Charlotte. She gave orders for a gurney and gowns to Orlando but forbade either Nurse Hynes or the faithful orderly from entering.

Charlotte and Matron tended Robert themselves, as they suspected he might be infectious, and wished to spare others from being exposed. After a quick examination, the women lifted his limp body onto the gurney.

Matron pulled a pair of shears from her pocket. "I will remove his clothing."

"No, Mum," Charlotte told her quietly. "This is my duty. I must do this."

Matron pursed her lips. "Indeed." She then stepped closer to the door and raised her voice. "Mr. Pyle! I must have a metal bin, with a lid, and some carbolic of acid. Do you understand?"

"Yes, Mum," came Orlando's muffled reply.

"Nurse Hynes?"

This answer was more firm, more accustomed to being addressed in such a tone of command. "Yes, Mum?"

"Place Mr. Pyle in quarantine, if you please. Delouse him, burn his clothes, and keep him under observation for three days. And have this room deloused as well."

"Yes, Mum. Where will you be?"

Her voice did not alter in any appreciable way, yet it echoed with a grim weight. "We shall be in the Moratorium tents. With Lieutenant Fitzgerald."

Those words slid into Charlotte's awareness, burning like an icy blade into her diaphragm. The Moratorium tents. Where they sent men to die.

Matron, not insensible to the younger woman's feelings, touched her on the arm. "There is yet hope, my dear. We must take him to the Moratorium as it is the only site we have that is fit for an infected man."

Blinking hard, Charlotte said, "Yes, Mum." She held out a hand for the shears. "May I, please?"

There began a strange period where Charlotte discovered that there was something akin to two of her living within her skin. One of her stood aside, in an attitude of quiet devotion. Charlotte was unaware of what exactly this part of her was doing, but she had a sense of prayer, of quietly, respectfully remembering the suffering patient before them. She clearly understood, however, that she dared not pray for herself, for her own selfish desires, but that her entreaties to God could only be for Robert, for the patient.

The other part of her was a focused, professional nurse. With Matron's scissors, Charlotte cut the clothing from Robert's feverish body and dropped the strips into the metal waste bin. She noted with a pang of sorrow that she must destroy the shirt she had so carefully mended. 'Now he will have nothing of me about him,' she thought, letting the shirt slip from her fingers to fall with a burbling splash in the carbolic acid.

Soon, Robert lay bare before her. She had dared to think of one day seeing him thus on their wedding night, but not in so helpless nor so vulnerable a manner. Her heart ached at the sight of his weakness, of his power of speech and cognition and action rent from him by the unthinkingly malign actions of this unknown bacillus.

Nor could she protect him, her true love. Matron stood patiently by, with clean bed clothing and a gown. Charlotte reached into her own blouse and drew forth a tiny cross on a chain. "My mother's," she said simply, unclasping the chain and transferring it to Robert's neck.

It had been a parting gift from her mother the day her parents had departed from England. Father had teased Mother about keeping their girl superstitious and pure, but Mother had only smiled and kissed her daughter. *"To keep you safe,"* she said with tears in her eyes.

"To keep him safe," Charlotte explained to Matron as they quickly bathed Robert in a solution of naphthalene, creosote, and iodoform to kill the lice. He shivered as they worked, but did not wake. She and Matron quickly dressed him in the clean gown and covered him with a sheet.

"Come now," Matron told her. "Let's be away before any cursed lice latch onto us."

The sojourn in the Moratorium became a test of her faith, of her belief in a kind and loving God. She'd had the faint inclination to question Him prior, but not the opportunity. With only herself, Matron, and their patient in that lonely, isolated tent, Charlotte had far too much time to ponder the wisdom of His ways. For it seemed Robert suffered the tortures of the damned. Charlotte knew Robert Fitzgerald for a good man...why should he suffer so? Even as she asked, she knew it was a fatuous question.

Job, too, had suffered, and God's only answer had been that the good man was but a utensil to be dealt with as the Lord pleased. She could not bear to watch Robert's afflictions and question the Lord's will at the same time.

It was clear by the second day that Fitzgerald had contracted typhus. If the chills and fever were not sign enough, then the body aches that afflicted him, muscle spasms that contorted his body, were indicative. Finally, however, it was the spots that appeared everywhere on his body save for his face and the palms of his hands that were the conclusive sign: tiny dots which might have been pricks from an imp wielding a red-hot pin.

Robert was only briefly lucid on the first day. She had shaved his head against the lice, and he was again burning with fever. She wiped him with a damp rag, and his eyes fluttered open. Dry lips moved, but no sound emerged. She hastily brought a metal cup to his mouth and allowed him to sip a tiny amount. "My Lady Sister," he rasped.

"My Knight," she replied, turning her head to hide the quick tears that flooded to her eyes. Quickly wiping her cheeks, she turned back to him. "Are you comfortable, sir?"

A tremulous smile drifted across his face. "Far too comfortable, it appears. Forgive me for not standing."

She took up the damp cloth again, bathing his chest. "I would forgive you anything, my love."

His eyes closed, were forced open again. "Were I to act in a way that required such forgiveness, I would be unworthy of your love."

Charlotte leaned forward, pressed her lips to his burning forehead. "Never," she whispered.

His hand reached for hers, but found instead the cross on its chain and held it up. With laboured effort, he made out the shape of the item so small in his hand. "From you?"

"It belonged to my mother. Now it is yours."

He stretched the chain tight, pressed the cross to his lips, and lay back as if that simple gesture had exhausted him. His fist rested on his chest, closed tight round the cross. "Thank you, my dear…dear… Charlotte."

His eyes closed again. She put her mouth beside his ear, and speaking in her native Russian, said in a low voice, *"I will love only you, Robert Fitzgerald, and no other."* It seemed he smiled, and then he was insensible again.

He awoke in tears.

He awoke in agony.

He tried to crawl away from the pain, but it clung to him like a ravaging demon. The pain was everywhere as if he were coated by burning pitch, as if it filled the spaces between his muscles and lungs and organs.

So he was in Hell.

In the sea of flames and blinding pain, there was one tiny oasis of comfort.

Something held his burning hand, the presence shining through his dark agony like a beacon, the touch cooling his fevered flesh. Something held cool metal to his mouth, and he drank.

An angel. There were angels in Hell?

The angel spoke, caressing his forehead. Again, the soft touch briefly drained the flames from his skin. He couldn't understand the angel's speech, but the tones were gentle. He fought the sheer agony to focus on the angel's words, and the angel spoke again. This time, he could understand the words, though they still sounded strange and not of this earth. "Hush, my love."

He was not aware he had been moaning, nearly shrieking. He clenched his jaws, and only whimpers escaped.

The angel bathed his brow with cool water

And then he slept.

The vigil was exhausting. August was fading into September, and the nights in the tent had become chilly. They slept in shifts and would keep each other company during the overlaps. Charlotte awoke on the seventh day to overhear Matron engaging in a spirited, whispered conversation through the flap of the tent with a bent silhouette that was clearly Dr Hartford, the Senior Physician in charge of Base Hospital No. 12.

Charlotte lay unmoving until the conversation was concluded with a sharp retort from Matron that rose to a low hiss. "Then send me packing back to Kensington, James! I have never troubled you for a thing, but I am insisting on this."

The silhouette of the Senior Physician bowed his head and retreated.

Charlotte sat up. It was nearly sundown; she had slept far longer than she planned. "How is Mr. Fitzgerald, Mum?"

"He is alive, Nurse," Matron snapped before catching herself. She came closer with a rueful smile. "Forgive me, Nurse Braninov."

"It is no matter, Matron," Charlotte said honestly. "We are both tired." She poured water into a basin, splashed her face, emptied and refilled the basin, holding it out for the older woman. "Perhaps this would refresh you."

Delicately, Matron washed her face and lowered herself heavily to her cot. The two nurses' cots were against either wall of the tent. Robert lay in the centre of the enclosure. They had moved him from the higher gurney and placed him on a simple cot, fearing he might fall whilst thrashing in his fever.

Charlotte glanced at Fitzgerald. When conscious, he had no appetite, and they had to be most forceful to get him to even drink a bit of broth. He had lost weight, and his collar bones were prominent under his gown.

"Rest yourself, Mum," Charlotte said to the older woman. "I can take over now."

Matron loosened her collar and eased off her thick-soled boots with a sigh. "What I would give for a bath." She lay back on the cot. After a moment, she said, "He caught it from that damned Russian diplomat."

"Mum?"

"That disgusting man your Robert cuffed about. I'm certain he had lice and they landed on Lieutenant Fitzgerald. Is it the fashion not to bathe in Moscow these days?"

"I do not know, Mum. It has been so very long since I was there." In spite of their conditions, Charlotte smiled at Matron's outrage. She removed a sweat-soaked sheet from Robert, who twitched without waking, and replaced it with clean linen. "Mum," she finally dared to say, "I know that it is irregular to have two nurses dedicated to caring for a single patient. I am exceedingly grateful for your—"

"Nonsense," Matron replied, with her eyes closed. "We have been exposed. We cannot risk exposing anyone else to the depredations of this disease." She added in an undertone, still vexed, "Beastly Bolshevik."

"Yes, Mum," Charlotte responded dutifully and looked down in silence at her Robert. She knew not whether he would live or die. The spots on his body had faded, but he was still wracked with muscular spasms, fever, and chills. From time to time, he cried out in pain, clutching his head. She could give him shots of morphine when the pains seemed at their worst, if only to reduce the suffering he felt. But for now, he was still, lost in something that surely was not sleep.

A small sob may have escaped Charlotte's lips, looking down at her love. She quickly stifled it as Matron said,

"Nurse Braninov, I have been told you have a lovely voice. Would you mind singing a bit? Hearing is the final sense to go, according to some. It might give Mr. Fitzgerald a measure of comfort to hear your voice. And I would be so grateful for the distraction."

And so Charlotte sang. She sang everything she could remember, even when Matron's breathing had deepened to an unladylike snore, when darkness was upon the land and the only illumination came from the anti-aircraft searchlights slicing through the cold air to stab into the clouds. She sang nursery rhymes and ballads of the Steppes. She sang hymns and popular songs she'd heard when at school in London. She sang until she could sing no more, but every sound that fell from her lips meant one thing only: *I love you, Robert.*

By the tenth day, the two women were haggard with fatigue, made edgy by their long confinement.

"How long can he go on?" Charlotte asked that morning at the end of her shift, striving to keep childish tears from her voice.

Matron's face settled into exceedingly grim lines. "We are approaching the crisis phase, Nurse Braninov." She lowered her voice. "I implore you to leave now. There is no profit in your staying. It can be a long and terrible death. I saw it many times in the camps during the Boer War."

Biting her lips, Charlotte simply shook her head.

Matron had expected as much. "Then rest, child. He and I shall both need your strength." So saying, she shooed Charlotte to her cot and watched her until the young woman fell asleep.

It was stuffy in the tent, and Charlotte awoke later, thirsty. She saw Matron crouched beside Robert in a posture that was nearly that of prayer. "You must live," she was whispering fiercely in the unresponsive man's ear. "You must live for Charlotte. I will not allow you to die, Lieutenant Fitzgerald. You will live!"

The sight was so altogether incongruous, it was impossible for Charlotte to believe that she was not dreaming, and her head fell back onto her pillow as sleep swept over her again.

The morning of the eleventh day, Matron bent over Fitzgerald and examined him minutely. She straightened up and looked Charlotte full in the face. "It is now time for you to leave this place, Nurse Braninov."

Charlotte shot a panicky look at Robert's cot. She could see him breathing. *Thank you, Merciful Father.*

"He will live, I judge," Matron said with a weary smile, and Charlotte's heart gave a sudden bound of joy. "And we, by the grace of God, are not infected either. Go, clean yourself, find fresh clothing. I will watch over him until you return. I will not have you enter this tent again until evening, is that understood?"

"Yes, Mum!"

"Rest now, Nurse Braninov. You have done well."

Impulsively, Charlotte rushed over and kissed the older nurse on the cheek as she wrapped her in a tight embrace. "Thank you, Mum. With all my heart, thank you!"

Embarrassed by this unexpected outpouring of affection, Matron pushed her away with gentle clumsiness, saying, "Go on, child, do not make me say it a second time."

Charlotte gave a deep curtsey, and with a relieved look at Robert, stepped out of the tent into the fresh air of the morning.

After the confinement of the past week and a half, the area around the hospital felt like a huge expanse of open air, while the sun was bright and harsh without the filtering effects of the canvas tent. Shielding her watering eyes with her hands, Charlotte stumbled along the duckboards almost drunkenly.

She arrived at her tent at the same time as Madame, who greeted her with effusive and almost understandable cries of delight. Kathleen, while not as loud, swept her round in a big hug before setting her back down on the cot.

"You scared the bejeezus out of me," the American girl said. Plying the other nurse with pastries and milk, the old Frenchwoman agreed.

Kathleen sat on the cot beside her friend, and casually plucked a croissant from Charlotte's hand, earning herself a reproving cuff from Madame. Ignoring the old woman, Kathleen went on, "We were all scared when we heard the Lieutenant had the typhus. I heard some of the doctors sayin' Matron saved the whole blasted Hospital when she quarantined the three of you." The croissant lay untouched in Kathleen's hand. "I was worried about you, I tell you."

Charlotte threw her arm around the other girl's big shoulders. Kathleen was no beauty, but she had a heart as fine as any Charlotte had ever known. "It's going to be all right now," she told her American friend. "Matron says Robert will live."

Now Kathleen crammed the croissant into her mouth. "I'm happy for you both," she managed around the bread.

Charlotte's wide smile suddenly turned into a jaw-cracking yawn. She covered her mouth with both hands. Both the nurses giggled like the girls they still were, and Madame patted her shoulder fondly, gesturing to the bed.

Kathleen hooked another pastry from the cart before saying, "I have to get. You look all done in, sister. Catch some sleep, and we'll talk tonight." Kathleen tipped the pastry at Madame as she walked out.

Charlotte stood to remove her soiled uniform. She'd essentially lived in it for the past ten days, and it was suddenly repugnant to her. She quickly peeled off the dirty garments, not even looking round to ensure her modesty was preserved. Madame gathered up the discarded clothing and said she would take it to the laundry. Charlotte nodded her thanks as she slipped into a clean uniform.

Madame had turned back the bed when Charlotte faced her again. *"The American girl, she aired your bedding every day,"* the old woman told her.

Yawning again, Charlotte slumped onto the cot and slid between the blissfully cool, clean sheets. Exhaustion seemed to be bubbling up from her very being. Relieved of the crushing fear for Robert, drained of the worry for his life, she felt empty and deflated, hardly able to keep herself upright.

Before she could say goodnight to Madame, Charlotte was asleep.

That evening, the Moratorium tent was empty. A young nurse in rubber boots and thick rubber gloves was scrubbing the floors with some substance that made Charlotte's eyes water.

Staring about the now vacant tent where she had expended such an immensity of hope and sorrow, Charlotte demanded in shock, "Where is Lieutenant Fitzgerald? Where is Matron?"

The nurse started to climb to her feet before replying. "No, stay there!" Charlotte barked. "Just answer me."

"Miss, Matron is in her tent. Was she who told me to clean this horrible place."

Charlotte hurried over to Matron's tent. As she arrived, the Senior Surgeon was taking his leave, a weary and grave expression upon his face. "Sir," she said most abruptly. "Where is Lieutenant Fitzgerald?"

"Fitzgerald?" It took him a moment to place the name. "The lad with typhus?"

"Yes, sir, the very one."

"He's been evacuated, Sister. Moved to recuperate in London. That was good work you did, Nurse. I doubt the man would have survived—"

She interrupted him, again in a manner that far more rude than was her customary way of speech. "But why, sir? He could return to his duties shortly, I am sure of it."

Matron had appeared beside Dr Hartford, saying, "A treaty signing is imminent in weeks, if not days hence."

Baffled, Charlotte looked to the old doctor for enlightenment. The surgeon obliged her by saying, "Each side will attempt to grasp every bit of land they can prior to signing the treaty. We expect to be deluged in wounded. We could not spare the bed, Sister." He added grudgingly, "Nor could we spare two trained nurses to tend to just one sick man."

He stepped past Charlotte. "Good evening to both of you. Pray rest well, for I fear you shall be needed on the morrow."

Charlotte stared after him with numb, impotent frustration. She then saw Alice standing near the entrance to the hospital proper, watching her. Undeniably, Alice was staring at her. There was a strange, triumphant expression of glee on the girl's face.

Charlotte took an involuntary step forward. She knew not when her hands clenched into fists.

"Nurse Braninov?" Matron's sharp voice pulled Charlotte up short. She looked up at the composed face of the older nurse, then back at the hospital entrance. Alice was gone. The stern old nurse swept back the flap of her tent and gestured inside. Numbly, Charlotte followed her.

And Matron held her while she wept.

Thus ended their war. Wars end in death, they end in despair. For many, there is the joy of having survived, but for some, the knowledge of those who were lost poisons the sweetness of life.

For Charlotte, the war ended in knowledge she'd never wanted. For as the weeks passed, and she waited some word from Robert—word that Matron assured her would come—Charlotte learned she could live with a broken heart.

The final surge of the wounded and maimed did descend upon them, and Charlotte discovered that she could still function as if she lived. She could assist the surgeons, she could eat the food that was placed in front of her, indeed, she could mimic life in many convincing ways. Yet every night, she fell asleep on a pillow that was wet with her tears, and she wondered how it was possible she could go on with the empty weight that had settled behind her breastbone, an emptiness so heavy her every step was an effort that made her gasp and pant at the end of a short walk.

Matron made inquiries. "He has been discharged into his father's care," was all she could sadly report.

When the Armistice was signed on the morning of November 11, 1918, there was dancing in the halls of Base Hospital No. 12. Wounded soldiers clanged bedpans together or threw bandages into the air like streamers. While the nurses gave each other giddy hugs and bestowed sisterly kisses upon the wounded men and the orderlies and the grandfatherly doctors, Charlotte moved silently and with studied purpose through the quiet back halls of the hospital. People ran past, shouting the happy news, and she would step to one side to not impede them. She had become skilled at not being observed as she moved from the surgery to her tent, where she would crawl into her cot and not speak.

Matron was waiting in one of those back hallways. She did not attempt to approach Charlotte but waited for her to draw near.

"Mum," Charlotte said mechanically, dipping her knees.

"Nurse Braninov," Matron replied in acknowledgement. She said nothing further, only gazed impassively at the young woman.

After sufficient time had passed, Charlotte curtseyed again and made as if to leave. "Mum."

"Stay a moment, Nurse Braninov," Matron directed her. Charlotte stood where she was, looking at the floor. "I am called to London," the older nurse announced. "There are many wounded men His Majesty desires should be brought home to mend. I will be assisting with the staffing and running of a hospital near High Castle."

"Yes, Mum." Charlotte felt exhausted. She ached for her tiny cot and the peaceful darkness she could find there.

"I am desirous that you come to London and work with me. You are a fine nurse, Charlotte. I would not see you waste your life in grief and regret."

Her words were only slightly penetrating the fog of Charlotte's weariness. "Mum?"

"Base Hospital No. 12 shall close before summer's end. These men will be shipped home. I would have you shutter this hospital and then join me in London as my senior nurse."

"London," Charlotte replied dully. "That's where Robert…"

"Lord Robert can go to the devil, for all I care," Matron replied with a quiet distaste. "If he has deceived and abandoned you, not only is he a scoundrel, but he is a fool as well, for you are one of the finest young women of my acquaintance."

Even though Matron spoke coldly of Robert, it was a cold that burned, and some of that heat began to reach Charlotte. "I had thought...of going back..." she murmured. English felt foreign to her, as well it should, but even the act of speech seemed unnatural. She had rarely uttered a spoken word these last weeks, she realized.

With great kindness, Matron said, "Your nation is in flames, Nurse Braninov, in subjugation to some mistaken ideal. Come, stay in London a while, at least until it is safe to return to your home."

Home. That word, that idea had lost its meaning. Robert was going to be her home. Where he was, was her heart and that would be their home. But no longer. That was the dream of a foolish girl who'd let herself be carried away by her foolish dreams.

"I...I would like that, Mum," Charlotte found herself saying.

Farewell

The hospital did not cease operation until the end of January. As a consequence, Charlotte had to endure another long winter in the drafty embrace of Base Hospital No. 12. With Matron's departure, Charlotte found herself working as the night shift supervisor. It was the equivalent of a brevet appointment in His Majesty's Army: additional responsibility with only a title, and no commensurate increase in position or recompense. They needed someone to fill the slot, as Robert might have said, and she was available.

Charlotte did not object to the hours, rarely noting the absence of Matron's occasionally forbidding presence. She didn't have to see Alice, indeed, she had overheard quite innocently that Alice had resigned and returned to England. And so there was only the Hospital, which suited her. It was quiet, and there were fewer people about during those hours, making them easier to avoid.

Except for Kathleen. Every other night or so, the American nurse would doggedly track down Charlotte. At first, Charlotte had tried to put her off by pretending there was work to be done that could not wait. Kathleen would simply pitch in, doing laundry, sorting supplies, washing bedpans. If there wasn't enough work to engage two pairs of hands, she found something productive to do nearby.

And she talked. As they worked, Kathleen would talk about her patients, about the weather. She would simply talk, and Charlotte would occasionally grunt in reply. Undeterred, Kathleen broadened her topics of conversation, once spending nearly 45 minutes expounding on the American President, Woodrow Wilson. That he'd finally put Americans into the fray and had helped drive the Germans to defeat was dandy, but otherwise, he wasn't worth a bucket of warm spit. *At least, I think she said 'spit',* Charlotte mused behind a placid expression.

Kathleen discussed the new influenza that had been seen among some of the American troops. It seemed awfully virulent. She thought they would have to keep an eye on it, and she asked Charlotte to report it to Dr Hartford. Charlotte nodded non-committally.

Kathleen was something of the bull mastiff in her personality. It was as if she had Charlotte in her jaws and would not release her until one of them was dead. When her Russian friend continued to maintain an aloof passivity in the face of perfectly reasonable conversational gambits, Kathleen shifted her mental grip and went for a new target. She began telling Charlotte about the ways in which she had changed.

"You never laugh anymore," the American said as they stood side by side, rinsing stinking bandages in vats of hot water. "You smile sometimes, but it's so fast I usually think I imagined it." The Russian girl glanced over but kept working. "You sleep all the time, too. But you have those dark circles under your eyes. You look like a raccoon."

Unable to bear it any longer, Charlotte threw her bandages into the sink, splashing hot, dirty water on them both. "Why are you here?" she demanded, her native accent deepening. "Why do you keep..." she searched for the English word. "Pestering me?"

Kathleen tossed her head, and some suds flew off her brow. She continued scrubbing at the bandages. The woman could *work*. "Because you're my friend, Charlotte," the big nurse said. "No man, good or bad, is gonna change that."

The simple statement stopped Charlotte, as if she'd been rapped on the sternum with a heavy bat. She held onto the edge of the crude sink with both hands, staring down into the water as if waiting for a revelatory vision. After a moment, she said in a low voice. "I am so tired. Of weeping."

"I know you are, honey," Kathleen replied.

"But, why would he leave me?" Charlotte said. She thought she might weep anew but strangely found herself dry-eyed. Her question was more from curiosity than from pain. Part of the anguish had been her bafflement.

"I didn't know him like you did, Cheri. I think, though, since I was on the outside of your little love bubble, I might have had a clearer look at him than you did."

The smile that had risen to Charlotte's lips at the term "love bubble" fell away. Wringing the bandages out in her strong hands, Kathleen went on, "I think he really did love you. He was true. I know how fellas can tell a girl what she wants to hear when he's sparkin' her, but I watched what he did."

Charlotte wasn't following everything Kathleen said, but she understood the meaning as Kathleen continued, "You have to do that on the farm. Don't matter what anybody tells you about their horse, you watch the horse, and let him tell you the kind of critter he is."

"So Robert was a good horse." She would have been surprised to know that there was a slight, slightly sad curve to her lips.

"Yes, ma'am," the American girl replied seriously.

"Back home, some of them ole boys will tell a girl just about anything to get you to drop your bloomers. Promise to marry you, other sweet soundin' lies. But Robert never did that, did he?"

"No, of course not. The very idea." She paused, thinking of a ladylike way to express herself that did not trespass upon vulgarity. "But I could feel that he wanted to, if you understand my meaning."

Now Kathleen chuffed. "He was a man, wasn't he? He had a pulse. He wanted to, but he never said a word about it, did he?"

"No," Charlotte repeated. "He treated me like…" *Like His Lady.* "Like a lady."

"He sure did. That's why I will not believe he just run off on you. Something must have happened to him. Don't know what. But it weren't 'cause of you or anything you did. And it weren't because he wanted that damned Alice girl instead."

Charlotte felt a full-faced smile rise to her lips, breaking free of the lingering sadness in her soul like a captured phoenix snapping its chains and flinging itself into the air with a cry of joy. The smile was at the sombreness of Kathleen's statement. She could always tell when the American girl was serious…her diction and grammar degraded, and Charlotte could imagine Kathleen in a corral from a dime-novel version of the American West, facing down some unscrupulous cattle baron, issuing an ultimatum as plainly and clearly as she could.

Focused on the washing, Kathleen said, more to herself than directly to Charlotte, "It just wasn't the time for you all. Time just wasn't right."

Charlotte put an arm around the big shoulders. "You are a good friend, Kathleen."

"I know. You're gonna miss me when I'm gone."

Charlotte collected the cleaned bandages and hung them on wooden racks to dry. "Where are you going?"

"Wyoming, Cheri. War's over. Nobody wants to pay to keep an American nurse out here in France, livin' the good life. It's near to scandalous."

Charlotte snorted a little laugh as she looked at her roughened hands and considered the plush accoutrement of their workplace; the heavy, now-rusting metal sinks, the single boiler for water, the cracked floor. "Yes, it has been the lap of luxury. I should hate to have to return to respectable employment."

"Hmmm," the American nurse grunted. "Besides. I didn't want to mention it, you feelin' so low about Robert. But there's a cowboy waitin' for me there."

Charlotte caught her breath, waiting for a shock of pain at the thought of her lost Robert and the unfairness of another's chance at happiness. The pain did not come. Instead, there was something like delight. Something like joy for her friend, who deserved so much that was good in the world. Had she, Charlotte wondered, had she simply been feeling morose because it had become a habit? Moving past that thought, she reached out and took both of Kathleen's hands in her own. "Oh, Kathy. That's wonderful. I'm so sorry I've been such a poor friend to you. You must have been bursting to tell me about it."

Kathleen shook her head. "Nah, I don't tell folks much of my business, anyway."

"Well, tell me," Charlotte said, grinning, feeling that empty weight behind her chest shift and lift. "I am your friend, after all."

The cowboy's name was Hector, but everyone called him Heck, naturally. He had seen Kathleen at a rodeo. "He busted a wrist showing off for me." It was something akin to love at first roping.

The American had not been exaggerating about her departure. She was due to return to the States by the end of the week. It would be a dreary Christmas without her at Base Hospital No. 12, but Charlotte was glad for her friend.

"So that's why you were pestering me," she exclaimed as she helped Kathleen pack a trunk. The word had no sting this time, either in the speaking or the hearing.

"Uh huh. I couldn't just run off without making sure you were going to be put right."

The depth of her friend's affection warmed Charlotte and shamed her a little. But Kathleen did not hold Charlotte's previous grief-stricken silence against her, nor mention it. Instead, she pressed a letter into Charlotte's hand. It had been carefully written in boxy print. "If I ever hear you got to America and you didn't come visit, we're gonna have words." She pointed to the paper. "This is my momma and daddy's address. That's my uncle's in Cheyenne. My brother is in the Army so I don't know where he'll be. And this is general delivery in Buckthorn. Our ranch is about 25 miles from town, but that's where we'll get our mail. Promise you'll write. . . I want to send you a wedding portrait."

"Of course," Charlotte assured her. She felt a prick of tears in her eyes, but these sprang from both elation for her friend and a bit of sorrow at seeing her go. They embraced. It was late, and Charlotte would soon start her shift. By the time she returned, the American girl would be gone. "I will miss you, Kathleen."

Kathleen's voice was hoarse. "I'll miss you, Cheri." She turned her head and wiped her nose on a sleeve. "I tell ya, I'll bet I'm the only cowgirl in Wyoming who's got a Russian Countess for a friend."

"And I'll be the only member of the Court with a cowgirl at my side."

Kathleen looked round their tent. Strangely, since the end of the war, it had become disorderly. It was dusty inside, and soot from the lanterns had marked the canvas. "We made a good team."

"You saved a lot of those boys, Kathy."

"We did. Together."

They embraced again, and then it was time for Charlotte to begin her shift.

Charlotte had begged a day of leave about a fortnight before Christmas. She was accompanied by Henry, the orderly, ("for protection," she had been told) as she rode to Paris in a double-decker bus filled with demobilizing soldiers. The city was mobbed, and a festive party-atmosphere filled the air. The approach of the holiday and the recent Armistice had renewed the hope of the citizens. Charlotte wore her nurse's uniform, for she honestly had no other decent clothing. All those she had brought with her from Russia she had long outgrown, and during her service with the Nursing Corps, she had no need for other garments.

At first, the nurse's uniform was a hindrance, as many soldiers and civilians stopped her in the station and on the streets of the City of Lights to give thanks for her efforts. She accepted them graciously, but as the morning was slipping away from her, she hurriedly sought out one bent old Frenchman for assistance. "Can you guide me to the Russian embassy?"

The old gentleman looked crestfallen. He explained he could not help her, but he seemed to take it upon himself, as a matter of national and personal pride, to provide her with an answer. He began laying hands upon the passers-by, importuning them in extremely rapid French. Charlotte stood by in growing embarrassment with Henry at her side. The English boy was entirely unable to fathom the source of the hubbub and more than a little bored of the tedium of travelling in a land where he did not speak the language.

In a matter of minutes, a French girl a year or two younger than Charlotte stood before them. She spoke in heavily accented English. "You need guide to embassy of the Russias?"

"Yes, please," Charlotte replied, also speaking in English. "We should be most grateful. I am Charlotte, and this is my friend, Henry."

Henry brightened considerably at the girl's appearance in their journey. She was clean, fresh-faced, a pretty if thin girl wearing a somewhat faded skirt and blouse with, of all things, giraffes embroidered upon the shoulders. Adding a bit of a swell's manner to his voice, the lad said, "Charmed."

The French girl returned his friendly gaze. "Aljean," she said, shaking hands with first Charlotte and then Henry. "Please, you come." She set off across the street and in completely the opposite direction as the nurse and the orderly followed her.

For a moment, Charlotte feared this might be a snare set for them by footpads or coshers, but Aljean led them straight and true to a row of fine homes not far from the Seine River. There was a sign above the entrance in Cyrillic identifying it as the Russian embassy, but jutting out from the wall hung a cloth banner declaring this an outpost of the People's Revolution.

She took a deep breath. "Merci," she said to their guide, then, seeing the look of disappointment upon Henry's face, decided to add, "Would you join us for some tea? It has been so long since we have experienced civilized dining."

Aljean glanced at Henry dubiously. "You were in the war?"

Charlotte answered for him. "He was right outside the front, at a Casualty Clearing Station near Messines." She urged the boy forward. "Do tell Miss Aljean about it. I shall be out shortly."

She left them talking as she strode toward the front of the house. From the well-laid out grounds to the delicately etched glass in the door, it was clear this had once been a fine residence, yet, the signs of neglect were obvious: the chipped, fading paint on the shutters, and the slightly overgrown walkway. There had been other signs in Paris of deprivation from the war, but most of the homes they had passed had been well tended, unlike this embassy.

She rapped on the brass knocker. When there was no answer, she pressed on the latch and pushed the door open. The room inside was foul with the stench of Russian cigarettes. She stood by the open door, hoping for some freshening breeze to clear the clouds of burnt tobacco. A thick-bodied woman sat behind a desk. She looked up without speaking.

"Is the Ambassador available?" Charlotte asked in her native Russian.

"There is no Ambassador," she was told. *"We are all the representatives of the People's Revolution."* There was little warmth in the woman's manner.

"I have —"

The People's Representative asked, *"Are you Red or White?"*

"Pardon?" Charlotte had a vague sense she'd heard the words before, but could not say under what circumstances or to what they referred beyond mere colour.

"You talk like a White," the woman sneered. *"We'll defeat you Kulaks."*

Although they were both speaking Russian, Charlotte could not make sense of what the woman was saying. Her lack of comprehension did not register nor deter the heavy-set woman. *"Even now, Comrade Trotsky leads brigades of brave workers against the lickspittle collaborators. It is the historic destiny of the proletariat to overcome the snares of the capitalists!"*

The woman was ranting as if she were on a street corner, when in fact only she and Charlotte were in the room. The woman stood and advanced around the desk. *"Who are your parents, White? Tell me, and we won't arrest you."*

Charlotte glanced round, first to ascertain no others had entered the dingy room, and second to assure herself she had not somehow stumbled into some surreal theatrical performance. Her fingers closed around the letter to her family and shoved it deeper into her handbag. *"I am leaving,"* she said, stepping for the door.

"It is your duty to help the People find every White and eliminate them like vermin!" The woman continued to rant as Charlotte walked away. Had the war made everyone mad, she wondered. She looked over her shoulder once, and the heavy-set woman was standing, no, posing at the entrance to the embassy. Insane, as if she were the star of her own private kinescope show.

Not everyone was unhinged, she decided with relief, seeing that Henry and Aljean were engaged in an energetic and slightly flirtatious discussion. Henry had lost all self-consciousness and was paying eager court to the French lass. The letter to her parents would have to wait. When she arrived in London, she would approach an English diplomat and ask him to forward it to the British embassy in Moscow. Perhaps the ambassador could get word to her family under the pretence of telling them about their daughter who had worked for the Nursing Service.

The encounter with the Bolshevik woman had

depressed her, and all she wished to do was go home. The image she held in her mind was that of her tent and the snug cot. Home, she realized. *I thought of the Base Hospital as home.* Whether it was home or not, she could not simply depart Paris. She had invited the young French girl to tea, and it would so disappoint Henry if they simply left the city.

Aljean knew of a small café near the River and gladly led the way, still chatting amiably with young Henry. The café, which proclaimed itself the *Gai Lapine* (or "Cheerful Rabbit," a most curious name), was a small establishment, set between a tailor and shoemaker.

Small though it was, the *Lapine* was crowded with both Parisians and a mixture of French and American soldiers, shoved up against the counter, hunched over their tables, even just outside the entrance, eating and drinking where they stood.

"The food must be very good here," Charlotte said, observing the crowds.

"Oh, oui, Madame," Aljean said, addressing Charlotte as if she were some elderly dowager. The French girl plunged into the packed customers, weaving among them with a grace that appeared to be born of much practice. Henry gamely followed, with less ease and many more apologies.

After her weeks of night duty and the general quiet of her existence, the noise of the crowd, and the closeness of their proximity felt suffocating to Charlotte. She hung back, and Henry noticed she was not with him. He turned and extricated himself from the sea of humanity. "Will you not take some tea with us, Miss?" he asked with touching concern.

"Just a roll, Henry," she said and pressed some money into his hand.

He glanced down at the bills and held them out to her.

"Miss, this is far too much."

Trying to hide a smile at his innocence, Charlotte closed his fingers over the francs. "Buy Aljean a nice lunch, Henry. For you, too."

"Oh, Miss." His face coloured.

"She's a very pleasant young woman. Do enjoy yourself."

"Miss...would it be proper?"

"I have no doubt, since you are a most proper young man." She gave him a playful shove. "Don't keep her waiting. I will meet you here in an hour."

"Miss, I should go with you."

She turned her head toward the River. It was nearly noon in Paris. The war had not killed her; her broken heart had not killed her. What did she have to fear, walking along the banks of the Seine? "I shall be very well." And to avoid further discussion, she stepped back out onto the footpath and began making deliberately for the river bank.

"One hour, Miss," Henry insisted to her back. She turned to wave and saw that Aljean had emerged from the restaurant to take Henry's hand and lead him inside. The French girl looked puzzled, and Henry bent his head closer to her as they walked, evidently explaining that Miss preferred to stroll the river.

The air was cold but clear. The streets were thick with motorcars, but here and there a horse-drawn wagon or two-wheeled cart could be seen. The horses looked thin and weary. The war had not been easy on them, either. Seeing the poor creatures made her think of Robert, and a bittersweet pang ran through her. He was ever solicitous of animals and those weaker than he, she remembered. The memory was overshadowed by her realization that she'd thought of Robert and had not wanted to double over weeping. She missed what they had shared (however briefly), and she regretted the loss of those dreams she had only dared to half-whisper to herself at night. But she was alive when so many others had died. She would live and she imagined she would love again, but perhaps never again with the wild intensity that had marked her feelings for Robert Fitzgerald.

So musing, she found herself among some stalls built against the wall along the river Seine. The little booths were stocked with old books. Each held its own proprietor, each one of the managers were different. Some appeared completely bored by the experience of being surrounded by literature; others had the look of ascetic monks as they bent over aged volumes, turning the pages with fingerless gloves. Still others flirted shamelessly with her and any other woman who passed by.

It was perfectly delightful. She stopped before one of the smaller stands, which was a cleverly built box, with walls that would swing out to reveal bookcases stuffed with every kind of book—intricately engraved leather bindings on classics in both French and English, tiny children's books, religious tomes. She liked the look of the man sitting there on a stool. He was one of the monk-class, it seemed, with a scarf around his neck and a bald spot lending him a tonsured air. There was something reverential in the gaze he cast over his little library before turning to her. "Mademoiselle, good day." He spoke in English, no doubt encouraged to do so by her uniform.

"Bon jour," she replied cheerfully, approaching the shelves.

"I have a fine set of Dickens," the monk suggested. "Most reasonably priced."

Dickens felt heavy. It seemed as if she were seeking nourishment, a healthy, yet refreshing meal for her mind. "No, too...ponderous." She browsed a bit more, inquiring about this book or that. The monk had voluble and decided opinions about each one.

A deep voice behind her rumbled, *"Tolstoy's last novel was prophecy."*

She turned. A large man was standing behind her, rather closer than propriety and the uncrowded book stall required. "Resurrection?" she asked.

The man came no closer but appeared to be browsing the book titles above her head. His neck was thick, and while the black seaman's sweater he wore could have accounted for the apparent bulk of his build, the corded muscles on the forearms that jutted from the pushed-up sleeves argued otherwise. *"Da,"* he replied carelessly, his eyes roving the shelves. Dark hair was thick on the back of his hands, and his lower face seemed to have been sketched in black pastel, so heavy was the shadow of a beard upon his skin. *"A man realizes his life has been lived at the expense of others, and only through his suffering does he purge himself of his sins."*

For a moment, Charlotte was tempted to laugh. *Resurrection* had been daring, in its day, with the scathing depictions of Russian Orthodox rituals and inept, corrupt priests, as well as the sordid lives it described. As a young woman, her knowledge of the novel had been cautionary, for unscrupulous young nobleman were known to begin discussions about the book with the ladies of the court, only to focus their conversation upon the most scandalous sections that dealt frankly with seduction and actual fornication. As a ploy to excite the passions of unwise or untutored girls, it was laughably transparent. She suspected the man behind her of attempting this same stratagem, hence her smile—until she realized he was speaking flawless Russian to her.

She turned to face him squarely. He towered over her

and did not look directly at her as he continued. *"A gentle lady should be careful about going to the Embassy. Landowners and members of the court have been arrested in Paris by the Commissars of the People's Republic and sent back to Moscow for trial."* Now he finally looked at her. His eyes were slanted at the edges—he had some Tartar blood in him. *"And they do not return."*

A shiver of energy rang through her. She was alert, poised as if she were in the snowy fields with her father, her rifle cocked and ready, waiting for the wolves to pass within range. This was no casual encounter.

"Why do you tell me this?" she asked, concentrating on the stranger, abstractly noting that the monk-like bookseller had closed his novel and was standing with his hand out of sight below the counter.

The dark stranger took a breath as if caught out in a lie. He reached out with that large hand and tapped the Nursing staff emblem on her hat. *"Scientific Socialism must make room for those who serve with their hearts."* There was a sense of tremendous, controlled power in the tap upon her hat. Faced with that strength, she found that she desired to have a rifle in her hands again, something for which she had not longed in years.

The man threw a few franc notes beside the bookseller, plucked a book from the shelf with what seemed to be no consideration at all, and walked away, further down the river, his bulky shape blending with the noon-time crowds and disappearing.

"Mademoiselle," the bookseller asked, moving his hand from behind the counter and coming toward, "are you unhurt? I can call the gendarmes."

She waved him away impolitely. *The damned Bolsheviks are everywhere,* she thought. *I hope the Czar's army scatters them to Siberia and beyond.* Charlotte looked about her with regret. A beautiful walk spoiled by someone's religious dedication to their anti-religious beliefs. Was there nothing that politics could not poison?

The ancient, dirty city of the Louvre and Notre Dame, Hugo and Pasteur, no longer felt safe to her. Until the troubles at home were settled, she would have to leave France as soon as she could.

Christmas, 1918, was bitterly cold. With the declining population of convalescing soldiers, one ward had been rehabilitated as a dormitory for the nurses, so they would not have to sleep shivering within the drafty canvas tents. Even so, by the middle of December, the nurse's ward was nearly empty, and Charlotte often slept alone with her cot pushed close to the stove.

On Christmas morning, Charlotte was the solitary occupant of the dormitory. Two nurses were on the day shift, and the other three had gone to Paris, where Charlotte had no desire to be. She waited with eagerness for Madame. Knowing it was a foolish and useless extravagance, Charlotte had located a pair of real silk stockings and wrapped them in a tidy packet for the regal old woman. Besides that, she'd acquired some thick men's gloves, socks, and a slightly soiled men's winter greatcoat for that worthy. Charlotte had said to herself as she wrapped the bundles, thinking of the thin and delicate silk, "The world does not all have to be useful," finishing the stocking's package with an especially intricate bow.

She stood on her toes and wiped frost from the uneven glass, peering out for the familiar sight of the French woman and her laundry cart. Madame was later than usual. Perhaps, Charlotte surmised, she was selling extra pastries this morning, providing a festive air to the blessed holiday for those unfortunate enough to still be on duty. Then she saw the old lady.

Madame pushed the cart slowly over the frozen mud, stopping often to catch her breath. It was clear she was making her usual rounds, but she lacked her usual brio. Charlotte hurried from the ward to greet her.

"Joyeux Noël!" she cried across the morning air.

Madame looked up and gave a tired smile. Drawing closer, Charlotte could see that there was a layer of ice on the woman's clothing, and under that, a carapace of mud. Good God, had the poor old thing slept outside? In a ditch, perhaps, in weather like this?

She took Madame's arm. *"Madame, you will come with me."* It happened without thought or consideration, it was simply the only possible action to take. In spite of Madame's relatively feeble protests, Charlotte guided the old woman into the warmth of the nurse's dormitory. After sitting her on a cot close to the fire, Charlotte hurried back out and dragged in her cart.

"Oh, lovely Miss," Madame said. *"You mustn't trouble yourself."* The ice on Madame's coat was melting, and the woman beneath sagged as if the inflexibility of the frozen garment had been the only thing holding her up.

"Forgive me for troubling you, Madame. As you see," Charlotte lied with guileless ease, *"I have been abandoned here on Christmas. I pray you would be so kind as to share the day with me."*

Madame's smile was brilliant and grateful. *"I would be honoured, Mademoiselle Charlotte."*

Charlotte insisted on bathing before setting out on their day, and would not do it alone. There were some rudimentary showers near the rear of the Hospital, which had seen duty delousing men from the front, but tubs were also present for allowing burned men to soak. Charlotte stoked the boilers, insisting Madame simply watch and talk with her, as she was a guest. She prepared two tubs, side by side, and begged Madame to join her. She turned her back to give the dignified old lady her privacy, dropped her own garments to the floor, and slid into the warmth of the bath.

She lay back in the embrace of the steaming water, her eyes closed, and listened. After a moment, she could hear Madame disrobing and easing with a surprised hiss into the tub. Then there followed a long sigh, a sound of such relief, contentment, and ease that Charlotte had to smile.

The young nurse had brought with her some scented soaps from Paris, and the two women giggled over them, holding each slippery shape to their noses to sample. The Russian girl finished her bath long before the old French woman. She climbed out and wrapped herself in a robe before refilling the elder's tub with more hot water. She insisted on washing Madame's long thick hair, and many rinsings were required to flush away the soap.

After towelling their hair dry, Charlotte gathered up the damp towels and their clothing into a bundle. In their robes and bare feet, the unlikely pair scampered down empty halls like naughty school children, avoiding any populated areas, and back to the ward to sit again on the cot by the stove.

"That felt most wondrous, Mademoiselle," Madame said. Her smile was genuine, but her eyes sagged with fatigue.

"I could nap," Charlotte said. *"It is so warm here. Do let's rest a while."* Without waiting for an answer, she gently eased Madame into a reclining position, and then took a blanket and stretched it over her guest, tucking it under her carefully. "I'm so pleased you stayed."

By the time Madame awoke several hours later, Charlotte had two sets of clean nurse's uniforms laid out for her. The French lady was much taller than she, so Kathleen's left behind skirt and blouse were put to good use. The older woman was thin, however, her frame more that of the Russian nurse, so Charlotte divided her own undergarments into two piles, and added one pile to the uniforms. Beside this she placed the wrapped presents.

Madame opened her eyes slowly, as if reluctant to leave the bliss and comfort of sleep. When she observed the clothing, and then the festively wrapped gifts, she looked up to Charlotte in alarm. *"Oh, Miss, you must not."*

Charlotte knelt beside her. *"Oh, Madame, you must."*

With tears in her eyes and trembling hands, Madame stroked the clean clothing. Charlotte helped her dress, and in a moment, the elderly French woman stood before her in the slightly large nurse's uniform, regal and radiating a quiet dignity that was not lessened by the appreciative smile upon her lips. She reached for Charlotte's hands and began to kneel. Charlotte grasped the skinny elbows and would not allow Madame to drop to her knees. Instead, she embraced the old woman, and whispered, *"Merry Christmas, my friend. I do this in His Name."*

Madame did not reply but clasped her tighter. Charlotte could feel her heaving breaths as she sobbed quietly. In time, the French woman seemed to master her emotions and stepped back from the young woman. As the old eyes were wiped, Charlotte motioned respectfully, *"I have your other clothing here, should there be something you require."*

"Merci," Madame said, and quickly sorted through the clothes that were nearer to rags. The stained chemise was in her hand, and then her thick-knuckled fingers were tearing at a seam. She plucked something shiny from within and showed it proudly to Charlotte. It was a simple gold band. *"My wedding ring."* She kissed the metal reverently and slipped it inside her blouse.

Charlotte had been issued a Book of Common Prayer by the English Army. She and Madame knelt before the stove, and Charlotte translated the Christmas Service from the English. Afterwards, they sang "Silent Night," their voices ringing through the empty ward. When the final notes of the hymn had faded away, Charlotte looked to her guest. *"I am famished. Let me fetch some tea, and I'll be right back."*

Charlotte had not been exaggerating. She was fiercely hungry and almost salivating. A quick stop at the mess procured a tray with two plates of bangers and mash, two large mugs of tea. The mess-men were accustomed to nurses eating at odd hours, and they cheerfully prepared the tray for her themselves, covering it with a clean hand towel to keep it warm during the chilly transit. She kissed each of the two wrinkled mess-men on the cheek, just to see them grin and blush.

Moving with practiced care so as not to spill the tea, she made her way quickly back to the ward. There she found a sentry pointing a rifle at Madame, who cowered on her cot.

Charlotte knew the sentry slightly. He was an American who'd come down with an ugly case of trench foot. He'd been left behind to mend, and, at a loss for employment for the recovering soldier, Dr Hartford had made him night watchman.

"Private...Jensen," Charlotte said, putting the tray on the ground near the stove.

"You got a trespasser here, Nurse," Jensen said. He spoke in that casual, abrupt way of other Americans that she sometimes found irritating.

"Nonsense," Charlotte said, pushing his rifle barrel away from Madame's midsection with one finger, a motion that Jensen did not resist. "This is my chaperone."

Jensen was no fool. "Chaperone, huh?"

Charlotte took Madame's hand and gently pulled the old woman to her feet. "Madame Bovary," she said by way of introduction.

Madame cut her eyes quickly at Charlotte, offering a very gracious curtsey. Charlotte went on in English, to Madame's incomprehension, "Madame Bovary will be staying here. It would be most unfitting for a young woman to be alone."

No fool he, neither was Jensen a heartless rascal. "Sure, Sister," he said with a wink. "I'll put it in the duty book. Everybody will know your Chaperone will be staying here with you. To keep you proper and all."

He held out his hand as if to shake Madame's own hand. "Sorry 'bout that, Madame Bovary."

Madame looked down at his hand and his open, good-natured countenance, and a radiant smile dimpled her face. She dug inside her cart and emerged with a pastry. Jensen received it, took a dubious bite, and then grinned, flakes of coarse sugar on his face. "That's real good!" He saluted her with the pastry, and walked away, shoving most of the treat in his mouth.

That evening, to Charlotte's surprise and delight, Jensen returned with some of his fellow ambulatory patients. The soldiers cheerfully pressed coins upon Madame and consumed her entire stock of pastries. A boy from Barbados had a tin whistle, while a lad from the hills of County Cork produced a small odd kind of stringed instrument. The duet played as a one-legged Arab coaxed an amazing variety of percussive sounds from the back of an over-turned canvas cot. The company sang hymns from their various homelands, laughing and dancing with both Madame and the young Russian nurse.

She only thought of Robert once, observing how he would have enjoyed the company. Private Jensen saw a shadowed look cross her face, and said kindly, "Ma'am, can we have this dance?" He was supporting the one-legged

Arab lad on his right shoulder, as the Arab shyly tried to escape. Of course, Charlotte had to accept, and there was more good-natured laughter at the sight of them dancing in such an ungainly, and yet holy fashion on this night, of all the nights in the year.

It was the finest Christmas Charlotte could have imagined.

In no time at all, it was January, and Base Hospital No. 12 came to the end of its existence. The weeks had passed quickly as men were made well enough to travel and sent on to recover closer to their homes and families.

Weekend nights, Jensen and the other soldiers would arrive at the dormitory, bringing more instruments, and the music and singing would begin. Madame had begun preparing more elaborate treats, which the soldiers cheerfully consumed. The boys were free with the money they paid the old French woman, perhaps seeing Madame's poverty, or more simply, feeling their good fortune at being alive, wanted to bless another if they could. Indeed, Madame began to accumulate a tidy sum, which Charlotte hoped would provide the old woman with the funds necessary to restart a new life in her shattered homeland.

There was a moment of awkwardness when Private Jensen, mistaking Charlotte's cordiality as something else, attempted to kiss her. She turned her face aside, and said, "Mr. Jensen, I do not…I cannot." Her voice failed her, and she stared forlornly at the floor.

That look of distress upon her face seemed to pierce him, for he was a decent fellow, and he stepped back so as to not impose upon her. "Sorry 'bout that, ma'am. I meant no impertinence."

"Thank you for the compliment, Mr. Jensen. And for your kindness."

"Sure, ma'am."

After that moment, he was never anything but genial and affable. He was, in spite of his bluff, abrupt way of speech, a gentleman. *He had not the breeding,* she thought, *nor the education, but in his heart he is noble none the less.*

The group of singers and players slowly decreased as their ranks were reduced by transfers to other locations or, in the case of a lucky few, outright discharge from the service. There had only been one death, that of the one-legged Arab boy. He was in the other ward, and she never knew his name. The soldiers, in their rough way, simply called him "Mohammed," but there was nothing of meanness in it. The poor, sweet fellow had developed a sepsis in his stump, and died quite suddenly of heart failure. There were no other members of his unit at hospital, so Jensen took it upon himself to arrange the funeral.

The American gathered the few remaining soldiers to provide an honour guard for their fallen brother. Dawn seemed the most fitting time for the ceremony, for every man among them wished to see their Arab friend off to a new beginning.

Charlotte and Madame met the soldiers at the graveside in their cleanest uniforms. The morning was clear and cold, and everyone's breath steamed upon the air. Watched by the required Army grave site registrars, Jensen and his fellows took up the canvas straps beneath the coffin to take Mohammed on his journey. The pallbearers were of all heights, and the exceedingly plain coffin was carried at a cant; yet for all the ungainliness of the procession, it possessed a dignity that humbled Charlotte. *These are such fine people,* she thought with pride as they approached. *God has graced me to serve among such as these.*

Jensen counted cadence as the men approached the

grave. After the men had carefully taken up their place on either side of the shallow cavity in the ground, he muttered, "Together now, boys," and called cadence again as their friend was laid to his final rest.

The soldiers recovered the canvas straps and wiped the sweat from their faces. For a moment, no one spoke. Madame broke the silence, her voice distinct and bright in the dawn. Charlotte translated for the others. "He was a sweet-hearted young man, with a generous spirit. Although we did not know him well, we loved him, and we shall miss him."

It was silent for a while after that. One of the soldiers said, "Amen," and crossed himself.

"Goodbye, kid," Jensen added and then barked, "Detail dismissed!" The men saluted as one and then made their way back into the warmth of Base Hospital No. 12.

Matron's letters had never been chatty. They were concisely detailed discussions about the issues she had encountered setting up the new rehabilitation centre. Charlotte wondered if the old nurse had spent so many years writing up reports that she had lost the knack for casual communication. Toward the end of December, the letters began to tend toward the terse, wondering when Charlotte would be able to come to England.

She shed no tears at leaving Base Hospital No. 12. There was nothing left to hold her in France any longer. The last of the patients had been shipped off, and her remaining tasks were largely administrative, overseeing the disposition of the remaining supplies and equipment at the hospital. Even the staff of whom she was so fond had gone. Old Gustav, released from his employ at the hospital, had paid a call on her and had made the acquaintance of Madame. He had known of the regal French woman, but not previously had the time nor opportunity to speak to her.

Now at liberty, Gustav found he had a great deal of desire to speak to Madame, and they were to be married in the spring. While to some the image of the short, stout little man and the tall, regal woman might have been comical, it made Charlotte beam with relief. She had been worried about how her dear Madame would get along and was pleased to know the old lady would not be alone.

Henry loaded Charlotte's bags into the back of a lorry in the cold of an early morning on the last day of January. Charlotte gazed at the single trunk and two travelling cases with bemusement. At age 18, they comprised her entire worldly goods. There might be some inheritance left for her in far Russia, but she could not be sure. She had been gone so long, in some ways Russia was the distant dream of a life lived by someone else.

"When must we leave?" she asked Henry, who seemed to have grown a few inches in the last two months.

"Whenever you like, Miss," he told her easily. His spots were clearing up, too. "The ferry to Dover runs almost every hour."

"Are you to see Miss Aljean today?" The young English lad and the thin French mademoiselle had made something of an impression on one another.

"Yes, Sister."

"I shan't be long."

"Don't hurry yourself, Miss."

She felt the need to take one last walk around the grounds. The weather was beastly cold, and she tucked her hands into her sleeves as she walked. Already, the Hospital was disappearing. All of the tents that had surrounded it were gone, and she believed she had seen farmers with plows at the far edge of the grounds, attempting to wrest the land back into a fit condition for the spring planting. There had been discussion by the local council of converting the Hospital building into a school, but that was mere talk. The structure had been hastily constructed, built to neither last nor long endure. Locals were casually filching lumber from the empty wards for use in rebuilding their own shattered homes.

How strange it is, she thought. So much of her life had changed here. Robert and Matron and Kathleen, Madame and nursing. She'd spent over three years at the Hospital, growing from a frightened girl into a young woman. She'd seen so much death, and yet, so much that was beautiful. Gazing at the shell of the hospital in the light of dawn, she could not help but think that soon there would be no sign she had ever been here. Any good she had done, as well as any injuries she had committed, would only be known in those hearts she had helped heal or had inadvertently hurt and, finally, known only in the mind of God. She, too, would carry the knowledge of these past days, with their gore and with their glory, inside her, and she wondered what that knowledge would do to her in the future.

The crossing was rough and cold, and by the time she had made the journey by train from Dover to London, it was late and Charlotte was knackered. Matron had arranged for a small flat near the rehabilitation hospital and the Russian nurse was most grateful for it. A silently surly man carried her bags up to the tiny room and left her in peace.

The room was not much wider than a hallway, with the small bed against one wall, a dirty window that looked out on a back street, and a closet of shelves that was barely six inches deep. A small tap and sink were on the other side of the window. The interior of the room was clean, and the linens on the bed were fresh, smelling faintly of bleach.

Eyes burning with fatigue, Charlotte eased off her boots and stretched out on the bed. It was the oddest sensation not to sink into the surface and have canvas press at her hips from either side and cradle her in the roughly woven embrace of the thick, unforgiving fabric. The bed upon which she now lay was likely a mean, cheap thing, but it was the very essence of luxury compared to where she had rested her head for the past three years. She could not remember the last time she had slept in a real bed such as this, a bed with sheets and a mattress and a duvet and a pillow. In time, sleep took her.

The next morning, after a hasty breakfast of gruel and a smallish poached egg provided by her landlady, Charlotte made her way to the King Edward Military Rehabilitation Hospital. It fronted onto Blackburn Street. Workmen on scaffolding busied themselves outside, plastering and painting in the cold air.

Inside, it was much the same. The tang of new paint was in the air, and there appeared to be nearly as many labourers as nurses walking the halls. Charlotte took herself to the front desk, where a young woman sat, marked by an alarming head of frizzy red hair that fought to escape from beneath her cap.

"Good morning," Charlotte said. "I am Nurse Braninov. I have an appointment to see Matron."

The frizzy-haired girl looked confused and hunted among her papers and notes. Her desk was untidy, and Charlotte hoped that the girl would get herself sorted before Matron made her rounds...she did so despise a lack of organization. "Hullo," the girl replied as she scrabbled through the litter of paper. "There we go. Nurse Brand-in-off."

Charlotte did not bother to correct her. "Yes."

The girl read from a piece of paper. "You need to see Nurse Peckham. Her office is at the end of the hall."

"Very well," Charlotte said, repressing a sigh of impatience. She followed the nurse's pointing finger and found a door with the words "Senior Nurse" painted on the glass. She stepped inside and repeated the introduction of herself and her orders to see Matron to yet another assistant.

This young woman in a nurse's uniform took her further back into the office and presented her to Nurse Peckham.

The Senior Nurse looked harried and fatigued, even though it was not yet 9 a.m. There were grey smudges under her eyes, and her mouth moved as if she were constantly speaking to herself.

"Mum, this is Nurse Braninov," the assistant said and withdrew.

Nurse Peckham looked up from her desk. "Oh, dear," she said.

Charlotte was led to Matron's room straight away. There were four beds in the room, and Matron's was the closest to the window. Matron was asleep when the Russian nurse peeked in. Her face was thinner, and the flesh sagged loosely upon her skull. Dear Matron's breathing was shallow, interrupted from time to time by a hitch in the movement of her abdomen, before resuming.

Nurse Peckham waited impassively while Charlotte took in the sight and then motioned her outside. Once in the hallway, Nurse Peckham said, "You had no idea." It was supposed to be a question but came out as a flat statement of fact.

"None," Charlotte admitted. "Who is attending upon

her?"

"The staff have been looking in on her."

"That is not sufficient." Charlotte may have spoken more forcefully than she intended. Passing nurses began to look at them and make inquiring noises among themselves. The Russian girl ignored them and focused her attention on the Senior Nurse. "I shall take charge of her care."

Nurse Peckham warmed to the exchange, replying tartly. "That is quite impossible, Nurse Braninov."

Charlotte faced her squarely. "I assure you, Senior Nurse, it is completely possible."

In the end, Charlotte had to take her protests to the head of the new rehabilitation hospital, Lord Jefferies. His Lordship was a fair complexioned man of about 35, with hair that was thinly distributed across his scalp. He was dressed in a staid business suit and looked up in understandable irritation as Charlotte and Senior Nurse Peckham were shown into his office.

"Well, now, what's this about?" he asked, glancing deliberately at the chronometer on his desktop.

As Nurse Peckham outlined their differences, Charlotte kept her eyes fixedly upon the director of the Hospital. Lord Jefferies glanced over at her from time to time, and then nodded.

"Impossible, Nurse Braninov."

Charlotte stood. "My Lord, Matron has a cancer. I would not have her in the care of"—she was about to say 'indifferent', but had not become so inflamed in her emotions as to speak intemperately, so she concluded with—"complete strangers."

Nurse Peckham hung back, giving that deference to a member of the Court which seemed to be bred into the middle class of England. As a member of the Russian court herself, having seen Lords and Counts aplenty, many of them in their cups or squabbling like fishwives over some insignificant slight to their person, Charlotte had far less awe of a Royal title than the Senior Nurse. She boldly stepped up to the director's desk, and would not look away. "My Lord, Matron served His Majesties George and Edward for years, and before that Her Majesty Victoria as well. The Crown owes a great debt to her."

Lord Jefferies took up a fountain pen and began spinning it on his fingers. "There is no question of gratitude, Nurse Braninov." He cocked an eyebrow at her. "There is simply no money in the King's purse to pay you to work here."

"I ask no payment. What I do, I do out of duty. And the deepest respect. And love."

His Lordship considered the short young woman before him. She stood as if ready for battle. He found the patience to try one last tack. "I understand Matron has no family. If you were a relative, I should have no problem acceding to your request."

At this, Nurse Peckham relaxed, seeing victory within her grasp. This outsider with her foreign accent would not burst into her hospital and tell her how to run it.

Charlotte bowed her head a moment. Her voice, when it emerged, was low, but distinct. "Lord Jefferies," she said. "It was only an accident of birth that separates Matron and myself. We have stood side by side amid the screams of the wounded and dying, with blood on our boots and drenching our clothing."

At this, Senior Nurse glanced over and regarded her warily. "You were in France, Miss?"

"I had the honour of serving under Matron for three years at Base Hospital No. 12, near Flanders. And for a short time at a CCS."

At a quizzical noise from Lord Jefferies, Nurse Peckham explained, "Casualty Clearing Station."

Charlotte went on, as much to the Senior Nurse as His Lordship. "In every one of those locations, my dear Matron showed me what true gallantry is made of and she breathed compassion wherever she walked. I hope one day to be as fine a woman of character as she. Matron is my mother in everything but name, sir."

The pen in Lord Jefferies' hand spun to a stop. He replaced the pen in its stand and said, "I regret I am unable to assist you, Miss Braninov. Senior Nurse Peckham will show you out. Good day."

His Lordship returned to his work, dismissing her from his awareness. Nurse Peckham opened the door pointedly. Mastering her outrage, Charlotte gave a sketchy curtsey (for it would serve nothing to treat Lord Jeffries with contempt), and strode out into the hall. Whom could she ask for assistance? She believed Dr Hartford, the Head Surgeon of Base Hospital No. 12, had offices in Kensington. He might be able to—

Nurse Peckham was at her side. "Pray, Miss, follow me."

Charlotte was startled out of her furious train of thought. "What may I do for you, Senior Nurse?"

"Pray, come with me, Nurse Braninov," the Senior Nurse replied, a trifle sharply and a little like Matron. "Let me show you where you may put your things."

"I beg your pardon?" the Russian girl said in confusion.

With a look of weary exasperation, Nurse Peckham took Charlotte by the arm and drew her down the hall. The other nurse's grasp was not harsh nor was her attitude angry; she merely seemed busy. "Did Matron teach you nothing, girl?" she said with a hint of a narrow smile. "Lord Jefferies may think he is head of the hospital, but it is the Senior Nurse who runs the bloody place. I would not allow a dog to die alone and friendless, had I anything to do with it, and I would not keep a Nurse from her Matron in those last days. I shall have one of the other students show you round. Do you comprehend my meaning, *Student Nurse* Braninov?"

Charlotte did not understand the Senior Nurse, not entirely, but she dipped her head and said with humble gratitude, "Yes, Mum."

"Good. Now, go along with you, girl. You have work to do."

Most of her time was spent in Matron's room. The old nurse had been heavily sedated against the pain of the invader that was consuming her from within. Often, Charlotte found herself lending a hand to the genuine student nurses who had been assigned to the other patients in the room. The girls all had stout hearts, if not the strong stomachs sometimes required for the work.

Charlotte turned from helping clean up an incontinent older woman to see Matron's eyes upon her. It was the first time her dear friend had been reasonably alert and conscious in days. "You have come," Matron observed in a husky voice.

"Yes, Mum," Charlotte answered, pouring some water. "So I have."

Sipping the water, Matron coughed and said, "Thank you, my dear. It is so delightful to see you again."

Charlotte took a chair and placed it close to the head of the bed. She did not wish to make Matron strain to see her or strain to speak. Nor did she wish their private conversations to be overheard. "You were ill in France." She tried not to make it sound like an accusation.

Matron smiled, perhaps a bit impishly. "I did not wish

to worry you. You had troubles enough of your own, Nurse Braninov."

"My troubles are very distant from here, Mum," Charlotte replied with a forced smile. "Are you quite comfortable? May I get you a hot water bottle for your feet?"

The patient waved that away as being of no importance, asking instead, "Has Peck been treating you well?"

"Senior Nurse Peckham has been splendid to me," was the honest answer.

"She's a bit of a stick," Matron offered and then yawned hugely before she could cover her mouth. Charlotte could not help but notice that her hand, once very strong and firm, had started to wither a bit, and was taking on a more claw-like appearance. "Pray forgive me?" the patient said, embarrassed.

"It's nothing, Mum," Charlotte told her.

"I'm very tired, Nurse. I shall rest a while."

"Yes, Mum. I shall sit with you for a time."

Matron nodded drowsily. Her hair had grown thinner now, and it was creating a kind of white halo about her head. Her eyes closed and her breathing slowed.

When Charlotte was sure that Matron was asleep, she slipped out of the room to fetch a hot water bottle for the patient. As she had suspected, the old nurse's feet were chilled.

After securing the bottle beneath Matron's bedding, Charlotte stood and stretched. It was nearly 2 o'clock in the afternoon. The student nurses bustled in and out of the room. They had their patients well in hand. She hailed one of the girls, a short, fattish, meek little thing whose name, she thought, was Agnes.

"Nurse Agnes, I must be absent for a few hours. Will you replenish Matron's hot water bottle before the end of your shift?"

Agnes bit her lip, and her eyes shifted in alarm from side to side. "Yes, Mum."

"Thank you." She felt a touch of compassion for the frightened-looking girl, who had been struggling to master the skills required to be a good nurse. "Would you care to join me for tea this evening?"

Again, the shifting eyes, and then, decisively. "Yes, Mum."

Taking up her handbag, Charlotte said, "I shall meet you in the canteen this evening, say, eight o'clock?"

Agnes nodded, and as Charlotte was leaving, she saw the girl drift over to Matron's bed and gently touch the shape of the hot water bottle. The sight soothed some of Charlotte's concern at leaving Matron, and she was able to walk from the hospital with a lighter heart.

Charlotte's errand at the Bank of England demanded more of her time than expected. Her father had deposited some valuables there for her when she started at boarding school, and she had been back but once to leave her nursing certificate in the vault.

Now she had need of capital. She had some savings from the pittance of a salary earned in France, but most of her pay she had donated to the Soldiers' Relief Society. During her time of service in the Great War, she had no need of the money, but now, caring for Matron, she required ready access to funds of her own.

She wore her nurse's uniform, for she had not yet bothered to purchase new clothing. Charlotte could not but see a concentration upon the latest fashion as frivolous, and in fact, she had been so long at the front and among uniformed personnel, that the Russian girl found the current styles a bit scandalous to her eye.

No matter, any of that. The Bank was an imposing edifice, with pillars out front and marble lions on lintels. The steps were worn to a concavity from the passage of decades of feet, and Charlotte added her small steps to the wear as she entered the building. It was oddly dark inside, in spite of the electric lamps that burned within.

A bank Manager was found who listened as she explained her errand. He apologetically verified her identity; fortunately, she still had her papers from Base Hospital No. 12, and these, along with her signature, were enough to ensure her access.

Handing her identity papers back to her, the Manager, a Mr. Ellis, gave a restrained smile. "You were much younger the last time I saw you."

"You remember me?" She was surprised.

"Oh, yes. You were here with a gentleman...your father, I seem to recall. The Count, was it not?"

"You have an excellent memory, sir."

He gave a modest gesture of acceptance. "One finds it useful in this occupation, Miss."

She had a memory, too, of a thin, bent man, like something out of Dickens, a clerk who had led them into the depths of the Bank, to the personal vaults. He had been frightening to her; made the 12-year-old Charlotte ashamed of herself for fearing him simply based on his hunched resemblance to a vulture. That dread was perhaps why she remembered him and not the professionally kind, personally bland Manager who sat before her. Mr. Ellis pressed a button, and a bell rang somewhere. She looked up, wondering if the Dickensian man would again be her guide, but was surprised to see a young man approaching with an expectant look.

He was perhaps a year or two older than she, with a bright face that was unlined with care or particular toil, wearing a suit that bespoke an attention to his appearance that was very different from the Manager's studied business attire.

"My assistant Mr. Matthews will take you to the vault, Miss Braninov."

Young Matthews inclined his head respectfully to her, taking the necessary documents from the Manager. "If you'll follow me, Miss," Matthews said cheerily.

Charlotte extended her hand to Mr. Ellis. "Thank you, sir."

"Of course, Miss. Would you see me on your way out, if it is no trouble?"

"Certainly, sir." She turned to follow the young assistant.

The trip to the private vaults was as she recalled. Mr. Matthews walked beside her, greeting other workers with an equal amount of cheerfulness as they wove deeper into the Bank. She found herself studying him as they progressed. She realized it was his face that had caught her attention. There was something about it.

"Have I some spinach in my teeth, Miss?" Matthews asked after a moment in that same buoyant tone.

"I beg your pardon, Mr. Matthews, I did not mean to stare."

"Well, as long as I wasn't looking freakish, stare all you like." The man's tone hardly ever changed. *How peculiar,* she thought.

He led her to a curtained alcove, which contained an electric lamp, a wooden table and matching chair. "Back in a tick," he announced as she seated herself. He returned shortly with a small metal box. He showed her the stamped numbers upon the latch, which matched those engraved upon her own key. She took the key and turned it in the lock. When the lock clicked open, he backed away. "I'll be right outside, if you need me, Miss."

Charlotte waited until the curtain closed back over the entrance before opening the lid of the metal box. She gazed at the contents, distracted. Some jewellery, some Russian gold pieces, some land deeds she supposed were worthless at the moment. The jewellery, she decided. She removed two bracelets and two pairs of earrings. She had no especial love for gems but knew the diamonds and emeralds on them ought to fetch a reasonable price.

After placing the items in her bag and relocking the metal box, Charlotte sat for a moment. The life-sounds of the bank were so different from either of the Hospitals. There was hushed conversation in the background, a faint, staccato arrhythmic noise she finally identified as typing. Drawers were closed, papers were moved. The Bank had none of the immediacy, none of the brutal vibrancy of life at Base Hospital No. 12, not even the pulse of the comparatively staid pace of King's Rehabilitation.

Then it came to her; what had bothered her about the assistant to the Manager. She gathered her things and opened the curtain. Mr. Matthews loitered a few aisles away, chatting up a young woman who was pushing a cart loaded with mail and parcels. At the sight of Charlotte, Mr. Matthews gaily excused himself and drew near. "Do you need something, Miss?"

"No, I am quite finished here. Thank you."

He took the metal box from her and handed it to a passing man. "Can you stow this for me, old boy?" The other man took the box without a word and continued on his way.

Mr. Matthews took his place beside her as they made their way out of the depths of the Bank and back toward the fading afternoon light. "I could not help overhearing Mr. Ellis say he had seen you years before."

"Yes, when I started at St. Theresa's."

"And here you are a nurse," he said. One would have to be blind to not recognize the uniform. "Where were you posted? In London?"

"France," she said after a short delay. "And you?"

"I was a staff officer to Brigadier General Thomas-Carr." He said it with a certain humility that rang somehow false to Charlotte.

She did not know the General in question, but she knew of "staff" officers. Robert had spoken of them. "The lads can't stand them. Nor can I blame them. The ruddy fools never come close enough to the front to get their uniforms dirty, yet without a second thought they issue orders that send the boys out to die in the mud."

Robert had not been a staff officer. He had been on the line, in that mud with his soldiers, bleeding as they had. Some of his division mates had come by to see him. Robert seemed humiliated by their compassion and shamed that he was unable to re-join them. Charlotte had seen some of his infantrymen with her own eyes and had even heard two of them in discussion as they left the hospital. The younger one had said, "The Lieutenant is well and truly buggered." "Aye," replied the older, expectorating contemplatively, "but 'tis no' his choice. He'd be with us if he could." "Aye," the other agreed as they moved out of earshot. "And he'd be a damned sight better than the lot we have now."

But Mr. Matthews was speaking to her, interrupting her reverie. "I say, Miss Braninov, there is a Monet exhibition at the Palace of Fine Arts. Would you care to see it?"

She looked at him, uncomprehending. It took her an embarrassingly long moment to understand that he was asking to pay a call on her. She took in his face, so open and unlined. She thought of the sprinkling of scars along the line of Robert's cheek, the deep wrinkles around Jensen's eyes and the slight jerkiness in the American's manner when he heard a loud noise. The word "Yes" almost left her lips. It might be lovely to spend time with someone without thinking of the war, or all that had been before. Then the word of acceptance faded. How could she spend time with this boy, this reasonably decent boy who had known nothing of the crucible? He was untried, and he was ignorant of those things she knew. "I cannot," Charlotte replied.

"Some other time, perhaps?" he offered brightly.

"I'm afraid not. Thank you for your assistance."

"Of course," he said with an easy smile before leaving her at Mr. Ellis' desk.

The Manager looked up from his work. "All is satisfactory, Miss Braninov?"

"Quite."

"You journeyed here by Tube?" At her nod, he said, "Miss, allow me to escort you to your stop." The man stood, took up his hat and umbrella. He offered her his arm, and they walked outside together, where Mr. Ellis opened the umbrella, a precaution that struck her as unnecessary.

As Charlotte was wondering about this excessively gentlemanly behaviour, Mr. Ellis spoke to her in a low voice. "May one be so bold as to offer unsolicited counsel?"

"Yes, of course."

Mr. Ellis leaned closer, lowering the umbrella over them a bit, creating a small bit of privacy against pedestrians who strolled past. "I have heard of events in your homeland," he said formally. "I would be so audacious as to surmise that you have visited the Bank to acquire certain valuables that might be exchanged for more liquid assets?"

She looked down at her feet. This blandly professional man was quite a bit more perceptive than she might have at first believed. "That surmise would be correct in essence."

"Do you have an agent who will perform the transaction for you, Miss Braninov?"

She did not. "I had thought to make my way to Fleetside."

"There is a man of my acquaintance, a Russian fellow, as it happens. He is, to my knowledge, a man both trustworthy and fair. I should be happy to recommend him to you."

Had she been older, or with Matron, there might have been some concern about collusion between the Manager and the mysterious Russian fellow, but as Charlotte was yet a young woman, the possibility did not occur to her. She possessed a nature that was kind and open, and it was unnatural for her to see the world as full of duplicity and sordidness, even after her time in the war. It was unnatural, then. It would not long be so. "Thank you, Mr. Ellis, that would be lovely."

The pawnbroker had a small shop with barred windows, set near a cigar store and a tiny millinery. She knocked on the door of the establishment, and after a moment, a round figure of a man slipped a bolt on the door and allowed her to enter. The round man re-bolted the door after she was inside.

She had expected a dank, mouldy interior, but was pleased to note the shop had a warm scent that made her think of her father's study. The round man watched her. "It's the tobacco," he said in a gravelly voice with the unmistakable accent of the streets of Moscow.

She addressed him in Russian. *"Sir, Mr. Ellis has recommended you to me."*

A pleased smile blossomed upon his face. The man had the oddest body. His torso was as round as a ball, with straight legs and arms that appeared to have been casually attached, the way a child might take an orange and make a doll by jabbing twigs into the skin. He gave a most courtly bow, graceful in spite of the strange configuration of his legs and torso. *"The good Mr. Ellis rang me to tell of your coming. Fedor Kamensky at your service,"* he told her, his Russian flawless in spite of his rough accent. He pulled a chair from behind a counter and urged her toward it. *"Please, sit."*

She cast a glance out his window, crowded with musical instruments and gewgaws. She had a sense the sun was setting. *"Sir, I cannot. I must get back to the hospital."*

He gave a thoroughly dramatic wince. *"Ah, my lady, can you not at least have tea with me? I have not heard the language of Mother Russia in many long nights."*

"Truly?"

He amended his statement lightly. *"Perhaps not that many long nights since. But, tell me, mistress, how may I assist you?"*

She removed the jewellery from her bag and laid them on a velvet surface under a lamp on the counter. Mr. Kamensky leaned forward and subjected them to a long inspection with a loupe. *"They are worth several thousand pounds,"* he declared. She caught her breath. She had known they were valuable but had not realized they had increased so. Fedor added, *"But I could offer no more than 500 pounds, mistress. It would be the same as stealing were I to do that."*

He left the bracelets upon the counter and stepped back, indicating she should retrieve them. She hesitated. *"You are kind, sir, to not press your advantage upon me. I do most fiercely need the money, and, as Baba Yaga said, a goose in the paddock always tastes better than those on the wing."*

Mr. Kamensky nodded along at the thought of the witch Baba Yaga, the sometimes wicked, sometimes helpful figure from the childhood myths they both shared. *"That is so. Perhaps I can find someone who would be more able to afford such fine work."* He raised the earrings. *"A hundred pounds for these, as good faith payment, mistress? If you can return in two days, I might have a buyer."*

"What if you cannot sell them?"

"I would keep the earrings, and pay you another fifty pounds."

Charlotte considered it. Even at the current depressed prices, it seemed a bit high for the simple earrings. *"I should think you would be the worse off in the bargain."*

Fedor Kamensky chuckled. *"Perhaps. But, mind, mistress, our friend Mr. Ellis would not have sent you to me if he did not trust you, as well. Consider it a mitzvah for a brave daughter of our homeland who strove to serve all men."*

She bowed her head. She would have to ask him later what a 'mitzvah' might be. The pawnbroker counted out some notes to her, and wrote a detailed receipt, signing it with a flourish. She swept both into her bag. *"Thank you, Mr. Kamensky. And when I return, I look forward to having tea with you, sir."*

She returned to the bank, where Mr. Ellis himself helped her restore the remaining jewellery to her private vault. In the privacy of the curtained alcove, Charlotte secreted the bills in her chemise. Mr. Ellis solicited the assistance of a young typist, who was able to direct Charlotte to a nearby women's clothing store, where she purchased two flannel gowns and several thick pairs of socks for Matron. While those packages were wrapped, she stepped over to the Underground Station and purchased a mixed bouquet of flowers. The bright, somehow cool scent of the daisies and roses filled her senses as she made her way back to the Hospital, their aroma pushing away the sooty air and occasional sharper stench of horse dung.

It was nearly 6 o'clock when she returned. Matron had awakened, and Agnes was helping her, rather ineptly, with a bedpan. Matron appeared tired and even a touch mortified by the ordeal. Charlotte put her packages in the bedside stand and told Agnes, "I'll finish up here."

After the necessaries were completed, Charlotte apologized to Matron. "I am so sorry to have not been back before you rose."

"It's nothing, Nurse Braninov."

"You must allow me to do something for you. Perhaps a sponge bath?"

The thought put the faintest of sparkles in Matron's eyes. "If it is not too much trouble, Nurse."

Charlotte replied with a serious look, "I was taught by my Matron, a most exacting instructor, that we must always do what is best for the patient." She quickly gathered the things she would need.

She placed a privacy screen around the bed, and as Matron began to tug at her shift, the old nurse said, "Do call that other girl back in. Someone might as well show her how to give a proper bath."

"Are you sure—" Charlotte began, then quickly closed her mouth at a sharp look from Matron. "Yes, Mum," the Russian nurse added in a familiar tone of obedience.

Agnes was down the hall, carefully writing in a chart. "Agnes," Charlotte called, and the student nurse looked up with concern. Charlotte softened her tone. "Would you be a dear and help me with Matron? She's quite a demanding handful."

"Yes, Mum," Agnes said, hastily closing the chart and toddling down the hall.

Lord, Charlotte thought, *she calls me Mum like I'm some elderly relation.* She found the observation amusing rather than discouraging, and ushered the chubby girl into the hospital room with a smile.

One she stepped behind the privacy screen, Charlotte's smile faltered, for Matron had disrobed, revealing stitches that stretched across her abdomen looking like nothing so much as a centipede that clung to the sagging flesh thereon. Agnes froze motionless where she was.

"Come now, girls," Matron chided. "You, Charlotte, I know you have seen far worse. Nurse Braninov was in France, did you know that, Student Nurse?"

Agnes realized Matron was speaking to her. "No, Mum."

"Listen to what she says, you will learn much." To Charlotte, she said drily, "Let's be about it, Nurse. I shall catch a chill."

"Yes, Mum."

"And I believe it is time for my morphine," Matron added in a casual tone.

"Yes, Mum, it certainly is." Charlotte found a vial and quietly administered the shot. Matron gave a long shuddering breath, and to her dismay, the Russian girl saw the tension leave the old nurse's frame. The old nurse had been in pain and had not mentioned it. Charlotte vowed to herself that she would never again allow Matron to miss a scheduled injection.

As the opiate eased her pain, it also relaxed Matron's iron grip on her self-possession. The old nurse began, very unexpectedly, to speak of herself. As the two nurses bathed her with great gentleness, Matron looked round at the ordinary hospital room, and said, "Oh, you girls wouldn't believe the nonsense we were taught when I was your age. Germ theory...you, girl, what is your name?"

Agnes squeaked, "Student Nurse Nichols, Mum."

"Who gave us germ theory, Student Nurse Nichols?"

"Louis Pasteur, Mum."

"Hmmm, yes." The old nurse looked down at her torso, her attention wandering. "It's a cancer of my female organs. I never used them for their intended purpose…as soon as their time was up, the ungrateful things go rogue like some wild elephant. I was in India, you know. Rode an elephant. It was after the Boer War."

"Indeed, ma'am," Charlotte commented, gently bathing the incisions. "How did you find the experience?"

"Very rocky. They seemed like the saddest animals. They were very intelligent. I hated to see them chained up. You must see them up close if you can."

"I hope to someday, Mum."

"The Boers. Poor ignorant folk. They were using cattle dung poultices on open wounds. I ask you. What would that cause?"

Agnes raised a hand timidly, as if in a classroom. "Gas Gangrene, Mum?"

"Yes. We know this now…but even so…putting something so filthy on a wound. Madness. There was typhus in the Boer War. Horrible thing. Horrible for your Robert."

Ignoring the curious look from Agnes, Charlotte shifted Matron's body to begin washing her more delicate areas. "Yes, Mum, but you saved him."

"Oh, no," Matron said. "It was love that saved him. Curious…it can't save everyone…but if they have love to hold on to…it gives one such strength."

"Yes, Mum."

"I loved all my girls. Even when I was harsh."

"We knew, Mum."

Matron asked anxiously, "Did you? That's wonderful. I should so hate to think you girls didn't know."

"It was never a secret, Mum. And we loved you back."

She patted Matron dry and the older woman reached

languidly for her hospital shift. "No, Mum," Charlotte said. "I found this for you." She presented the two wrapped bundles.

Matron fumbled with the strings, lacking either the strength or the dexterity to open them, and extended the packages to Agnes. "Would you please, dear?" Even as the old nurse did that, Charlotte could not but admire the way she was taking every opportunity to teach the chubby little nurse.

Agnes' face grew red as she took the presents. Perceiving that the young woman grew anxious when she felt observed, Charlotte gathered up the sponges and towels and emptied the basin to clean later. When she turned back, Agnes had dutifully untied the strings (placing them carefully to one side) and peeled back the paper to reveal the brightly coloured fabric within.

The narcotic effects of the morphine must have been fading, for Matron turned a stony eye upon Charlotte at the sight of the gowns. "There was another thing your Matron, a most exacting teacher, told you, did she not, Nurse Braninov?"

The flush in Agnes' cheeks had barely started to fade, and it returned at the chilly sound of Matron's voice. Blithely, Charlotte replied, "My Matron taught me so many valuable lessons, Mum, I am quite sure I don't know the one to which you refer."

"Your Matron was most specific about not giving presents to one's patients." As an aside, she explained to Agnes, "A nurse can beggar herself doing that—"

Agnes interrupted in a regretful tone, "But you're just not a patient, Mum, you are Nurse Braninov's mother. This is what I was told." At the look of utter confusion on Matron's face, Agnes sought confirmation from Charlotte. "I was not mistaken, was I?"

With great equanimity, the Russian nurse responded, "No, you are entirely correct, dear Agnes. Thus, my Matron's exacting injunction does not apply, does it, Mum?"

For a moment, Matron's voice did not appear equal to the task of speech. Her mouth attempted to form a reply, found it insufficient and endeavoured another before she gave up the attempt and simply swallowed hard. After a long breath, the fine old nurse said in a voice that lacked its earlier crispness, "I suppose, in that case, the injunction is not applicable." Rallying, she directed an additional edict to Agnes, "Mind you, the other commands provided by Nurse Braninov's Matron do continue to hold sway, for they are wise and useful in almost all cases."

"Yes, Mum," Agnes replied smartly. She extended the two unwrapped packages. "Which one do you like? They're both lovely."

Matron's voice still seemed a bit unsteady. "Which. Which do you like, my dear?"

Agnes brightened at being asked her opinion. "Oh, I should say the green, Mum, for it matches your eyes."

"The green is lovely. Would you help me put it on?"

The two girls carefully slipped the flannel gown over Matron's head and tugged it down her body. Charlotte produced some lotion, and applied it to Matron's feet, over her protests. "I've got the feet of an old draft horse," she said, trying to shoo the girls away. Charlotte would not be deterred from massaging Matron's left foot, nor would Agnes, who knelt at the end of the bed and took the older nurse's other foot in her hands and aped the motions of the Russian girl.

After wiping Matron's skin, Charlotte rolled the socks onto her old feet. The patient lay back on her pillows with a smile. "That was lovely, girls, just lovely. Come,

Charlotte, sit beside me."

Agnes hurried to bring a chair for Charlotte, who sat facing the old nurse. Matron reached out and took her hand. "Thank you so much. Daughter."

Charlotte took the thin, wrinkled hand in both of hers. "You are welcome, Mother."

Matron closed her eyes. They sat that way in companionable silence until Agnes blurted, "I do hope that someday I shall have a daughter like you, Nurse Braninov."

Without opening her eyes, Matron said, "Only if you are very fortunate."

"Yes, Mum," Agnes agreed, adding after a pause, "But, begging your pardon, I should hope she would not call me 'Matron.'"

"It suits me," Matron answered with a small smile.

There was no question that Matron was failing. Nourishment did not interest her, and little save the morphine gave her relief. Charlotte thought the old nurse did find comfort in her presence. Thus, the Russian nurse was torn when she found it both convenient and necessary to share her care of Matron with Agnes. The fat little nurse was a dear thing, if a bit timid, but she cheerfully kept watch over "Charlotte's Mum" while Charlotte crept away to sleep, eat, and bathe.

It was good for both the young nurse and the old. Matron, even from her sickbed, was a fount of experience and knowledge, and Agnes eagerly hearkened to every pearl of wisdom that fell from that worthy's lips.

For herself, Charlotte did return to see her Mr. Kamensky. He produced samovars of hot, sweet tea, and plied her with small sandwiches. He had been able to find a buyer for her goods, he told her, but he regretted the price was not as high as he hoped.

"2500 pounds," he said between sips of the tea. *"Based on my description, that is the most they are willing to offer. Alas, there are a number of our people exiled here, fleeing from the Reds, and for many, their only wealth is what they could carry upon them. Fine Russian jewellery is not nearly as rare as it once was."*

After making arrangements to return in a few days with good Mr. Ellis from the Bank of England to allow the buyers to inspect the jewellery, Charlotte asked Fedor, "Sir, who are the Reds?"

Kamensky sputtered dramatically—for he was a fellow given to dramatic sweeps and flourishes, she noticed—before saying, *"You do not know?"*

"Truly, sir, I do not. I have been in England or at the Front, for the last eight years. I have heard little since Lenin's revolt, and even less of that was good." As she spoke, she was trying to remember the last letter she had received from her family. She thought there might be a one stored in her trunk in the tiny flat she was renting. She could not be sure.

"The Reds are what the Bolsheviks call themselves. They battle the Whites, the supporters of the Czar, for control of our homes."

"Reds, Whites. What does it mean?"

"Who can say? Red for the stout blood of the working man, the Whites for the purity of their cause?" Fedor lowered his teacup, going on in English as if the words were too unpleasant for their own tongue. "It is very ugly, Nurse Braninov. Biblical. Brother against brother, servants against their masters, sons striking down their fathers."

This was troubling news. "The Reds...do they raise their hands against anyone who is of the Royal House?"

"Most, Mistress. If one is a member of Court, one is presumed to be a White. Some have joined the Reds, but...I have heard many do so under duress."

The tea in her cup had gone cold, the sweetness was now cloying. She set the cup aside as Fedor went on.

"The Reds, I have been told, will coerce cooperation from military men by taking their families hostage. With a sword at the throat of a man's wife, a husband will do a great many things to save her."

Shocked, Charlotte snapped, "That is barbarous."

Kamensky agreed, sorrowful. "Yes, Mistress, it is deeply barbarous and unworthy of civilized men. And, I regret to say, for every barbarity the Reds perpetrate, the Whites respond in kind."

"For ideas," she muttered in disgust. "They are killing each other for an idea, are they not?"

"Perhaps," he suggested. "But, are not ideas what move us through the world? You had an idea about your earrings, and it brought you here."

"But not to kill you."

"No, Mistress. That is not an idea which occurs to you. But it might occur to another, and move him to action."

She now wished they had not commenced this disagreeable topic of conversation. It did remind her, however, that she needed an additional favour. "Do you know of anyone who is travelling to Russia? I must get a letter to my family."

"I would advise against that, Mistress. Letters could be intercepted. Used against one's family."

"I must try. I must let them know I am alive."

Kamensky bowed his head a moment. "Very well, Mistress. Bring the letter with you when we exchange your jewellery, and I shall do my best to see it delivered."

It was clear that Matron's death was near. Charlotte had seen the end before, in France, usually more swiftly. But the final weakness was upon the old nurse, and with that loss of strength came an emotional frailty, made all the more awful by the weight that had slipped from her, leaving only folds of skin where once had been strength and vitality.

"What shall you do?" Senior Nurse Peckham asked Charlotte, looking in on Matron one spring day. The patient lay upon her bed, wearing the other flannel gown, this one in a rather proud shade of yellow. Fresh flowers sprouted from vases at either end of the bed, the blossoms brought by both Agnes and Charlotte. For all the daisies and lilies brightened the room with their colour and fragrance, the woman sleeping upon the bed resembled nothing so much as the cheapest of waxworks in the mould of her dear teacher.

"Mum, I do not know. I dare not return to my home. I do have some resources, and I suppose for now I will have to establish myself in London."

Nurse Peckham took in the room, her mouth moving as it always did. "I believe Matron had hoped to have you work with her here."

"That was my understanding."

"Would you consider joining my staff? The girls speak highly of you. It would appear you are an excellent teacher."

Charlotte could not hide her surprise as she turned to the thin Senior Nurse. "That is a generous offer, Mum."

"Not as generous as one might suppose," Nurse Peckham replied flatly. "As you are not a credentialed instructor, you would hire on at the wages of any other nurse. I would expect you to work with the Student Nurses during their floor rotations. You have seen wounds and injuries of which they could scarcely conceive. They would need your experience. It would be a very trying employment, Nurse Braninov."

Charlotte withdrew to the hallway. "Truly, you are kind, Miss Peckham. May I beg your leave for some time to consider this kind offer?" She gave the slightest of gestures toward the hospital bed they had both been observing.

"Certainly. When your affairs are in order, see me, and I should be happy to discuss this matter further."

"Thank you, Mum."

Senior Nurse left her without any additional word of farewell. There was no rudeness intended, it was simply her way, and Charlotte gave it no further thought.

Agnes joined her just before tea. "Sorry I'm late, luv! The old sailor in seventeen was passing a stone. It was most awful to hear."

Charlotte nodded, distractedly, and thanked her. "I'll be back by seven at the latest. Matron has slept most of the day."

The stout little nurse reached out to touch Charlotte's hand. Her shyness had retreated a bit at a time since she and Charlotte had become friends. "I am sorry, dear. Do you think it will be long now?"

Charlotte shook her head. "Not long at all. I will return as soon as it is possible."

She had an appointment with Mr. Kamensky that afternoon. Mr. Ellis had excused himself from the Bank and insisted on accompanying her to the pawnbroker's tiny establishment.

The buyer was already there when they arrived, a tall, stiff woman in a travelling suit that had been the fashion thirty years before. She wore a hat with a half-veil across her face, and there was a waist-coated man at her side. The man was shorter than the stiff, tall woman, and had very fine hands.

Kamensky greeted Charlotte in an oddly formal manner. As she was in a hurry, Charlotte gave it no thought but simply complied with his directions, laying the jewellery upon the black cloth counter. The waist-coated man stepped forward, produced a magnifying glass, and examined the bracelet and other items minutely.

It was a most awkward interval, for no one spoke. The tall woman's head almost reached the roof of the little shop, and her eyes were hidden in shadow. She seemed to be studying the rafters.

After some long moments of silence, Mr. Ellis offered, "It is an uncommonly fine evening."

"Indeed," agreed Mr. Kamensky.

Their conversational inventiveness at an end, they lapsed into silence. Finally, the waist-coated man straightened up, replaced the examining glass in his waistcoat, and nodded his head.

The tall woman opened a bag and withdrew a thick collection of pound notes. She passed them to Mr. Ellis, and, uttering the first words Charlotte had heard her speak, said, "I loathe doing business with Jews."

Mr. Ellis looked up from counting the notes. Kamensky glanced away, as if embarrassed.

Charlotte felt her face growing hot. She had heard sentiments like this, far more poisonously expressed, in the Tsar's court, and her father had pointed out to her that the Bolsheviks also blamed the ills of their country on the Jews. Yet, good Kamensky had been nothing but kind and forthright in his treatment of her. And this strange woman had the gall to insult the man in his own establishment.

"You need not do business with a Jew," Charlotte said, pulling the notes from Mr. Ellis and thrusting them into the startled woman's hand. "Indeed, I should wonder that as fine a gentleman as Mr. Kamensky would be willing to do business with a person as ill-mannered and poorly bred as yourself."

At this, a look of alarm crossed the waist coated man's face, and Charlotte had the sudden understanding that her belongings were going very cheaply indeed. She did not hold Mr. Kamensky accountable for this in any way, nor would she ever.

"Let us not give way to hasty speech," the waist-coated man said. He had a high, reedy voice.

Fedor said to Charlotte in Russian, *"There is no need for disputation. It is a part of being among the Gentiles."*

The waist-coated man continued, saying to the tall woman, "These are exquisite pieces of work, Lady Dalingworth. It would be a shame to lose them over…a religious disagreement."

The tall woman bent down, towered over Charlotte. The Russian girl felt that the woman had done this often, leaning over other girls like some huge praying mantis. Charlotte's eyes blazed and she would not look away from the insufferably rude woman.

"I do beg your pardon, Mr. Kamensky." Her voice dripped with insincerity. "I meant no offence."

Kamensky replied in a tone as equally devoid of honest regret or emotion, "Of course, Lady Dalingworth, and there was none taken."

Her Ladyship extended the bills to Mr. Ellis, and then passed several more notes to Mr. Kamensky. "For your trouble. Sir."

Kamensky bowed and slid the money over to Mr. Ellis, saying, "I have not been troubled in the least."

Mr. Ellis recounted the money, wrote out a receipt, and showed it to Charlotte. The amount read 3000 pounds. He passed the receipt to Lady Dalingworth's man, who examined it briefly before tucking it into his jacket and sweeping the jewels into a small, black fabric bag.

Charlotte felt the slightest twinge at seeing the bracelet disappear. As a child, she had worn it when playing dress up, before her mother had caught and scolded her for doing so. The little girl had merely wanted to be as refined and beautiful as her mother, for just a little while. Now, the time for childish things had passed, and the bracelet was no longer a magical totem to transport her to a glittering realm where she was adored and desired. That bit of be-jewelled metalwork had become simply a tool, a utilitarian device to enable Charlotte to continue caring for Matron.

Mr. Kamensky escorted Lady Dalingworth and her functionary to the door with the utmost courtesy. After he had closed and locked the door, he turned to Charlotte, and said quietly, *"Thank you for speaking so kindly of me. You are young, Mistress Braninov. You will have to decide whether it is better to ignore the droning of imbeciles like Lady Dalingworth, or to address it directly."*

Charlotte inclined her head. *"I could not let her speak so about you."*

"I ask you, most respectfully, do you think it changed her mind or did it just make you feel better about yourself?"

The question could have been slighting, but it was spoken with such sorrow that any protest of Charlotte's withered in her throat. *"I do not know. I suppose…both."*

Mr. Ellis looked on, uncomprehending, although he could not fail to see the sadness upon Fedor's face. Kamensky continued, *"I have lived all over Europe, my dear Mistress Braninov. Nowhere have my words changed the heart of a Jew-hater."*

"But you are everything a gentleman should be!" Charlotte insisted.

It was Mr. Kamensky's turn to incline his head. *"I strive to be so. And it is by my actions that I can call 'friend' a man who once referred to me as a 'filthy Jew.'"* His eyes cut toward Mr. Ellis.

"Surely not, sir!"

"As long as one does not have to actually get to know the subject

of one's hate...one's hate can continue to live in safe and ignorant comfort."

Charlotte thought on this a moment, then said with a tone of great respect, *"You are a wise man, Master Kamensky."*

"I am but a fool, however since I know it, that knowledge makes me appear wise."

She took his hand. "Thank you for your services, sir."

With a click of the heels so familiar to her from the court of the Tsar, he bent over her hand. "I am ever at your service, Contessa Braninov."

When Mr. Kamensky had released her hand, Mr. Ellis counted the notes into Charlotte's hand. He coughed discreetly when he finished. "There is the matter of Mr. Kamensky's fee. Ten percent was the agreed-upon recompense."

Three hundred pounds, Charlotte peeled off five one-hundred-pound notes and placed them next to Fedor. "You did far more than was asked of you, sir. Please, accept this with my thanks."

"Yes, Mistress Braninov."

She then counted out an additional three hundred pounds and offered it to Mr. Ellis. "For your kind counsel, sir."

The banker seemed positively shocked. "I could not. I could never."

Placing the notes directly in his hand, Charlotte said, "Then, please, sir, give it to the poor. I planned on leaving this shop with two thousand, two hundred pounds, and that is what I shall do."

Kamensky made an impatient gesture to his friend. "Come, now, Ellis, I know your wife has her charities. Do not be so churlish as to deny Mistress Braninov's generosity."

"Well very," Mr. Ellis said, folding the notes and

placing them in a large wallet. "But they shall be donated in Miss Braninov's name. I will insist upon it."

Kamensky offered tea, but Charlotte graciously declined, saying, "I have a patient in the last stages. I must attend to her."

Mr. Ellis escorted her back to the Bank, where the money was deposited and recorded. He offered to walk her back to the hospital, but as she did not wish to be slowed by his presence, she begged off. She had not taken two steps away from Mr. Ellis before she recalled the letter to her parents. She spun around and approached the banker's desk again.

He looked up with a pleased expression, reaching for the hat he had just set down. "Have you changed your mind, then?"

"Oh, no, sir, I have come to ask another favour of you." She gave him the letter, explaining that good Mr. Kamensky might have a way to get it to Russia.

Mr. Ellis took the letter as if receiving a holy commission. He placed it within his vest, saying, "I shall deliver it this very evening."

Thanking him effusively, Charlotte took her leave. She felt she had been away from Hospital too long, and she did not wish to miss an instant with Matron—the moments they had left were growing fewer and fewer.

In her last days, Matron asked Charlotte to read from the Bible. The old nurse would listen until she fell asleep, but had the habit of awakening at odd intervals, ready to discuss the text.

"Paul is such a paradox, is he not?" Matron asked Charlotte with no preamble. Charlotte put down the tray she was holding to go and sit beside the bed.

"How do you mean, Mum?" Charlotte asked, turning

her chair to exclude the other patients from the conversation. The three beds in the room were occupied, and the young Russian nurse had discovered she possessed a kind of jealousy of her time with the old nurse and found a fierce resentment of outsiders, no matter how well-intentioned, who attempted to join their conversation. She made allowances for Agnes, of course, for she seemed truly fond of Matron, but anyone else received only the sight of Charlotte's back.

"He was such a Pharisee, even after he had met the Risen One. So exacting about what we must do, just as the Pharisees had been in their time. He exchanged one set of rules, it seems, for another."

"I cannot say it had occurred to me, Mum."

"Of course not, dear." Matron paused for breath. Her breathing was becoming more difficult, as the recurrent mass in her abdomen had begun to press against her diaphragm. "You are young, and your heart is good. You are not so in need of Paul's strictures as those of us who have lost our way."

Surely Matron could not be speaking of herself? Charlotte attempted to move on to a more pleasant topic. "You said he was a paradox. How did you mean?"

"For all of his Pharisaic tendencies, Paul could still speak undeniable truths. We do see but through a glass darkly, my dear."

"Yes, Mum. I can only hope that is true."

"Oh, it is, dear Charlotte. The things I have heard the dying say—but Paul spoke the finest truth. That love is the highest of all. Love...true love...it allows one to endure much, to bear the refining fire that burns away the dross, to leave us as the purer beings our Father intended." Matron took the young nurse's hand. "I see so much that is good and lovely in you, daughter. Yet I fear you have only begun your time in the fire."

At that Charlotte drew back involuntarily, just the smallest flinch. These words, from a dying woman, sounded almost like a curse, and there was a still the tiniest part within the young nurse that was a small girl who listened to the stories the peasant women told and half-believed themselves.

With her feeble strength, Matron clung to the younger woman's hand. "I only tell you this because I see that God has a great design in store for you. He will make you into a sword of destiny, my love. You must know this, for you will be plunged into the fire and then thrown upon the anvil and hammered. It will go on until you have been forged into an implement worthy of His Hand."

Charlotte's earlier stab of fear faded, with sorrow stepping up to fill its place. Her dear Matron was truly in her final days and had begun raving. Yet…the ravaged old nurse spoke only with quiet conviction, lacking the breathless urgency of the deranged, the fevered need to impact their truth on a disbelieving world.

"I hope I shall prove worthy," Charlotte finally said.

"None of us are, Cheri." Matron was quiet, breathing hard. Charlotte thought she had gone to sleep, when Matron added, "It is in our imperfect struggles to be worthy that we prove we may just deserve His Grace."

"Yes, Mum." Charlotte would have to think on this. She was no student of divinity, but she was fairly certain that Matron's statements might be doctrinally suspect. Yet, she wondered, could a doctrine become an anchor? The Boche had their doctrines, and it led them to rain death upon millions and to bring ruin to their own people and lands. Perhaps a doctrine that could not encourage nor embrace doubt and questions was a doctrine that was fundamentally too fragile to survive.

Matron interrupted her musings by asking, "What time is it, Nurse Braninov?"

Charlotte stirred herself and checked the heavy chronometer over the nurse's station. "Nearly 11 p.m., Mum."

Matron's face was very white, and her eyes were very green. "I am so deeply tired, dear. I think I shall sleep for a while. You should rest as well."

"I'm fine, Mum—"

The green eyes sharpened their focus on the young nurse. "You have already been far longer at your shift than you should. I have heard Nurse Agnes passing by. She is adequate for attending a sleeping patient."

Matron's voice lacked something of the volume of her old self, but the tone of command rang through nonetheless. Charlotte stood, and gave a curtsey. "Yes, Mum, as you say."

"Very well," Matron replied drily, but with a look of impish delight in her eyes. "I shall speak to you again in the morning."

"Thank you, Mum."

"And do not forget what I have said, Daughter."

"I shall remember your words, always, Mother," Charlotte replied lightly.

Matron settled back into her bed, uttering an unmistakable noise of doubt as she did. "See that you do."

When Charlotte returned, freshly bathed and in a clean uniform at nearly 5am, Agnes met her at the door to the room. On sighting the Russian girl, tears rippled over the doughy cheeks. "She is gone, Nurse Charlotte. Your mother has passed."

Charlotte attempted to step around the girl. "Where is she? You must let me see her."

Swallowing back a sob, Agnes said, "She is gone, Cheri."

Charlotte knew not what to say. Like an apparition, Senior Nurse Peckham appeared at her side. "We have removed Matron's body from the room." Charlotte nodded, knowing this would be the proper course, as the other patients would only be further distressed by the laying out of the deceased in the hospital room. "You may be assured that Matron's remains are being treated with every respect."

"Yes, Mum, of that I have no doubt." Charlotte felt tears pressing against her eyes, but willed them away. She would not crumple now, not here before the other students or the patients.

Senior Nurse gazed upon both young girls. Charlotte, she knew, had seen death many times and in many hideous guises. Agnes, poor brave young thing, had perhaps not the Russian nurse's breadth of experience with such events, but a stout and kind heart. Still, they were both just girls, and she knew the fondness they had shared for the departed. "Nurses, I would have you join me in my office."

"Now?" Agnes asked in a fog of incomprehension.

Senior Nurse Peckham's tart reply left no room for misunderstanding. "Now."

The Senior Nurse directed another student to take charge of the patients in the room where Matron had died, then beckoned the two to follow her. They numbly walked behind their superior to her offices.

Once inside the Senior Nurse's office, they were bade sit. Nurse Peckham's assistant brought in tea on a tray and closed the door when she departed. The Senior Nurse herself poured them tea.

Agnes sniffled over her cup. Charlotte held herself very upright, allowing herself only tightly controlled movements as she took tiny, token sips.

Senior Nurse, as was her custom, began with no preamble. "Matron appointed me the executor of her estate. She wished for her body to be donated to the Royal College of Surgeons, for anything they might learn from her illness."

Agnes gave a kind of hiccup. "She was a fine lady of medicine, after all."

"Indeed," agreed Nurse Peckham. "She has also left a bequest for the Hospital, to care for wounded soldiers, and a gift for both of you, as well." She took sealed envelopes from her desk drawer and distributed them to each of the girls. "Matron's solicitor will be in touch shortly."

Charlotte took the envelope from the Senior Nurse. It was a simple, even cheap bit of white paper. She could not bear to read the contents now. The very idea of Matron remembering the young girl who had been a stranger to her only four years before nearly broke the Russian nurse's resolve not to weep.

"I would have you young ladies return to your homes now. Nor do I wish to see you here until the memorial service for Matron. Do we have an understanding?" She inspected the young women, each in their turn, to ensure they had clearly comprehended her. "Your pay will not be affected by this absence; Lord Jeffries can be most liberal when he least expects it."

The two nurses muttered their thanks. They stood to rise, obviously drained by the emotional toll of the night's events. Senior Nurse stopped them at the door to her office, her mouth working as she sought the best way to express herself. "I expect you to be strong, ladies. Matron would require no less. And yet...do allow yourselves to grieve. It is one way to honour those we have loved and lost."

Charlotte held out her hand to the Senior Nurse. "Thank you for your kindness during this difficult time, Nurse Peckham."

"We have lost a dear friend today," the other said, clasping Charlotte's hand firmly before releasing it. "You may not know how dear. Matron was my teacher, as well, and I should say I am no less indebted to her than you. Nor was I any less fond of her than yourselves."

The two nurses murmured mechanically, "Yes, Mum."

"She chose her own time to die," Nurse Peckham went on. "I have seen it before. She waited until you were away, Charlotte, for she did not wish to leave you with the sight of her passing."

What an extraordinary thing to say, Charlotte mused. Yet, she knew the Senior Nurse to be a woman of many years' experience in Hospital. If it were true...then human beings might have much more control over their comings and goings in the world than she previously suspected. "Matron was ever concerned about the well-being of others."

"Even if it briefly injured them," Senior Nurse agreed. "Now, ladies, you must be on your way."

Charlotte sat on the bed in her small flat. It was nearly 7 a. m., and she could hear the other tenants moving about as the last of them hurried to leave for jobs at shops and offices and garages. She simply slumped there in the confines of the tiny room, and in time she awoke, lying on her side, still dressed. It was quieter in the flat now, although she could hear the noises of cleaning downstairs, and faintly, a snatch of whistling.

She pushed herself upright with a sigh of disappointment at her carelessness, for she had wrinkled her uniform as she had slept. There was a sharp-edged jab in her side, and she pulled Matron's envelope from her waist pocket.

Charlotte turned the envelope in her hands. How dreadfully curious, this would be the last communication she ever received from the dear old nurse. For a time, the young woman simply sat on her bed, letting the envelope dance and glide to the random movements of her fingers.

It was something as fundamental as needing to visit the loo that moved her to practicalities. She laid the envelope on the bed and used the water closet down the hall. When she returned to the little room, the sealed missive seemed to be taunting her. Charlotte sat on the far end of the bed, examining it until she thought, in a tone that sounded a bit like her departed friend and teacher, *Oh, for Heaven's sake, just open it.*

She slit the end of the sealed envelope with a tiny pair of manicure scissors and shook out the letter within. Even as it fell into her lap, she could see the precise, clear handwriting upon the sheet that identified it, more surely than a signature, as having come from Matron.

The contents were brief, but they filled Charlotte's heart. She read:

My dearest Cheri-

These few words will not be sufficient to tell you with what regard I hold you, nor how humbled I have been by your generosity of spirit. I had seen that generosity in the turmoil of France but never imagined that I would be the recipient of such loving kindness in my last days.

I dare to believe that I go on to a better place, and thus I have few qualms about leaving the world. One regret I take with me is the knowledge that I shall not be able to watch you continue to grow into the strong, vital woman I know you will become.

If an old nurse may be presumptuous enough to offer advice, I would say this: never let the cruelty or indifference of others cause you to shut yourself off from love. I write this with a bitter tear in my eye, for this wisdom came too late to me, and I would not have you, my dear Daughter, live that way.

We shall meet again, Charlotte. God bless you and keep you until that time.

Charlotte took several deep, heaving breaths as she read. The letter was signed, *With great admiration, respect, and my deepest love, Matron.*

She closed her eyes for a moment, and pressed the letter to her lips, uttering a silent prayer for Matron, commending her to the keeping of her Father and His Son.

Charlotte's eyes were heavy again, and clutching the letter in one hand, she drew the coverlet over her shoulders and slept.

The next three days passed in a quiet kind of greyness. Charlotte slept, and she remembered to eat once or twice a day. A letter arrived by post, notifying her of the memorial for Matron in the Hospital Chapel on the coming Friday, two days hence. A hasty postscript from Agnes included the unsurprising information that location had been expressly chosen by the deceased.

On the fourth day, Charlotte ventured out, her best uniform folded over her arm. Travelling as she had, and certainly lacking servants, her clothing had begun to look a bit tatty. She was hoping to find a laundress who would make the uniform spotless and do it in less than a day. The Russian Nurse would not appear at the service unless she could do so in a manner to give honour and credit to her teacher.

The land-lady directed her to an establishment near Victoria Station. "Business fellows pass by all the time and need to look sharp. Ask for Lucy…tell her I sent you.

And...I am sorry to hear the old lady died." The landlady, a hard-muscled thing with bad feet who winced when she climbed the stairs could not keep the hopeful tone out of her voice when she asked, "Are you planning to stay on, Miss?"

It was a most inappropriate question to ask at this delicate time. Charlotte, recalling Mr. Kamensky's observations on the inadequacy of mere words changing a person's heart, refrained from chiding the woman. Charlotte sensed clearly that her landlady was only just barely surviving. The lodgers in her house kept her from penury and allowed her the dignity of maintaining herself and not relying upon the charity of others. "I do not know," she finally replied. "I have been offered a position at Hospital. I will surely remain for some time yet."

A relieved grimace passed over the woman's face, which she tried to force back into a semblance of respectful consideration for Charlotte's loss before saying. "We can chat about it at a more convenient time."

"Yes, thank you."

Stepping out of the row house after so many days in her room or asleep, the young woman was briefly staggered by the open space that yawned around her and the noise that pelted her ears. She kept her head down, focusing on the paved footpath, trying to narrow her attention to only that which was directly in front of her to keep the very bustle of London from overwhelming her. Even though it was but ten o'clock in the morning and the streets were not yet filled with throngs of those going to and fro, the numbers of people around her seemed immense. Charlotte stopped for a moment in the entryway of a building to catch her breath.

A middle-aged woman hailed her. "Are you well, dear?"

"Yes," Charlotte told her, then fanned herself. "I

became overheated for a moment. It will pass."

The kind woman lingered a moment more to ensure Charlotte was truly in possession of herself, and then went on her way. It was better after that. The air, while it had the usual tang of the streets, the sharpness of horse dung mixed with the flat reek of the smoky exhaust from motor cars, still was cool on her face this morning, and that seemed to help.

She passed two small children in shapeless white gowns playing on a stoop. One of them, a girl, Charlotte thought, looked up as she passed. The little girl favoured the nurse with a delighted smile as if she had been waiting all day to see the young woman walk by. The little girl held up a tattered doll. The Russian nurse could think of nothing to do other than nod approvingly and say, "What a pretty dolly," before continuing on her way.

It was as simple as a dirty child in a stained jumper giving a complete stranger a smile, but Charlotte found her grey mood beginning to lift. With her uniform slung over one arm, she strolled along and found herself beginning to become aware of the tiny bits of beauty along her route. There high up on a wall was a collection of twigs, and the most brilliant jay flew into it with something in its beak. The jay's head moved in a blur of motion. Charlotte fancied she could hear faint, demanding cheeps. And over there, in a small window set in grey masonry, someone had glued bits of coloured glass to the window in fantastical shapes and placed a lit electric bulb behind it, so the light sprung forth into separate beams of colour reaching out like blossoms that faded into nothingness.

A faint, contented smile graced her lips as she made her way toward the Underground Station at Victoria. Was it simply health and youth asserting their power over events, or was it an act of will, a decision about that to which she would give her attention to that had lightened her burdens? Perhaps it was a combination of both, for mastery over her outlook was a lesson she would be forced to recall again and again.

Nearing the station, Charlotte found the swarms of people were less daunting to her. She let her gaze drift over them, and allowed the different features of the passers-by to catch her eye. The white-haired man with the ruddy, wrinkled face. The fretful young woman she supposed was a maid. The focused face of what must surely be a businessman, striding to some important appointment. She let the faces and bodies slide past her without concern, without judgment, with nothing more than a silent prayer for their well-being.

At the entrance to the Underground Station, she paused. The lights had flickered, and the stairs were briefly dark. The would-be passengers queued up and something about the line of people waiting patiently to descend into the dimness below the streets made her think of one of the stories that Robert had told her, about the way the soldiers lined up in the rear of the squalid trench, waiting for the men in front to move enough for them to take their own place at the wall facing the enemy.

How peculiar, she thought, to associate these men and women, going about their lives, with the soldiers she had served so long. She supposed she might see such similarities for a while, until the weight and habit of life in peacetime slowly overcame the long practice of seeing the world in terms of the constant enemy; the dark predator stalking among the beds to snatch the unprotected, and life a fragile thing that must be shielded from the jackal Death. She welcomed the advent of that time when she would be more aware of life, and of living, than she was of the constant presence of death.

So thinking, she joined the queue and waited her turn to descend into the underworld.

After asking a newsboy for directions, she found the laundress. Recalling her own time assisting with the bedding at Base Hospital No. 12, she had been expecting an open, steamy shop like their own facilities, and was surprised to discover a bright, tidy establishment, the walls covered with white squares of tile no larger than a shilling piece. There was simply a counter in the front, where customers waited to be served. When they had been assisted, their clothing was whisked away through a door in the rear of the shop.

As her landlady had said, business was brisk, and there were several people ahead of her in line. Charlotte did not mind the delay. It gave her mind time to wander. The Underground was quite a centre of commerce. She decided she would purchase some flowers at the stand across the tracks, and then take herself out to lunch. She had eaten so little in the past three days, and she observed within herself a most indelicate yearning for large portions of beef and potatoes, bread and stewed tomatoes, to be finished off by a large mug of coffee and a slice of pie. Berry pie, she decided, wondering where she might find a meal of such prodigious portions. A working-man's café, she supposed, but perhaps her appearance at lower-class eatery could cause a scandal. Charlotte realized with amusement she really didn't give a tinker's damn about anyone who might be scandalized.

So smiling, she stepped up to the counter. "Good day. I was told to ask for Lucy."

The woman behind the counter, a spinsterish thirty-year-old of medium height with pronounced freckles on her cheeks, looked up. "Pardon, Miss, but are you Nurse

Brand…Branin…"

"Braninov," Charlotte pronounced for her.

"Aye, that's it. That's a tough one. Foreign, eh?"

"Russian," Charlotte admitted. "And you are—"

"Lucy, Miss Braninov." She gestured toward a large Bakelite phone that sat in a prominent place of honour along the back wall next to the door. "Estelle rang me, said you might be dropping in."

"That was kind of her."

Lucy held out her hands, and Charlotte, realizing what the laundress wanted, draped the uniform garments on the counter. "Yeah, she's a queer old bird," Lucy commented as she inspected the heavy blouse and skirt. "Hard as a frozen pond one minute, then sweet as an old milk cow the next." Flipping the skirt over to check the hem for mud, she added, "A funeral, I think I heard."

"A memorial."

"Same thing, at least you'll be indoors."

"Would you be able to clean and press these by tomorrow?"

Lucy looked over her shoulder at a series of tickets pinned to a wire that ran along the back wall above the phone. "Hmmm, that could be dodgy." Catching sight of the look of dismay that sprang to Charlotte's face, Lucy rolled the uniform into a cylinder and tucked it into a small bag that she set aside. "Don't you worry, luv, I'll do it myself tonight. It will be done in a tick, and you'll look right smart for the service tomorrow. It will be ready first thing in the morning. Seven o'clock."

"That would be awfully kind of you," Charlotte said, taking her receipt.

"Maybe you'll meet a nice fellow at the service. If he has a friend, bring them both by." Lucy gave an off-kilter smile that made her look suddenly young and hopeful.

Charlotte decided if she did meet a nice fellow, she would certainly introduce him to Lucy straight away, as she had no interest in making the acquaintance of any gentleman, no matter how nice he might be.

There was no time to linger, for more customers pressed behind her. Repeating her thanks to Lucy, Charlotte left the laundry and began looking for the way across the tracks to the flower stand. She made her way along the corridor near the tracks, and again let her eyes take in the faces of those around her. This time she found that she was evaluating their health. The old woman who shuffled along with a tremor in her hands: palsy, and probably a stroke. The florid, heavy-faced husband with a hitch in his step: the gout, and he should cease to partake of both wine and red meat so freely. She gave a shake of her head, half-amused, half-annoyed that she was so unable to leave nursing behind.

There was a walkway built over the railroad tracks. It was not so crowded, and she was able to move quickly to the other side. She was planning the next day while she briskly set out for the flower shop. As Matron has delighted in her dressing gowns in green and yellow, she would order a bouquet in those hues to be collected in the morning after she had picked up the cleaned uniform. *Perhaps Lucy has somewhere that I might change, and I could leave directly for Hospital.*

So thinking, she let her eyes drift across the moving mass of Londoners. And there she saw Robert.

Her heart gave a stutter before she looked away, furious with whatever youthful part of herself still wanted to imagine that she might one day see Mr. Fitzgerald again. Her eyes had lit upon a handsome man with some faint resemblance to Robert. She made herself look again to confirm this.

But it was Robert. Thinner, yes, still looking a bit ill, but she knew him. She knew the way he stood, the hair that insisted on falling over one side of his forehead, the line of his jaw—ah, how her fingers trembled with the desire to stroke his face.

He lingered near a fountain just down from the flower shop as people moved past him. He seemed to be looking for someone. His attitude was anxious.

Charlotte was moving toward him, she knew not when her feet had begun to carry her toward her love. She could not think, for too many thoughts were racing through her mind. *How had he come to be here? What could he say about his absence? Is he well? Am I being a fool?* Questions dashed and flared through her, the intensity of them blazing like sputtering rockets against a black night, crashing and colliding against one another, so that she was nearly insensible to all but their blinding presence.

The Russian nurse approached the English soldier. He was not in uniform, she could see now as she drew nearer, but wore a tailored suit which only seemed to emphasize the sickly thinness of his body.

"Robert," Charlotte said. Her voice was thick, husky with longing.

He looked around, startled, slowly realizing who had spoken to him. "Pardon?" he said, looking down at her.

Her vision swam. "Do you not know me, Mr. Fitzgerald?" Charlotte became aware her breath was coming in short bursts. She was almost panting. Three men nearby were watching her and Robert, and she had the sense they were with him. They were younger, perhaps their second year in University.

A troubled look crossed his face, causing the sprinkling of scars upon the left side of his face to leap forward into harsh relief. "Are we acquainted, Miss?"

The boys from University laughed uneasily, a trifle guiltily, it seemed to her. She spared them a glance if only to turn her face from Robert and allow her a moment to wipe her eyes. The youths looked away, and one of them stared past her as if looking for succour.

She followed his gaze, and there, emerging from a news stand, was Alice and beside her a man she recognized as Nigel. They were idly chatting about something and glanced toward the fountain where Robert stood. Perhaps not recognizing the nurse with whom she had shared a tent in those awful weeks another world away, Alice gave a happy wave toward them.

Breath hitched in the Russian nurse's throat. She was the daughter of Count Alexander Braninov, a proud soldier and loyal son of Russia, and the daughter, by spilt blood and much heart-rending toil, of dear Matron. She would not disgrace either of them by creating a public spectacle. Charlotte composed herself. "Forgive me, sir. I was mistaken. I regret troubling you."

She turned on her heel as sharply as if she had been on parade at Nursing School, and walked away with her back straight and her head held high.

England had once seemed like a land of promise. Matron gone, Robert truly lost to her. Now this cold and gloomy land, with its dull food and dirty streets, felt like a prison.

She was wearing a crisp, newly cleaned nurse's uniform. The laundress had been as good as her word, and the uniform had been ready at 7 am. Lucy had clucked over how drawn Charlotte had appeared, and forced her to submit to a touch-up with some cosmetics. It mattered not to the Russian girl.

From there, she had paused briefly at the Hospital

Chapel and said her own private farewell to Matron before the service had started. She slipped silently away to pay a call on Matron's solicitor, who was taken aback at her breach of decorum. But after a few moments reflection, the lawyer had agreed to transfer the whole of the inheritance that Matron intended for Charlotte instead to Agnes.

In time, she found herself at Victoria Station, in the queue for boarding passes. The attendant, a man with a faint harelip, asked, "Where to, Miss?"

Charlotte said, "Dover. May I purchase passage on the ferry here, as well?"

The attendant didn't need to scan his fares or schedules to answer her. "Yes, Miss. Dover train departs every hour. The next one is boarding now. Ferry passage will be an extra three pounds."

She opened her bag. Inside, was nearly five hundred pounds. Another 1500 pounds were in a money belt under her garments, along with her jewellery. She had been to the bank, spoken to Mr. Ellis and removed her funds. She had paid a farewell call on Mr. Kamensky, who had wept and begged her not to go. *"You cannot know what it is like, Mistress! Your family...they may already be dead. What good would you do, dying to search for the buried?"* She promised him she would be careful, but she would not be dissuaded.

She paid the fare, took the two passes, and tucked the handbag more tightly under her arm. She found the train and stepped onto her car without a look backward.

From Dover, she could take the ferry to France. In France, she would be able to find a train into the continent, and then, north to Russia. To the only home and whatever family Charlotte had left.

Epilogue

Orlando could see Master Robert was upset when the group returned from their drive. The patient was agitated, looking about him as if searching for something he'd lost. Lady Alice and Lord Nigel were on either side of him, guiding him carefully into the drawing room with many soothing words. Behind them came Robert's brother Stephen and his two equally useless fellow students, looking bored and inconvenienced by life as was their usual affectation.

"There now, old boy, you needn't worry yourself about it," Nigel was saying.

Robert's hand went to his shirt front and clutched at something through the fabric. Orlando knew what it was he held clenched in his fist. "But...she said she knew me, Nigel. And...and I am sure I knew her."

Alice laid her hand on his arm, "Robert, perhaps it was one of the girls who helped you after you were wounded." It took much of Orlando's self-possession to not allow a twitch of repugnance to appear on his ugly face.

Nigel had his friend by the other arm and was steering him toward a chair that faced the garden. Spying Orlando, he said, "I say, old man, I think we could all use a touch of brandy." The little man removed his apron and silver-polishing gloves and quickly loaded a just-polished tray with a bottle and glasses enough for all.

The younger Lord Fitzgerald could not be induced to sit. Miss Alice took him by the arm again. "The Doctors said you would have trouble remembering every little thing, Robert. Is that not so, Nigel?"

With the faintest hesitation, Nigel replied, "That is so. You were awfully ill, Fitz. You do remember that, don't you?"

Hand still at his chest, Robert answered vaguely, "Yes."

Taking the bottle from the tray and pouring two glasses, Nigel went on, "Well, then, that very wise physician did tell us all that memory loss is one symptom of typhus." He pressed a filled glass on Robert, who took it with his free hand. Nigel took a hasty sip of the brandy before adding with an odd sort of cheerfulness, "And he did say it was only temporary. That you may yet recover your complete memory of that time."

Miss Alice held out her hand, waiting for a glass. Orlando quickly filled the snifter and passed it to her. She took it without looking at him and stepped closer to Robert. Glancing at Nigel, she interjected, "He said it was only a possibility. I think we should put those awful days of the war far behind us."

She set her glass upon the top of the pianoforte and Orlando sighed inwardly. That would be another hour of rubbing the cherry wood with beeswax to remove the ring left by the base of the snifter. The noble young woman gazed upon Fitzgerald with a playful air of disappointment.

"Oh, look at you, Robert." She began patting his clothes, tidying him up as if he were a child. "I know you don't feel your best these days, but we can cast our eyes forward to a happy future, can we not?" Teasingly, she tugged at the hand that was pinned to his chest. "Come now, Robert, let us throw off those disturbing memories of when you were so nearly taken from us."

The young Lieutenant allowed his hand to be pulled away from his chest. Lady Alice daringly reached inside his collar and tugged on the chain that encircled Robert's neck. A tiny gold cross dangled from her finger, just under his chin. "You don't need to wear this silly thing any longer, do you?" Her fingers tightened on the chain. "Let's put it away, darling."

The noise that torn out of Fitzgerald was guttural, primal, and seemed to erupt from the deepest part of his being. *"NO!"* he roared. It was a growl and at the same time a sound of pain, bringing goose flesh to Orlando's arms. He had heard a man in the trenches make almost the same noise when gutted in his sleep by a Hun's bayonet.

Fitzgerald's hand snapped around and closed over Alice's smaller one, trapping it there. She squealed, struggling against his grip. "Robert, you're hurting me!"

Nigel shoved his empty glass at Orlando and moved between the other two. "Now, Fitz, no one is going to take it."

Robert's head whipped round. For a moment, he glared fiercely at his friend. Calmly, Nigel placed a gentle hand on the clutching fist. "I assure you, no one is going to take it. You are frightening Alice."

Indeed, tears were standing in Alice's eyes and her face had gone very pale. Robert blinked, exhaled harshly, and suddenly released her. She drew back, cradling her hand.

Fitzgerald paid her no heed. He fingered the end of the

chain before lifting the tiny cross to visually confirm it was still in place. He tucked it into his shirt without a word and sat in the chair facing the garden. He would not speak, and both the shaken Miss Alice and the thoughtful Lord Nigel left shortly thereafter.

Robert was distressed for the rest of the afternoon, and nothing would serve to restore him to peace. He shut himself up in his room, and Orlando had dared much to unlock the door from without and let himself in. He found his master sitting on the bed, knees drawn up and arms wrapped around them, rocking back and forth, saying in a soft, almost sing-song voice, "I do know her."

None of Orlando's entreaties or blandishments would distract the man he had served so faithfully during their time at Base Hospital No. 12. "Come now, sir, how about some tea? Mrs. Temple made her fruit tarts, wouldn't those be nice?" Even the cook's biscuits had not the power to relieve Robert of the nameless grief that possessed him.

Fitzgerald continued to rock as the tea grew cold and the filling in the tarts congealed. Orlando could not bear to leave him in such a state, nor could he any longer be party to such an iniquitous deception of the best man he had ever served. The little man that Charlotte Braninov had come to see as a dwarven warrior set his tray down with finality, muttering, "Bugger it." Knowing it would be the end of his position, he absented the room for a moment, only to return with a small sweets-tin which he placed in front of the stricken younger man.

Robert stopped rocking and looked at the metal box with idle curiosity. Orlando lifted the lid and removed from within a small photograph of a young woman who smiled reluctantly at the camera. "Sir, is this the young lady you saw today?"

The younger man took the photo in both hands,

holding it as carefully as one would a wounded bird. "Yes," he breathed.

Orlando sat on the bed at his master's feet. "Her name is Charlotte Braninov, sir. You loved her."

Mr. Pyle told him everything, or, that is, everything Orlando knew. He had only observed, as servants were taught to do, and he had never presumed to question the young Lieutenant about his feelings for the Russian nurse. Yet, even these careful, correct descriptions were enough, for each recollection of that faithful man was as a net cast into the darkened ocean of Robert's memory, each one hauling up a rich harvest of personal recall, full of both detail and emotion, until Fitzgerald found himself slumping exhausted on the floor.

"Did she love me, then, Orlando?"

The old fellow stood erect, as if at attention and testifying for his very life. "Oh, sir. With all her heart or I am no judge."

Robert dragged his sleeve across his eyes. The revived memories had the freshness of recent experience, although months had passed since they had actually occurred. He felt keenly the loss of Ignace and his little cat, the warmth of Charlotte's gaze, the touch of her lips upon his. He pulled himself to his feet. "While I shave and bathe, do send for Lord Nigel. There are questions I must ask him."

"Of course, sir. I shall be tendering my resignation from your service once I do so, sir."

Robert turned and looked on the little man with great fondness. "You shall do no such thing, dear fellow, unless it is your wish. I have no desire to lose the companionship of such a good man as yourself."

There was a longer pause than was customary before Orlando replied, "Very good, sir."

Nigel returned late that evening. The maid let him into the house, and he found his own way back through the house, as befitted a long-time friend of the family. The elder Lord Fitzgerald was hunting in Scotland, leaving the mansion empty save for Robert and his brother, and, of course, the servants. Stephen was away, probably revelling in the less savoury parts of Piccadilly with his fellow students.

Lord Smythe-Worthington located Robert in his room. Orlando was clearing away some dishes. Robert wore some simple lounging slacks and shirt. He looked up at Nigel's entrance and said with a smile, "I would have dressed had I known."

Nigel himself wore a complete suit of evening clothes, as he had only just come from the opera. He returned Robert's smile gratefully, for this simple jest brought some of his old friend back.

Without preamble, Robert pushed a Kodachrome snapshot toward Nigel. "That is her."

He lifted the photograph. It was a slightly blurred photo of four people playing cards outside on a blanket. Robert, the servant Orlando, and two women in nurse's uniforms. One was a rather formidable older woman and the other was an exotically beautiful young woman, who was gazing not at the camera, but at Robert.

"Yes," Nigel said simply, returning the photo to his friend. Robert took the thin piece of paper carefully and squared it on the desk in front of him, as if to ensure he could see it in the best light. Nigel then addressed Orlando without accusation or rancour, merely stating a simple fact. "Lord Fitzgerald will have you sacked."

Robert raised his head from contemplation of the photograph. "Orlando is my personal attendant. Lord

Fitzgerald shall have nothing to say in the matter." The tone was also Robert of old. Commanding, direct. He looked now at his friend. "Why did you not tell me, Nigel?"

Now Lord Smythe-Worthington felt uneasy. He had no good answer to this query. "I...I did not know what to do. Rob, you were so ill, you hardly knew me. Lord Fitzgerald insisted we not discuss your time in the Army. Dr Evans told us the strain could cause you further distress. Your father was concerned—"

"My father's concern for me has ever been tinged with his own self-interest," Robert said flatly. He tapped his finger on the desk slowly and distinctly, but not, his friend noticed, upon the photograph itself. "This woman walks in my dreams, Nigel. I thought I was going mad to dream of such an angel every night. Miss Braninov was the angel that saved me."

It was said with such simple, honest force that Nigel felt the kind of shame he had not experienced since he was a boy and had been caught tormenting the simpleton son of a grocer. "I am sorry, Fitz. I truly meant no harm."

Robert looked away from him, as if master his emotions. "You must find her, Nigel. She cannot...she must not think that I do not care. She must know how much I care."

"I will ask about her for you," Nigel answered without elaboration.

There was nothing more to be said. All three men in the room knew that Nigel, as had his father, was already immersed in "the Great Game," that murky and often ungentlemanly world where the interests of His Majesty's government were pursued and enforced by means that were best not spoken of aloud. The pawns of the great game were everywhere, even if unknowing of their position on the board, and the younger Lord Smythe-Worthington had the resources to locate the Russian nurse if anyone did.

It was nearly a week before Nigel returned with word. During that time, Robert pored over the contents of the sweets-tin, for it contained small mementos and tokens of his time in France, and most especially of Charlotte. A folded card with her oddly slanted handwriting. A tiny flower. Photographs. A scrap of fabric, he learned, that had cradled Ignace and his wee kitten, Nell.

Each day, his memory became sharper, clearer, and more and more of his life began to make sense to him. He commented to Mr. Pyle on the third day, "I did not care for Miss Alice, did I?"

Orlando said carefully, "You were cordial without being familiar, sir."

Fitzgerald remembered pursuing her through the tents on the night of the aerial bombing, when she had run mad with fear. "She was a bloody nuisance."

"Aye, sir," Orlando replied without committing himself one way or the other.

Robert would see no one while waiting for Nigel. He sent Alice away whenever she called and exiled his brother Stephen to lodgings in the city. He took long walks round the grounds, exhausting himself. He would sleep for a time, but then the restless energy would overtake him, and he would be up pacing again.

When Nigel appeared at his door on the sixth day, Robert knew that he brought ill tidings.

Without asking him in, the young Lieutenant said, "Where is she?"

Nigel removed his hat and stepped inside. They'd been friends a long time. "She's dead, Robert." Fitzgerald shook his head, denying Nigel's words. "She took a train to

Dover. The ferry to France. From there, we have her on several trains to Russia." Lord Smythe-Worthington sat heavily on a chair in the entry. "It was madness," he went on, rushing his words. "Russia is on fire, and she went straight into the inferno."

"You don't know she's dead," Robert insisted.

"Her train was stopped by the Bolsheviks, Fitz. They shot everyone on board." He shook his head, staring down at his hands. "Everyone," he repeated.

"Sir," Orlando began, but Robert held up a quieting finger before sitting opposite Nigel. He was silent for a long time.

No one spoke. Nigel looked at the floor miserably. Finally, Robert stood with great deliberateness, as if trying not to further damage an already cracked vessel. Softly he said, "My Lord, Mr. Pyle will show you out. Good night."

It might have been the huge row that brought Nigel back to the house some days later. Since receiving the news about Miss Charlotte, Robert had retired to his room, spending most of the time in the dark. Orlando could not be sure, but he had the sense his master was praying as he grieved. This period of mourning was interrupted by Lord Fitzgerald, who had returned early from his hunting trip and was in receipt of a startling communication from Miss Alice.

The elder Lord Fitzgerald, a few inches shorter than his son, but a thickly shouldered bull of a man, thundered into the house that evening, barely stopping to kick off his boots and hurl his jacket at the butler before stomping into Robert's room.

Orlando was in the servant's quarters, tending to Robert's shoes and brushing his top hat, for they had been shut up in storage for several years while his master had been in France, and were in deplorable condition. Normally, had the little man been inclined to eavesdrop, he would have had to strain to hear, but there was no need for such subterfuge when Lord Fitzgerald had his Irish up.

"Damn you, boy!" the older Fitzgerald roared by way of greeting. "What is this I have heard from Miss Alice? You have refused her entry to this house?"

"Indeed I have, sir," Robert replied in a voice that trembled from the effort to remain civil. "I have no wish to keep company with her any longer, sir."

"I would have you keep company with the lady, you pup. I will have you marry the wench for the honour it brings our house and I will accept no other answer!"

Mr. Pyle could hear the sound of Robert leaping to his feet. "And I tell you I will be damned and in Hell before I would marry such a scheming creature! She would have used her wiles to mislead a sick man to achieve her ends and you would have aided her in this deception!"

Something crashed in Robert's room. "I will not allow you to dishonour the name of Fitzgerald, boy! This defiance will not do, I tell you, it will not do, sir!"

And now Robert proved he had inherited in some measure both the temper and the volume of his father, for the walls fairly shook when he replied heatedly, "I faithfully fulfilled the King's Commission by sending his soldiers to die in the god-bedamned mud of France! What will not do is you treating me as your chattel and as a child, sir!"

The elder Lord Fitzgerald attempted to respond, but Robert countered, louder, if possible, than before. "You would sell your oldest son into a marriage of convenience merely to advance your own ambitions and to hell with love? What kind of man are you, sir? What wound has ripped the heart from you?"

There was another crash that made Orlando flinch, the

sound of Robert's bedroom door being flung open. "You are no son of mine! I will not have you in this house, sir!"

"As you wish, sir! And that will be the last direction of yours I shall follow!"

Nigel appeared less than an hour later. It was full dark outside, and as had been his custom these past seven days, Robert sat in the darkened house, with but a single candle burning.

Orlando showed Lord Nigel right in and then quickly retired to the pantry before returning with a tray and three glasses of whiskey.

"It seems this is a night of some import," Nigel commented.

"Indeed. I am barred from my father's house." Robert looked around. "It never was much of a home to me. I think…I felt more at peace in France."

Nigel took two glasses from the tray, handed one to his friend. "You appear much recovered, old boy."

Robert lifted the tumbler, but did not drink. "I feel as if I am reborn. As myself. Amazing how memory of the past anchors one in the present." At the moment, he looked very old to Orlando. It was surely a trick of the shadows and the ravages of his recent illness. Robert said to Nigel, "I am almost the man I was, yet…I am not whole. For my angel is in heaven."

Nigel nodded, regret plain upon his face.

Robert raised his glass. "To Charlotte Braninov. The woman I loved as I have loved no other. The angel who saved me."

Nigel lifted his glass in response, and Orlando took up the third glass of whiskey and held it high, saying, "To Miss Braninov, a fine young lady."

The men drained their glasses solemnly. Robert stood, walked into the great room, and threw his glass into the fireplace. The glass shattered like his hopes.

Nigel and Orlando followed him in and propelled their glasses into the cold hearth.

"Where can you send me, Nigel?"

"Pardon?"

"I cannot stay in England. I must leave, for a while at least. Surely, there is some place for a broken man in the Great Game?"

Nigel took in his friend's face slowly. "I can make some inquiries. A man of your family connections could be useful." He smiled knowingly. "Your father may withhold your inheritance, but he cannot deny your title."

"Do with me what you will. There is nothing for me here now." Robert turned away from him to look into the cold ashes of the fire. Burnt, yet cold and dark as his dying dreams.

As Robert Fitzgerald considered the blackness of his future, thirteen hundred miles to the east, one of the few survivors of the Smolensk train massacre awoke to begin her day, hours before dawn.

She had been sleeping on the factory floor, covered with a mismatched assortment of blankets, amid a pile of equally weary co-workers. She climbed to her feet, still wearing her boots and her nurse's uniform. In the dimness, she looked down at the now stained and wrinkled uniform. In her fatigue, thoughts repeated themselves often. She mused, not for the first time, how odd it was that a simple thing could both save you, and yet enslave you. It was the nurse's uniform that had kept her from being shot in the back of the head like the other unfortunate passengers of the ill-fated train, and now, it was the nurse's uniform that held her here, a captive of the Red Army, forced to tend their wounded under the most appalling, ill-equipped conditions.

She yet lived, but she knew not for how long. She had seen how careless the Reds were of the lives of their people and how insane were the dictates of their government. None were safe in the madhouse that Lenin was creating. If her time came, she swore she would not go quietly or compliantly. She would not succumb to the lies around her, even if only she knew she had resisted to the last.

She took a long breath, trying to ignore the stench of unwashed bodies around her. Wrapping a thin blanket tightly around her shoulders, Charlotte Braninov shuffled toward the distant ward and an unknown future.

End of Book One

Thanks for reading the first book in my **By the Hands of Men** series.

If you could stop by Amazon and leave a review, you'd be doing me a great favour. The more reviews, the more visible my books will be to other readers.

And, if you'd care to come along on my continuing journey as a writer and learn more about the stories I discover as we go, head over to **roymgriffis.com** and sign up for my mailing list.

Keep reading for a special preview of
Charlotte: Through the Ocean of Fire
Book Two of the **By the Hands of Men** saga

To the Motherland

The ferry from Dover was an older, steam-driven vessel with two decks. The lower, more protected from the wind and the waves, housed an odd assortment of motorized Lorries and a variety of horse-driven conveyances; the upper was for passengers. The upper floor was for passengers. Nearly half of that deck was enclosed with a roof and windows, with wooden shutters offering protection against inclement weather, with the other half open to the air. Hard wooden benches were the only seating available.

There was a tiny tea room just a bit larger than a coffin within the enclosed section. It was run by a stout, terse elderly woman with some unfortunate hairs on her chin. Braced against the swaying of the ferry, she offered tea that was only slightly warmer than tepid and a few forlorn biscuits. As she slopped tea into a heavy mug for Charlotte, the elderly woman cast a thoughtful eye out toward the sea. "Freshening wind," she commented, the meaning of the words lost on the young nurse.

Charlotte followed the woman's gaze. Outside, darkness was moving across the rolling water as the sun dropped in the sky. It would be night before the ferry made port.

"It will get rough," the other woman explained, taking a few coins from Charlotte and giving her a dispirited bun of some sort. "Hold on tight to your tea and bring the mug back when you're done."

The snapping wind off the English Channel made it too cold to sit outside, and already there were chilled passengers trooping up from below to find shelter. Charlotte took a seat on the inner corner of one of the wooden benches, reasoning it would be warmer. She found she hated the idea of being cold, even a little. After but a minute or two, she reluctantly shifted over to the outside corner, near the bulkhead, as the flood of passengers had to pass right by her to get to the tea room, and most of them could not help but jostle her elbow or knee as the ferry moved with the waves.

She wedged herself into the corner of the bench. Here, farther from the centre of the labouring vessel, the roll and pitch was noticeably more pronounced, and the tea in her mug began to slosh alarmingly. To keep it from spilling over her, Charlotte gulped down several mouthfuls in a very unladylike manner. Crooking one arm around the back of the bench, clutching her mug and bun in the other hand, she settled down for the crossing to France.

Under other circumstances, the motion of the ship might have been enjoyable, even a bit of a lark, for in some ways it reminded her of being a girl. As the ship rose on the water at the crest of a wave, she had the giddy weightless feeling that she remembered from being at the top of the swing. But her heart was heavy, and she had not the lightness of soul to find pleasure in such simple things. As the light outside disappeared, Charlotte drew into herself and endured the trip to Calais.

Through the Ocean of Fire

She was relieved to see that it was fully dark when the ferry arrived in Le Havre. Numbly queuing up with the other departing passengers, she felt an ache as if a healing wound had been struck anew. For seeing Robert as she had, just for the barest of moments, resurrected in her those emotions she hoped had been buried in toil and effort. Their new birth was as painful to her as their death had been. Yet something else weighted her feet as she shuffled down the cast-iron gangplank toward the dockside and France.

Shame. Charlotte felt ashamed for having been gulled by Robert Fitzgerald. It was obvious now, here in the cold French night; the man had never cared for her. When she had approached him at the Underground that morning, he feigned lack of all knowledge of her, whilst his companions laughed uneasily, clearly fearing a scene. She had believed him lost to her, and the sight of his dear face, his familiar form, awakened in her a longing to feel his arms about her once more. She had wanted to lay down her burdens and rest awhile in his embrace, shielded as she had once been during those terrible days of the Great War. The hope had risen in her like a surging wave, catching her unaware, and, thus, to be spurned by him so was as if that flood of hope had crashed into the most impenetrable of dams, and was flung back upon itself in a swirling, confused, and useless chaos of emotion that had nowhere to go.

"Mademoiselle?"

Charlotte lifted her head. She found herself the only passenger in the ferry terminal. It was an open kind of hall, with dirty floors and a handful of worn wooden benches. An elderly porter peered at her with curiosity. The porter was slightly hunched, perhaps from a lifetime spent lifting travellers' bags. Wisps of white hair drifted out from beneath his official black cap, the brim a touch low over his eyebrows.

"Mademoiselle," the porter repeated again. "Are you well?"

"Perfectly," Charlotte lied automatically as she gathered her wits. She had no luggage, bringing nothing from her life in England except the clothes she wore and some valuables secreted about her person. "The railway station. Is it close?"

The porter reflected the question not at all. *"Oui.* He gave her clear directions to the station, which was not far from the terminal. She thanked him and started for the door to the street.

She paused, her hand upon the brass push rail, looking out into the night-darkened street. Streetlamps gave illumination, but, she imagined, no heat. She quailed at the idea of walking through the cold. She should find a room and sleep for a while; yet if she did, that meant she would have to see France in warm light of day. France, where she had known and loved a man she thought had loved her.

For a moment, Charlotte wanted to weep. She felt the porter's curious eyes upon her and asked impulsively, "Do you know where I might find a room for the night?"

The hunched porter's face grew thoughtful. "Yes. It's not far. He took a key from his pocket, locked the ticket office, and walked toward her. "Allow me to show you, Mademoiselle. Rene Decouleur, at your service."

Monsieur Decouleur held the door for her, gesturing to the street outside. Charlotte took a reluctant step onto the cobbled street, waiting while the porter locked that door as well. "This way, Mademoiselle," he said, setting off slowly up the street to the east. Charlotte fell into step beside him.

The shops that lined the north side of the street were dark, as were most of the homes that lay above them. To the south were docks and quays, where vessels of every kind rocked gently in the tide. Small sailboats, punts, fishing vessels, tugs, all seemed bereft of purpose and life save the rhythmic sounds of rigging creaking or the splash of water upon their hulls. Looking about with dull curiosity, Charlotte noticed that there was very little outward sign of the Great War's impact upon the city. "The war," she said, not intending to speak aloud. "It did not reach here?"

"No, Mademoiselle. Our soldiers...many left and did not return. They lie where they fell, farther to the east. Monsieur Decouleur did not glance up as he toiled along over the uneven stones that made up the street. "Our city was most fortunate. His voice was flat. At another time, Charlotte might have observed that the porter did not truly think his city had been blessed, but she was not capable of such insights on this night.

Now she could perceive lights ahead of them on the street. It was a yellowish glow, as from lanterns or poorly powered electric lights. As they drew closer to the source of the illumination, she could see open shutters over thick windows and the heavy rounded stones that made up the structure of the place, with dark, thick wooden beams jutting out over the street.

Rene led her inside, where she hesitated a moment, realizing the shop was a tavern. Some gnarled figures sat around tables, mugs and food in front of them as they yarned and argued. Glancing round at the dim interior, Charlotte wondered how long it had been here on the waterfront. *Henry V might have stopped here on his way to Agincourt*, she guessed, her weary mind dancing to avoid the question of whether she were wise to enter this place.

A tiny yet fat woman came round from behind the long counter. She wore heavy trousers, like a working man, and a sailor's top. Spying Monsieur Decouleur, the little fat woman began to speak at him in very rapid French. Charlotte's command of French had been shaped around more polite discourse, as fitted a young lady, and she was unable to entirely decipher the idiom in which the little woman spoke. The porter was able to slip a random sentence or two into the raging stream of the interrogation directed at him. Charlotte did catch the occasional word, such as "nurse," at which point Monsieur Decouleur turned to look more closely at her in evident surprise. She was then also able to quite clearly hear the description "idiot" directed at her guide.

Dismissing the porter to a table, the proprietress approached Charlotte and looked up at her. "I have a room," she said in heavily accented English, pointing overhead. "You would like?"

"Yes, please, just for tonight. Charlotte shivered, and added, "Do you have extra blankets."

"Oui. Yes. The fat woman darted behind the bar, pulled a mug of beer, and shoved it at the porter. Then she looked about the tavern, as if gauging her choices. She took Charlotte by the elbow. "You follow.

The fat woman plunged through a small door behind the bar, which immediately presented a set of narrow stairs leading upward into a dim unknown. The little fat woman lit a candle. "Come, come," she said impatiently.

The weak flame of the candle showed the rough, unplastered walls on either side as if they were heavy charcoal sketches; too, it revealed the thick heavy planks that made up the steps. Charlotte unconsciously lifted the hem of her uniform skirt as she slowly followed the tavern keeper upward.

The room that was presented to Charlotte was compact, with the roof slanting downward over the narrow bed. There was a small window along one wall. The taverness leaned over the bed muttering. She struck the mattress several times, and waved Charlotte closer. "No cooties," she said with pride. Then, thrusting the light into Charlotte's hands, she quickly stripped the sheet and case for the pillow and remade the bed with fresh linen from another room. The fabric was greyish from much use, but smelled quite clean. The good woman stopped once to stand at the top of the stairs to listen. As there were no sounds of riot or breakage coming from below, she returned to the room where Charlotte waited numbly with the candle in her hand.

With no delicacy at all, the little fat woman pointed to a ceramic jug beside a small wardrobe. "Chamber pot. The privy, she explained, was in the yard in back of the building, and was nothing a cultured lady would wish to use. She also took pains to demonstrate the lock on the door.

"I sleep there, Mademoiselle," the woman said, pointing to a similar room on the other side of the stairs. The two rooms shared a wall, apparently, for she added, "If you need me, knock on the wall."

Charlotte felt fatigue beginning to swallow her as if she were sinking into the constricting maw of some great black beast. "Merci, Madame," she remembered to say.

The fat little woman waved it away. "Helene," she said, indicating herself as if her identity were of no great importance.

Reaching into a side pocket of her heavy skirt, Charlotte found a few coins. "Please, let me pay you now."

"Four francs," Helene said.

Damn. She had neglected to exchange her English currency before leaving. "I have only pounds," she apologized.

"Half-pound," Helene said casually. "Breakfast, too. We

have good ham today."

Charlotte dropped two coins into Helene's hand. As they disappeared into the French woman's pants pocket, Helene made a noise, "Tch," before hurrying over to her own room and returning with an armload of coverlets. "Gets cold," she commented in her clipped French, mindful of Charlotte's apparent difficulties with the language, spreading the roughly-made blankets over the bed.

Madame Helene stood in the doorway, surveying her work with a critical eye. She nodded to herself, satisfied. "*Bonne nuit*, Mademoiselle," she said. "Sleep well. Then she turned abruptly and darted down the stairs to return to the tavern.

Charlotte moved toward the door to the room, closed it, and turned the lock. She set the candle upon the stand beside the bed. She longed to simply tumble into the bed, but dared not. As she had no other clothing with her, she would be forced to travel in the wrinkled uniform if she gave in to the urge. Some atavistic sense warned her against appearing that way in public, not for the sake of propriety, but of safety. A woman traveling in such a condition would attract unwanted attention, if not from meddling officials and minor functionaries, then from less savoury types. A woman who looked downtrodden seemed to inspire in certain kinds of men the desire to tread upon her in her misery.

She sat upon the bed to pull off her boots before wearily removing her uniform skirt, jacket, and blouse, draping them with care over the chest against the wall. A small belt round her waist, heavy with jewellery, she placed under the bedclothes. Wearing only her chemise, without the heavy serge Charlotte began to shiver where she stood patting flat the fabric of her uniform and tending to the pleats of the jacket. That task done, she scurried across the room and slipped beneath the heavy layer of blankets that covered the small bed.

Charlotte uttered an unbecoming oath as the bare skin of her legs made contact with the chilly sheets, and she curled herself into a tight ball, drawing her legs up under her chemise and wrapping her arms about her knees. For a few more miserable minutes, she shivered, but slowly her body heat began to warm the bedclothes, and with relief the Russian girl stretched her limbs.

She leaned over and snuffed out the candle. The wick glowed red in the gloom, and gradually faded, leaving on the faintest trace of harsh smoke in the air, which dissipated rapidly.

Alone now in the darkness of the room, the only noise about her the muted, relatively sedate revelry from downstairs, Charlotte's thoughts could turn, against her will, to recollections of the events of the day past.

She could see Robert's expression as he contrived ignorance of her. See it, yes, but she felt anew the stunned confusion she had experienced, then the burning shame at being so publicly scorned.

The memories plagued her. She could not thrust them from her by a simple act of will. Perhaps if she were not so weary, so sick at heart, she might have turned to more drastic, less useful remedies such as dressing and going downstairs to seek a liquid anodyne to her pain. But the idea of moving, of continued consciousness, was abhorrent to her.

All she could do was pray. "Father," she said aloud, her hand reaching by habit for a small gold cross that had long hung about her neck, but finding it not, for that tiny piece of gold work had been given, along with her heart, to Robert Fitzgerald. The awareness of the absence of the cross made tears prickle in her eyes. She clenched her hands tightly together, as if to stop them from questing for the missing jewellery. "Father," she said again, "thank you for my safe journey. Shield me, I pray, from these thoughts that bedevil me. Her voice caught, and she made a noise like a hiccup as she fought to keep from weeping. In a quieter, more determined tone, she continued. "Bless Matron. Bless Mother and Father. Bless the brave and true soldiers, everywhere. She murmured on, asking her Lord's blessings on everyone she could remember.

She was growing warmer now, drowsy. "Bless Mr. Fitzgerald," she breathed softly. Charlotte could not invoke the name of God to curse one who had wronged her. It felt wrong—blasphemous, even. "Bless Mr. Fitzgerald that he may come to know You," she uttered, her thoughts slowly scattering, the thread of them unravelling as sleep took her.

By the Hands of Men

Book Two

Charlotte: Through the Ocean of Fire

"Through the Ocean of Fire" is the second volume of the **By the Hands of Men** series. Historical fiction by Roy M. Griffis, the epic sweeps across four continents in a gripping tale of fate, loss, redemption, and love.

Head to Amazon now and grab the next book in the saga that readers have called "Extraordinary," "Amazing," and "Compelling."

The complete **By the Hands of Men** series

Book One **The Old World**
Book Two **Charlotte: Through the Ocean of Fire**
Book Three **Robert: The Ingenuities of Hell**
Book Four **Charlotte: The Blind Machinery of the World**
Book Five **Robert: The Wrath of a Righteous Man**
Book Six **Ringside at the Circus of the Fallen**

Afterword

Nobody writes a novel by themselves. *Somebody* was warming William Shakespeare's ale, and James Joyce had lovely Nora bringing him rashers of bacon, among other treats, while he toiled over the adventures of Leopold Bloom.

I am indebted, first, to my earlier readers like Kia Heavey, Jamie Wilson, Ruth Rice, and John Earle (among many others) whose enthusiasm for the developing novel made it much easier to drag myself up at 4 am to write before getting ready for work. A special tip of the hat to Professor Meg Blair (trauma nurse, educator, and contributor to many nursing text books), who gave my revisions a final editorial review.

The research itself was not difficult, for a great deal has been written about the First World War. One of my personal skirmishes was the need to resist the temptation to turn this into a text full of fascinating historical fact, rather than the story of two people who find one another and discover love in the most difficult of circumstances.

I would be remiss if I did not mention the generous assistance provided by Ms. Nelle Fairchild Rote. This remarkable woman grew up hearing about an aunt, Helen Fairchild, an American Nurse who died in France during the Great War one decade before Ms. Rote was born. With a lifelong interest in her aunt's letters from the War, Ms. Rote spent years accumulating documents about her aunt, along with a trove of historical data which culminated in an extraordinary self-published work titled *Nurse Helen Fairchild World War I*.

It would be impossible for me to recommend this book highly enough. The breadth of detail about the times that her aunt would have lived through is impressive, but Ms Rote went further, and imaginatively crafted additional letters for the book in her aunt's voice to better and more immediately convey the events and emotions of serving under such difficult conditions. It truly is a work of both love and art. The text is unfortunately out of print, which is a shame, because it belongs on the shelf of any history lover, whether they wish to know more about the war, or about the women who served so well and so selflessly. Ms. Rote, at 88, welcomes correspondence (elle12@ptd.net).

Finally, of course, my thanks to my family for their understanding while I was immersed in writing this book and the rest in the series: especially my son, Cameron, for his willingness to forgo snorkelling and other Dadman delights to give me a day to work on the novel, and to my lovely wife, Alisa, for her constant encouragement and support.

A note about the cover

The image of the beautiful woman on the cover is that of an actual nurse, Florence Ethel Spalding, a young Australian who, among her other posts, served aboard the Hospital ships at the Gallipoli landings. Film and history students know what a deadly encounter that was for the Allies. Her photo is used by the kind permission of the Manly (Australia) Library Local Studies department.

ROY M. GRIFFIS

Storyteller